"I'm *what?*"

"Take it easy, Maxine. You're just the kind of woman I need to get my family to—"

"I heard that part. What I want to know is what you *meant*."

Despite her scorn, the idea uttered in jest was seeping deeper into his consciousness. Maxine was the perfect candidate for a make-believe bride.

"I can't imagine you're talking about a real marriage," she said.

"No way." He shuddered. "I could just call my folks and *tell* them I'm married. *Voilà!* Inheritance released."

She said, as if curiosity had gotten the best of her, "So give me details."

"No details. I'll just tell my mom I'm married. She'll swoon with delight and declare the terms of the will fulfilled. If worst comes to worst, I'll let my mom speak to my blushing bride. That'll be you."

She grimaced, reflected, then said, "All right."

Being nobody's fool, he didn't push it. He gave her a thumbs-up and crossed to the bottle of champagne chilling in a silver bucket.

At which point Maxine aimed a forefinger at his sleek back, cocked her thumb and silently mouthed a single word: *Gotcha!*

Dear Reader,

I can't tell you how long I've wanted to tell the story of Randy Taggart, the spoiled brat in *Fireworks!,* book one of my TAGGARTS OF TEXAS miniseries. But for Rand to grow up and find his own true love, Thom T., the Taggart patriarch, had to grow old—make that older, because he was no teenager to begin with.

How to give Thom T. his due? The question stumped me for a long time, but the answer came to me in a flash.

So here it is, book five in the further adventures of the Taggarts. I hope you like the way I've handled Thom T.'s "little problem." I also hope those of you who remember the other Taggart men—Jesse James, Daniel Boone and Trey Smith—will enjoy catching up on their lives and the lives of their wives and children.

For me, this book was a joyful homecoming. I hope it pleases you, too.

Ruth Jean Dale

HITCHED!
Ruth Jean Dale

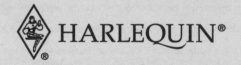

HARLEQUIN®

TORONTO • NEW YORK • LONDON
AMSTERDAM • PARIS • SYDNEY • HAMBURG
STOCKHOLM • ATHENS • TOKYO • MILAN • MADRID
PRAGUE • WARSAW • BUDAPEST • AUCKLAND

ISBN 0-373-70933-1

HITCHED!

Visit us at www.eHarlequin.com

Printed in U.S.A.

ABOUT THE AUTHOR

Ruth Jean Dale lives in a Colorado pine forest within shouting distance of Pikes Peak. She is surrounded by two dogs, two cats, a husband (her one and only) and a passel of grown children and grandchildren. A former newspaper reporter and editor, she is living her dream: writing romance novels for Harlequin. As she says with typical understatement, "It doesn't get any better than this!"

Books by Ruth Jean Dale

HARLEQUIN SUPERROMANCE
678—KIDS, CRITTERS AND CUPID
687—THE CUPID CHRONICLES
788—CUPID'S REVENGE
853—FAMILY SECRETS

Other "Taggarts of Texas" books:

HARLEQUIN ROMANCE
3205—FIREWORKS!
3242—SHOWDOWN!

HARLEQUIN TEMPTATION
413—THE RED-BLOODED YANKEE!

HARLEQUIN HISTORICALS
768—LEGEND

Don't miss any of our special offers. Write to us at the following address for information on our newest releases.

Harlequin Reader Service
U.S.: 3010 Walden Ave., P.O. Box 1325, Buffalo, NY 14269
Canadian: P.O. Box 609, Fort Erie, Ont. L2A 5X3

PROLOGUE

DEAD OR ALIVE, Thom T. Taggart spoke for himself.

But considering that the crusty rancher had been laid to rest less than two hours earlier, his appearance on the forty-two-inch television screen set up special for the occasion in the parlor of the Rocking T Ranch near Showdown, Texas, elicited a collective gasp from the assembled audience.

The old Texas rancher and oilman, spiffy in a dark Western-cut suit and string tie, sat in his wheelchair, holding up a copy of the *San Antonio Star*. He pointed to the date and his lined face creased in a broad grin.

"Howdy, y'all," he drawled. "As you can plainly see, today is my birthday. Seems only fittin' to make my final will and testament before y'all show up to surprise me." He winked, letting everyone in on the joke. "Not that I ain't fixin' to live to be a hundred like I always said, 'cause I am."

At that point, Kit McCrae Taggart began to sniffle. Her husband, Boone, patted her hand in an attempt to comfort. She gave him a grateful glance and tried to swallow back her tears.

Thom T., all-unknowing, went on. "Folks, it's been a great life—still is, even if I am mostly stuck in this dang chair these days. I may not be as spry as I usta, but I'm still of sound mind.'' His familiar hearty laughter filled the room. ''That bein' the case, I'll be gol-darned if I'll let the government get its hands on a penny more a'what I got than it deserves. So here goes.''

It took a lot of hard swallowing and throat-clearing for his nearest and dearest to maintain their poise. Those who shared the Taggart blood had come to hear their departed patriarch's final words and receive his final bequests.

That included Jesse James and Meg Randall Taggart, who were accompanied by thirteen-year-old daughter, Clementine. Daniel Boone and wife, Kit McCrae Taggart, who were present with their son, Travis, nine, and daughter, Cherish, three. And shirttail relation Thomas Trenton Taggart Smith, always called ''Trey,'' had come with his wife, the former Rachel Cox, and their eight-year-old twins, Thom T. and Taggart Smith.

Only Meg and Jesse's twenty-one-year-old, Thomas Randall Taggart, Thom T.'s great-grandson and namesake—''Rand'' to friends but still called ''Randy'' by the family—was missing.

On-screen, Thom T. harrumphed. ''As for Randy—'' He let out a huge sigh. ''I told that boy's other great-grandpa not to leave him all that money on his twenty-first birthday, but would the old fool listen to me? The boy probably won't even show up for my funeral, but what the hey—I love him anyway. I admit I been hornswoggled now and again,

but not this time. That boy's better than you know—
better than he knows.''

Thom T. took a deep breath as if to steel himself
for their disapproval. "That's why I'm leavin' my
first great-grandchild my dearest possession, my
heart and soul—the Rockin' T Ranch. I'm talkin' the
whole kit 'n' caboodle, folks.''

This produced a ripple of surprise from the observers. Thom T. reacted as if he'd heard them from
the grave. "Yep, I know I always said Jesse would
get the Rockin' T," he stated, defending his change
of heart, "but he's got the Hells Bells Ranch and he
don't need this place, too. What'a you say to that,
boy?''

"You got that right, Grandpa.'' Jesse's voice was
muffled and he stared straight at the television screen
as if holding himself together with spit and baling
wire. "I don't *need* anything.''

Thom T. nodded as though he'd heard. "I guess I
could leave the home place to Boone, but he's a big-
shot lawyer and politician so he don't want nothin'
to do with ranchin'—am I wrong about that, Dan'l
Boone?''

"Never, Grandpa.'' Boone's voice was uncharac-
teristically tight. "I don't recall the last time you
were wrong—about anything.''

"And Trey,'' Thom T. went on. "He lives a'way
out in California and is always tryin' t'get his neck
broke doin' that movie stuff.'' He chortled. "Besides, he's a damnyankee and don't want nothin' to
do with no ranch in Texas.''

Tough-guy Trey, eyes bright with unshed tears,

joined in the old rancher's gleeful laughter. Trey, the man who could fling himself down a flight of stairs or jump off a cliff into a damp sponge without a second thought, radiated pain.

Thom T. sobered. "I been worryin' over this for quite a spell," he admitted. "I finally decided to let the chips fall where they want to. But the ranch ain't comin' easy to Randy. To get it, the boy's gotta prove he's worthy. He's gotta get hitched and become a productive member of society. And he's gotta do it by his thirtieth birthday because I ain't made outa patience."

"Fat chance," the boy's father muttered darkly.

Meg gave her husband a quelling glance. "Show a little respect, Jesse. He's your own son, after all."

Jesse rolled his eyes but subsided.

Thom T. blithely went on. "And since the lawyers pissed and moaned about how they was supposed to know if Randy had met my requirements, I told 'em to let you three couples decide—yes, you folks sittin' in front'a this TV sniffling, because if you're seein' this tape, I'm pushin' up daisies."

"Oh, Thom T.!" Kit's voice was somewhere between a moan and a gasp. Tears streamed down her cheeks, but she was smiling. "You old sweetheart. You know us better than we know ourselves."

Rachel's smile trembled. "He always did," she said. "I hope he knew how much we all c-cared for—" She couldn't go on.

Thom T., of course, didn't hear her but sounded as if he had. "Get holda yourselfs, the whole buncha y'all," he commanded, his expression stern. "That boy and his wife have gotta *love* each other—that's the most important thing. Then they gotta convince his ma and pa and his two aunts and uncles that it's a *real* marriage, not one'a them make-believe deals just to get his hands on the ranch. Not that he's likely to go to any trouble, since his other great-grandpa left him more money than he'll be able to spend if he lives as long as I have.''

The old man's mouth curved down unhappily. ''If I was gonna be around, I'd fix young Randy up with the right gal like I done Boone and Jesse and Trey. Unfortunately at my age I cain't count on wakin' up tomorrow, let alone bein' around long enough to whip my great-grandkids into shape. I'll just have to count on luck, God willin' and the creeks don't rise.''

There wasn't a dry eye in the house by now. This did not deter the no-longer present Thom T.

''A'course,'' he continued in a musing tone, ''there's always the risk that Randy won't ever want the Rockin' T.'' His tone revealed pain at such a prospect. ''I thought a'that, too. If Randy don't claim this place by his thirtieth birthday, it goes to the Texas Sunny Days Nudist Colony. They been tryin' to buy it for years anyway.''

Thom T. then proceeded to parcel out oil wells, oil and mineral rights, valuable Western paintings and sculptures, stocks and bonds—all the trappings of a rich but modest man. Beneficiaries included not only his loved ones but also those who had served him in his declining years—although judging by his image on the screen, he hadn't declined nearly as much as his advanced age would suggest.

Unluckily the man who'd vowed to see a hundred

had expired just ten days short of his goal. As everyone present knew, he'd been wrong about Randy not attending the funeral. The boy had, and he'd been as torn up as the rest of them. He just hadn't hung around for the reading—or viewing—of the will.

Even his mother had to admit that Randy *did* have more money than was good for him, and he wasn't interested in anyone's opinion about what to do with it. Now it looked as if the Rocking T Ranch, its history and all it had meant to the Taggart family and this part of Texas, would inevitably be overrun by a swarm of naked sun worshipers.

Or so Jesse predicted later over a beer with Boone and Trey.

"He's my son and I love him," Jesse said darkly. "But he's only twenty-one years old and he's got the bit between his teeth. At this point, I don't know if he'll ever be the man me 'n' Thom T. want him to."

He sighed and lifted his can of beer. "What the hell. Here's to the Rocking T."

Boone clicked his can against his brother's. "Here's to Randy. May he do the right thing, and do it in time."

"And here's to Thom T. Taggart." Trey added his can to the cluster above the small table. "That old fox was smarter than all three of us put together. He pulled strings his entire life, as we can all attest—to our great good fortune. It wouldn't surprise me any if he's still pulling strings from the great beyond."

Three hard, handsome, successful men drank to that.

CHAPTER ONE

Eight years later

DOWN TO HIS last hundred thousand in ready cash, Rand Taggart boarded a small Alar Airlines jet in Chicago on a pleasant September afternoon. The day was the only thing that *was* pleasant, unfortunately, for he was bound for San Antonio and a heaping helping of crow. Even a smile from the pretty blond flight attendant didn't lighten his mood.

Helluva note when a good-lookin' woman fails to arouse my baser instincts, he thought glumly, stowing his leather flight bag and briefcase in the overhead compartment in the small first-class section. The best he could manage for her was a nod.

The fact was, he'd rather eat a bug than face what awaited him in Texas: telling his parents that he'd spent, given away and been scammed out of millions of dollars—the latter by his old college roommate, of whom they'd never approved anyway. Then, while they were still in shock, the unmarried ne'er-do-well son would try to coax them into helping him break his great-grandfather's will.

The mind reeled. Nevertheless he had to do it before he could go after his onetime friend. He wanted

his money back, but he wanted to get his hands on
the perpetrator almost as much.

"Excuse me."

He turned to find a gray-haired woman standing
in the aisle, trying to juggle a large travel bag and a
child. She appeared flustered.

"Young man, could you help me get this bag into
the overhead bin?" she asked.

"Sure thing." He rose and hoisted the bag easily
next to his in the open bin. "Anything else I can do
for you, ma'am?" He managed a grin for the kid.
Only two or three years old, he guessed, although he
was no expert on children. The little girl looked back
at him with unblinking blue eyes, her mouth turned
down petulantly.

"Nothing. Thanks for your help." The woman set
the child into the seat in the last row, directly behind
Rand's. "I hope Jessica won't be a bother on the
flight. She's cross because she didn't get her nap today. With luck she'll sleep all the way to San Antonio."

"Yes, ma'am," Rand said. If he'd been wearing
a hat, he'd have tipped it politely. Good manners
died hard, even when you were mired in a slough of
despond.

Other passengers were trekking down the narrow
aisles. Rand seated himself in his usual window seat
and ignored them, along with the whole routine of
boarding. It wasn't that he minded flying; God knows
he'd done enough of it in the past eight years. Trips
to Europe, the Caribbean, back and forth from coast
to coast…

He'd hopped a plane and traveled three thousand miles to dine in Pasadena at the mom-'n'-pop café that served up his favorite pizza, the one with cashew nuts mixed in with the meat and veggies. He'd flown to Pamplona for the running of the bulls and to Acapulco for cliff diving, to Japan to buy pearls and to Florida to give them to a woman he hardly knew.

He'd thought the money would last forever.

It hadn't…but it would have lasted a helluva lot longer if he hadn't renewed acquaintances with good old Bill Overton. Now Rand either had to get married with lightning speed—God forbid!—or convince his parents, his aunts and his uncles to back his attempt to break the will of Great-grandpa Taggart.

Fat chance, he muttered. They'd want to hear chapter and verse on how he was able to throw away the millions left to him by his *other* great-grandpa, John Hayslip Randall IV, of the Boston banking Randalls. There'd be richly deserved lectures about *responsibility* and *duty* and *obligation,* and a whole lot of "I told you so's."

The worst part of it was, they couldn't say anything to him that he hadn't already said to himself, and in much harsher terms than *they'd* use. He was fairly certain most of them still loved him, which was more than he did at this sorry point.

Nevertheless the Rocking T Ranch had suddenly become his only source of ready cash while he tried to recover his lost fortune—he should live so long. This time he intended to use his head to manage his money—quite a change from the last go-round. At twenty-nine, he knew better than anyone that it was damn well time for him to grow up.

He'd already been thinking along these lines before Bill Overton had revealed himself for the dirty dog he was. Why did Rand always have to learn the hard way?

Time crawled past. Now that he was committed, all he wanted was to get to Texas and get this over with. At last the line of passengers slowed to a trickle, then stopped altogether. Maybe he was going to luck out for once, he thought with the faintest flicker of optimism. Maybe he'd have this entire two-seat row to himself. If he did, it would be the first positive thing that had happened to him since—

"I'm sorry?"

At the soft words, he forced his attention away from the window, where he'd been idly watching the usual bustle of the ground crew. A woman stood in the aisle, regarding him coolly from behind the most unattractive pair of eyeglasses he'd ever seen.

The rest of her wasn't very impressive, either. Her neat brown dress hung around her waist like a sack with a string tied round the middle. The garment buttoned all the way up to her chin, and elbow-length sleeves dangled limply around her arms.

Her features were regular, but bland to the point of invisibility. Eyes of a nondescript brown were magnified by those miserable glasses, and her hair, an equally ordinary brown, was slicked back to her nape and tied with a droopy bow.

She licked colorless lips. "Uh, I'm sorry?" she

said again, making a question out of words that would normally be an apology.

"For...?" Rand encouraged her to elaborate, since he had no idea what she was getting at.

"I think you're in my seat?"

"No way." Rand fished into his hip pocket and extracted his ticket. "I always get a window seat. See, right here—" He broke off, staring at his ticket: aisle seat. Even his travel agent had it in for him these days.

"If it's a problem, I don't mind trading." The woman sounded anxious about it, though. "Really, it's no problem at all." Bending, she hoisted a large garment bag.

"Let me do that," Rand said quickly, scooting over and out into the aisle. "Go ahead." He gestured toward the window seat. "It's all yours."

"If you're sure you don't mind..." She gave him an agitated glance and relinquished her bag to his care. "Thank you so much."

He swung the ungainly piece of luggage into place, surprised that it weighed considerably less than he'd expected. Apparently she believed in traveling light. After sitting down in the detested aisle seat, he squirmed around to locate the safety belt. To his displeasure, she spoke again.

"I'm Maxine Rafferty." Turning awkwardly against the confines of her seat belt, she offered her hand.

"Rand Taggart." He barely touched her hand with his. He wasn't in the mood to get friendly with anyone on this trip and those feelings had nothing to do with her lack of appeal. He'd have felt the same no matter who took his window seat.

She chewed on her lip with even, white teeth. "Are you going to San Antonio, too?" she asked.

He nodded. That was where this plane was headed, so what did she think?

Her smile was strained. "I really hate to fly," she said suddenly. "Something bad always happens. The last time, the plane sat on the runway for four hours. It was awful."

"I can see how it would be." He should be kind and supportive, but all he wanted was for her to shut up and let him return to his brooding.

Seemingly she caught on, for with a distracted frown she turned back to the window. This left Rand free to resume his dark thoughts, the darkest of which was the absolute certainty that the six people who held his fate in their hands were gonna turn him down cold.

Okay, so he hadn't exactly been leading that productive life Thom T. had envisioned for him—the word *wastrel* leaped to mind. Once he reached his parents' ranch in the Texas Hill Country, he'd have to talk fast. He could count on his mother, of course, but his father...

Jesse James Taggart was not a man who made a lot of allowances, and especially not for his son. Rand had never been able to please his father, had never even come close to living up to the Taggart name. Early on, he'd quit trying.

The flight attendant's voice came over the intercom, reciting the usual safety instructions while the plane rolled away from the jetport. He didn't listen to what she was saying because he could have given the spiel for her he'd heard it so many times. Strapped into his seat, he waited until they were airborne before leaning back with a sigh.

In so doing, his elbow extended into the aisle and somebody smacked into it. Rand yanked his arm aside, automatically mumbling a ''Sorry'' and glancing up.

The guy never even saw him, probably didn't even realize what had happened. Rand had just a glimpse of a set, white face and blazing eyes. Several years of sometimes-fast living immediately told him that the man's expression owed more than a little to the use of booze, pills, illegal drugs, something along those lines.

The guy was probably rushing to the postage-stamp-size rest room to ingest illegal substances. Rand hoped no one was unfortunate enough to already be crammed in there, because this guy was in a *big* hurry. Whatever. Rand had more important things to worry about.

The die was cast. Nothing could stop the fate flying toward him at breakneck speed.

''*THIS IS A HIJACKING!*'' A rough male voice sliced through the flight attendant's smooth recitation. ''Everybody stay where you are and nobody will get hurt.''

The flight attendant's voice shot up into a squawk of protest and the intercom went dead.

Ha, ha, Maxine thought crossly. *Just what I need—a comedian serving the pretzels.*

She glanced at the darkly handsome man in the aisle seat, curious to know how he'd react to this less-than-funny prank. His eyes were closed, so perhaps he was sleeping. That gave her an opportunity to admire him for just a moment.

Rand Taggart wore a butter-soft leather jacket, a shirt with an expensive logo, khaki trousers and pricey leather sneakers. And he wore it all with the kind of nonchalant grace that shouted "Money!" without him ever opening his mouth.

It was more than that, though; the photograph definitely hadn't done him justice. He was so damn good-looking that she'd caught her breath in surprise at first sight of him. He had a square-jawed suntanned face, dark hair that curled slightly around his ears and temples, long-lashed eyes a shade of blue-gray she'd never encountered…

And a natural arrogance not unexpected, under the circumstances. Nevertheless she was determined to strike up a conversation with him. After taking off her eyeglasses, she rubbed idly at the bridge of a nose unaccustomed to their weight. No way did she intend to waste this flight to San Antonio, especially at first-class prices, when she'd gone to so much trouble to—

The intercom opened again in a hail of static. *"We're being hijacked!"* the flight attendant shrieked. "This is not a joke!" A series of grunts and gasps and the sounds of a scuffle followed.

Rand sat bolt upright. "I close my eyes for five

minutes and we're being hijacked?'' he demanded. Half rising, he looked about.

Maxine stayed where she was, aware of the increasingly anxious buzz around her. People were confused, their voices growing louder in alarm. From the row of seats directly behind, a child let out a screech that cut through Maxine like a blade.

Even so, she refused to believe the plane was actually being hijacked. No way! She'd been nervous about booking this flight, but fear of flying wasn't why. Normally as subtle as a sledgehammer, she'd set herself a task that depended on subtlety. She wouldn't allow herself to be distracted by—

"Hijacked! The hell you say!" This new, masculine voice came from behind the open curtains separating first and tourist classes. "Don't worry, Robyn, somebody's gettin' cute. We'll see if the FAA thinks it's so damn funny."

Rand sat down suddenly, his arm pressing Maxine back against her seat. "There's a guy with a gun comin' up the aisle," he said, a touch of Southern steel creeping into his mid-Atlantic accent. "Lean back and keep quiet. Don't do *anything* to attract attention."

The flight attendant's shaky voice rose above the babble with a boost from the intercom. "Please, keep calm and nobody will be hurt. Do everything they say."

"How the hell many are there?" Rand muttered, not turning to see. "Jeez, I don't believe this!"

A man shoved past, heading for the front of the plane. Turning at the forward seat in first class, he glared back at the hapless passengers. Maxine caught her breath on a little moan at the sight of the guy's menacing expression.

It didn't help that he was waving a pistol around in one hand while exhibiting a hand grenade in the other. "Everybody shut up!" he roared, red-rimmed eyes glowing. "Next person who opens his mouth will get a grenade shoved down his throat."

Maxine snapped her teeth together with a click. In her immediate vicinity, all sound ceased except for the snuffling of the child in the seat behind. Those in tourist class apparently couldn't hear the man's warning, though, for it was beginning to sound like pandemonium back there.

"Goddammit!" The hijacker strode back down the aisle, still brandishing his weapons. Rand leaned slightly in, his shoulder touching hers until the man had gone past.

"Two of them." He was looking at her, but she knew he was thinking out loud. "I hope to God nobody gets any bright—"

The intercom crackled and a new voice came on, a voice rough and threatening. "You people shut up and listen! We've got guns and grenades and we're ready to use them unless we get some damn cooperation!"

He'd convinced Maxine, and everybody else, as well, it seemed. Suddenly she could have heard a pin drop. There was something utterly persuasive about his threats. Wide-eyed, she couldn't help counting on Rand Taggart for reassurance. He shook his head in silent warning, then took her hand and squeezed it.

He must think she was on the verge of hysteria or something. She wasn't *that* weak or stupid…but there was some comfort to be found in his steady grip nonetheless. She didn't pull away.

"Listen up," the disembodied voice continued. "I've got a gun pointed straight at the captain's head and my partner will keep you folks in line out there or else—you got that? Try anything and I will surely shoot the shit outa this pilot, in which case we're all dead meat." He didn't sound as if he cared.

The intercom went dead. Rand grimaced. "I'm taking him at his word," he said. "If everybody keeps cool, we should be all right."

Small comfort. "Do you think—"

The intercom cut her off. "This is your captain speaking."

Maxine felt a leap of hope at the new, confident voice—hope dashed by his next words.

"If everybody will just remain calm and cooperative, I'm sure we can work something out with these gentlemen. The seat-belt sign will remain on and I'd personally appreciate it if you'd all stay buckled up. Mr.…?"

"Smart-ass," the other voice snarled. The sound of a blow, a groan.

When the pilot spoke again, his voice was no longer calm and assured. "This gentleman h-has instructed me to, uh, has given me a new flight plan. Sit tight and pray. We have plenty of fuel and no intention of doing anything foolish."

"Oh, gosh…" Maxi swallowed hard. "This isn't sounding very good."

THE WOMAN in the front row likely agreed, because she burst into hysterical sobs. Rand didn't say a word, just leaned back and closed his eyes. At least his own problems were taking a back seat, what with overwrought passengers, weeping children and erratic flying patterns.

Not that there was a helluva lot he could do, which was frustrating. Beyond occasional comforting words for the woman in the seat next to him—Maxine something-or-other—he was powerless. When this whole thing started, what little color she had in her face had disappeared, apparently never to return.

"Can't we *do* anything?" she finally blurted at him.

"Like what?" She must be nuts.

"You're a man. Men are supposed to know these things."

He felt his temper soar. "If you think I'm gonna get shot trying to be a hero, you've got the wrong guy."

"I probably do." She settled back, radiating disapproval.

Well, hell. What did she expect? Now he had something new to brood about.

Around them, many of the passengers were climbing beyond the point of no return on the hysteria scale. Maxine, although she'd shown no signs of losing it, was obviously scared to death. Hell, so was he. He should be more understanding.

He kept his voice low and easy. "Did you say you live in San Antonio?"

She gave him a startled glance and shook her head.

"Maxine," he said reproachfully, "I can't take your mind off your troubles if you refuse to talk."

She responded with a quick, uncertain smile. She really did have a nice mouth—wide, full lipped. Almost lush. It was a wonder he hadn't noticed that before.

"I live in Chicago," she said a bit vaguely. "Mostly."

"Are you going to visit friends in Texas, then?"

"No. I have a job interview there." She licked her lips nervously. "What do you do, Rand?"

"As little as possible."

"Ah." Her expression seemed to relax a little. "Independently wealthy, I suppose."

"Depends on what you mean by *wealthy*. He kept his tone neutral. He didn't intend to tell this stranger that he'd probably thrown away more money than she'd ever see. "I'm on my way to visit my family."

"Parents?"

"That's right. And two aunts and uncles who live nearby."

"Do you have a close family?"

"Close enough, I guess. How about you? Do you have much family?"

"One sister, and she's…well, she's kind of in trouble at the moment."

"That's too bad." He didn't want to pursue this line of questioning. He wasn't particularly interested in her *or* her sister, would never see her again once this was over. He had plenty of problems of his own without getting caught up in hers.

But looking into her vulnerable face, he couldn't

bring himself to break off the conversation. At a loss, he finally said, "I have a sister, too."

"Has she ever been in trouble?"

Rand laughed. "Clementine? She's been in trouble since the day she was born, but probably not the kind of trouble you mean."

"Clementine. I don't believe I've ever heard of anyone with that name. Except, 'Oh, my darling,' of course."

"She used to hate it, but now that she's older, she kind of likes it."

"Older like...?"

"She's twenty-one." He knew she wasn't interested in hearing about his sister, but he was struggling to keep the conversation going. "How old are you?" About his age, he figured.

"I'm twenty-five."

"No kidding." *Idiot. You can't tell her you thought she was at least five years older than that.* Damn shame Clemmie couldn't get hold of Maxine for a few hours and do something about that frumpy exterior.

"Excuse me, sir."

Rand glanced around to find one of the ashen-faced flight attendants standing in the aisle, holding a basket with cans of soda and tiny bags of pretzels. "Would either of you care for a drink or a snack? It's not much, but this was supposed to be a short flight."

"They wouldn't let you use that big cart, huh?" Rand guessed.

She nodded. "He said if they needed to get

through the plane in a hurry, they didn't want *that* thing in the way.''

''Which makes sense, I suppose.'' He took a couple of cans from the basket and handed one to Maxine. ''How's it going up front?''

The flight attendant licked her lips. ''Okay, I guess. They're obviously doing drugs, though, and you never know where that will lead.'' She made a face.

''Maybe if they get enough of that junk in them, they'll fall asleep.''

''God, I hope so, but it just seems to make them more squirrelly.''

The beefy man across the aisle—an insurance salesman from Dubuque, Rand recalled, Larry something-or-other—leaned into the quietly spoken conversation. ''Why doesn't the captain do something?'' he demanded, his face reddening. ''We've got them outnumbered, for God's sake.''

The woman in the maroon-and-gold Alar uniform was rendered speechless by this asinine criticism, so Rand jumped in.

''Good idea. You make the first move.''

''Me? I—we—ah...'' The man's bluff had been called and his bravado evaporated.

A bit of color had returned to the flight attendant's cheeks and she gave Rand a grateful glance before moving on.

Rand turned around to Maxine, who studied him without expression.

''Maybe we should gang up on those hijackers,'' she said defiantly. ''If we're going to die anyway—''

"Nobody's going to die," he said, appalled.

"Is that a promise?"

"It's a prediction. Why don't we just settle down and—"

"May I have your attention, ladies and gentlemen." The pilot's voice burst from the intercom. "Time to buckle up. We'll be landing in about twenty minutes at—"

The sound was cut off to a chorus of *"Landing where?"* Maxine and Rand looked at each other. He smiled. She didn't.

"See?" he said encouragingly. "In an hour we'll be off this plane and going about our business again."

"From your lips to God's ear," she said with feeling. "In the meantime, keep talking, will you? Tell me the story of your life…anything to keep my mind off *them.*"

THE HIJACKERS apparently changed their minds with disturbing frequency because minutes stretched into hours while the plane continued on a meandering course through the sky. After a while, Rand found himself running out of things to say and he still couldn't loosen Maxine up enough to do more than nod or answer "Yes" or "No." She did show an annoying tendency to ask personal questions, however, which he turned aside with growing impatience.

He wasn't a man who talked about his personal business, especially when he was ashamed of it.

The hijackers took turns exploding out of the cockpit to wave guns and grenades around, to make threats. Singly, they'd stalk to the back of the plane, get everybody all worked up to screaming and crying, then turn and stalk back, to disappear inside the cockpit again.

Finally the insurance man across the way got fed up for real. "We *really* oughta rush 'em," he whispered hoarsely to Rand. "They're gonna get us if we don't get them first."

That thought had occurred to Rand, too, but had quickly perished. Whatever those two hijackers were doing in the cockpit wasn't making them sleepy it was making them mean—make that meaner. They gave every indication that they'd as soon shoot the passengers as keep an eye on them.

"Take it easy," he tried to calm the jittery man. "Nobody's been hurt yet. Why start something we may not be able to finish?"

"Yeah, well…" The man subsided, mumbling.

The next time one of the gunmen appeared, he took one look at the insurance salesman, apparently didn't like what he saw, raised his pistol and fired point-blank.

At the same instant, the plane banked into a sharp descent, throwing the gunman off-balance. The bullet *panged* into a vacant seat in the first row, sparing the insurance salesman. The first-class cabin erupted in shrieks and cries, so the hijacker fired a couple more shots after the first, playing hell with the upholstery.

Rand shoved Maxine against the window and turned to shield her with his body. In the aisle, the hijacker was swearing and making all kinds of threats, ending with a bellowed, "You think I don't know what's going on out here? You want to jump me, right? Try it! I'm *begging* you to try it! Hell, I might just throw this grenade and get it over with."

Fully believing the end was near either from bullet, grenade or a crash landing, Rand braced himself for the worst. So much for his own petty problems. He wasn't going to live long enough to—

The wheels slammed down onto solid earth. The plane vaulted into the air and landed again, heavily. The odor of burning rubber permeated the cabin.

"Please!" The word was just a gasp from Maxine. "You're crushing me! Let me up!"

Why the hell not? If the hijacker hadn't thrown the grenade by now, maybe he wouldn't. "Sorry." Rand straightened. A quick glance forward produced an exclamation of astonishment.

The hijacker wasn't there. And hurtling past the window was a landscape Rand didn't recognize: sand and cactus and a few stunted trees.

But first things first. "You okay?" he asked Maxine. "I didn't mean to crush you but I was afraid—"

"Shit!" The insurance salesman was hyperventilating. "He's crazy! Did you see that? He tried to shoot me!"

Rand grimaced. "Buck up, fella. You survived to tell about it."

The man groaned. "I think I'm gonna be sick." He stumbled to his feet and staggered forward to the rest room, bouncing side to side with the motion of the plane.

Into a tense silence, a petulant voice intruded. "Grandma, I'm hungry!"

Jessica, the little girl in the seat behind them. A tug on his sleeve made Rand start; the child stood in the aisle, looking up at him plaintively.

Maxine's smile didn't mask her concern. "Honey, you have to sit down." She dug around in her shoulder bag. "Here." She held up a candy bar. "You can have this if you'll get back into your seat and—"

"Jessica!" The little girl's grandmother sounded panicky. "Get back in this seat at once!"

"Choc-late!" Jessica escaped her grandmother's clutches and lunged for the chocolate bar. She grabbed it, then fumbled at the wrapper.

Rand tried to take it from the chubby hands. "Let me help you, hon."

"No, let *me* help."

The hijacker had crept up on them all unseen. Now he reached for the candy bar.

Jeez, this guy would take candy from babies? Talk about rotten!

Jessica lunged for the chocolate. "Mine!" she screamed, holding the bar in both hands and backing away. She whirled around, then dashed down the aisle as fast as her chubby little legs would carry her.

The gunman straightened, swaying with the roll of the plane, and his arm came up. All Rand could see was the revolver rising, a finger already tightening on the trigger.

CHAPTER TWO

JESSICA'S GRANDMOTHER let out a bloodcurdling screech and leaped into the aisle, blocking it. Her frantic gaze met that of the gunman and she screamed again. She turned, then stumbled after Jessica, blundering into the curtain.

"Crazy old bat." All the gunman's attention was riveted on the floundering woman. His lip curled and he squeezed the trigger.

Rand acted purely on instinct. Grabbing the gun hand, he shoved it up and the bullet whistled harmlessly into the overhead luggage bin. Struggling into the aisle, he wrestled for the gun, slowly forcing the hijacker back.

In the cramped space, the man teetered, swore. Balance gone, he made a panicky grab for the last straw—Rand, who fought off the grasping hands.

The hijacker toppled backward, bouncing off the metal arm of a seat on his way down. He landed flat on his back, his head striking the floor with a solid *thump*. The gun popped free, ending up at Rand's feet. The hijacker didn't move.

Breathing hard, Rand bent to retrieve the weapon. The plane lurched, bounced, skidded, knocking him to his hands and knees—but he had the gun. He struggled up, to find Maxine kneeling in the aisle seat. Her eyes behind the ugly glasses were wide and scared.

She gave voice to the obvious. "You could have been killed!"

"You wanted me to do something, didn't you?"

The insurance guy, back from the rest room, pointed to the unconscious man in the aisle. "He's out cold. One down and one to go!"

Rand hefted the comforting weight of the pistol in his hand. He didn't give a hoot in hell what the insurance guy had to say but for some reason thought Maxine's opinion might be useful. "Now what?"

"How about this," she responded promptly. "You stand in the entryway beside the cockpit." She'd obviously given their situation some thought. "I'll scream my head off, and when the other hijacker comes out to see what's going on, you get the drop on him."

Rand groaned. This sounded like a recipe for disaster. "There's gotta be an easier way."

She crossed her arms over her chest and glared at him. "You think of it, then. This plane is going to stop soon and when the guy up front sees what you've done to his partner—" She made an appropriate slashing motion across her own throat, complete with sound effects.

Her point was well taken. A gun battle inside an airplane would not be a good idea. After a moment's consideration, he said, "You sure this'll work?"

"As sure as you were that we'd be off this plane three hours ago."

She had him there. "Lacking a better idea…"

The level of hysterical wailing in tourist class steadily increased, although first-class passengers appeared too stunned to join in. Jessica's shrieks soared above all else, but he deliberately shut out the racket. "You." He indicated the insurance agent. "Keep an eye on that guy. If he so much as blinks, slug him."

"Hard enough to make him see stars for a month," the man promised. He dragged a heavy hardcover book out of his seat pocket and held it at the ready.

"All set?" Rand looked at Maxine.

She took a deep breath and nodded. The woman wasn't short on nerve.

Satisfied, Rand stepped over the unconscious hijacker, then crept toward the front of the airplane. The revolver gave him confidence, although he hadn't held one in years. His father and great-grandfather had taken pains to teach him how to handle firearms when he was just a kid, before the days of political correctness.

The plane came to a final grinding stop. Holding his breath, Rand placed an ear flat against the cockpit door and strained to hear. Nothing. He turned and positioned himself to the side, where he'd be hidden when the door opened. Maxine, standing near the flight attendants' galley on the left, looked to him for a signal.

He nodded and she nearly split his eardrums.

"Eeeee…! No! Stop! Don't come any closer! I'm warning you! Aaargh! Eeeeee…!"

The cockpit door slammed open so hard that it

banged against the barrel of Rand's pistol. For a moment he couldn't see Maxine and terror swamped him. If he screwed up and she was the one who got hurt—

"Dammit, what's goin' on out here? I've had just about enough of—"

Rand shoved the door with all his strength and raised the pistol, fully prepared to shoot the crap out of the hijacker. Instead, he looked into the blank face of a man who didn't know what had hit him…a man slowly crumpling, knocked silly when the heavy door connected solidly with his head.

The insurance salesman rushed up "We got him!"

The pilot barged through the door, rumpled and a bit crazed. Dried blood crusted his forehead, but he didn't appear to be seriously hurt. He stopped short at the sight of his tormentor sprawled on the floor. "What the hell!"

The co-pilot joined them, taking everything in at a glance. "Where's the other one?" he demanded.

"In first class, dead to the world." The insurance guy pointed.

Rand finally got a word in edgewise. "Where are we?"

"Mexico," the pilot said. "It's a miracle we're still alive. Those guys wanted to go to Argentina. By the time they finally agreed to a fuel stop, things were getting desperate." He slapped the other pilot on the shoulder. "It's a damn good thing you remembered this old airport, Joe."

The co-pilot shrugged. "My dad used to fly in and out of here in the fifties. This place was an early

Cancún, apparently." He didn't look as if he fully believed what had happened, even now. "We'd better get the door open and see what the hell we've landed in."

Rand had more immediate concerns. Where was Maxine? Still hiding in the galley? "Here." He thrust the revolver into the salesman's hand. "Take over."

Turning away, he finally spotted Maxine struggling up the rapidly filling aisle. She was lugging her suitcase and his, his briefcase slung over her shoulder. He pushed his way to meet her, so relieved that he nearly put an arm around her.

She leaned close to be heard. "I don't know about you, but I want *out* of here."

"You and me both." But now new worries set in. Neither friends nor family were aware he was on this plane and publicity was the last thing he wanted. Was there a way to avoid all the hoopla surrounding a hijacking?

"When the door opens..." she began.

"Just part of the crowd." He tried to shield her from the press of frantic passengers stumbling over the unconscious man in the aisle as if they didn't even know who he was.

Suddenly the airplane door blew. Instead of leading the charge to escape, Rand stepped aside, drawing Maxine with him. A dozen or so passengers rushed to the opening where the door had been.

No jetway awaited them, just a too-short metal stairway leading down to a graveled field. The first step was a good six feet below the door, but that merely slowed the stampede instead of stopping it.

Two Mexican officials trying to climb into the plane were instead shoved out of the way by the mob. At the first break in the exodus, they tried again with better results. Shouting in a mixture of Spanish and broken English, gesturing grandly, they forced the passengers back until they could drag the two still-unconscious hijackers to the door and pass them down to colleagues waiting on the stairs.

By then, the flight attendants had gained the upper hand, and the evacuation proceeded in a more orderly manner. When the time came, Rand moved into the line, drawing Maxine with him. At the door, he lowered her to the first step, tossed out the luggage and leaped down beside her. When they reached solid ground again, dry heat hit him a hammer blow.

Even in growing darkness, he could easily see that they'd landed in the middle of nowhere. Off to his right, a few lights glowed in the distance, evidence of civilization. Other than that, all he could make out was a small concrete block building at the edge of the field and an overabundance of cactus and rocks.

The pilot had it right; this *was* insane. The hijacked plane, on the small size by commercial standards, dwarfed the two private planes parked nearby at the edge of what appeared to be a vast network of crumbling pavement.

Maxine's whole body sagged. "I never thought we'd get off that airplane alive."

He slid an arm around her shoulders and squeezed.

"Hey, don't cave now. You were great. Hell, *we* were great."

She managed a shaky smile. "We weren't bad at that. Do you suppose—"

"That way, *señor*." A uniformed Mexican official bustled up, indicating that they should join the flow of passengers toward a metal shack on the edge of the field. "My colleagues wait to interview all the passengers. We must determine the facts surrounding this crime."

Rand and Maxine exchanged dubious glances. "We don't know a thing, but we're happy to cooperate," he assured the officer. Once out of earshot, he had a different message for her.

"Look," he said in a low voice, "I don't want to get any more mixed up in this than I have to. I'm going to ask that insurance guy if he'll take the responsibility for bringing down the bad guys."

"You'll never get away with it."

"I will if you'll go along with me. Nobody really saw what happened except you, me and that salesman. Jessica and her grandmother were heading the other direction, if you recall, and those up front were cowering, not watching."

"Yes, but—"

"Maxine, please do this."

"Why? You did a brave thing. You should get credit for it."

"It wasn't brave—it was an automatic reflex. I don't *want* credit."

"Or publicity, apparently."

"That, too." She was shrewd, that one. "Will you stick with me on this?"

She drew in a deep breath. "Okay," she relented. "If you can get that guy from Dubuque to lie through his teeth, I suppose it's the *least* I can do."

"Thanks. He's right over there, so how about you watch the luggage while I talk to him." The salesman wasn't going to be a problem, though. He already half believed he'd pulled off the rescue all by himself.

WHEN RAND TOLD the authorities, innocent locals because the big-city boys hadn't yet arrived on the scene, that the villains were brought down by the heroic actions of the insurance salesman from Dubuque, nobody questioned this version of events. Maxine, however, gave him a look that he found almost…calculating.

IN THE DEAD OF NIGHT, Maxine and Rand followed their luggage onto the last of three aged buses for the short ride into the village of Platillo Volante. Exhausted and unhappy, the Alar passengers settled into their seats with barely a murmur.

When the pilot rose at the front of the bus, nobody seemed to care much. Clinging to a pole while the bus careered down the rocky road, he called for attention.

Someone at the back of the bus roused enough to shout a question. "What time will we be taking off tomorrow? I gotta get home to Texas."

"Uh, that's what I have to talk to you about."

Dead silence greeted this announcement. In the third seat from the front, Rand and Maxine exchanged startled glances.

The pilot continued. "I regret to inform you that the plane was damaged in landing. It looks like…it looks like we'll have to bus you folks out of here."

"Bus us out of here!"

"To the nearest decent airport," the pilot elaborated. "Alar Airlines will send in a crew to fix the plane, but it would be too dangerous to have passengers on board when we take her up, even if you wanted to wait around."

"Where's the nearest decent airport, then?"

The pilot squirmed. "They tell me that Platillo Volante is only a few hours from Tijuana. Alar Airlines will send nice, air-conditioned buses to transport us there just as soon as arrangements can be made. In the meantime, you'll be staying at the best hotel in town."

"To hell with this," Rand muttered to Maxine. "I don't have time to sit around in Podunk, Mexico."

"What makes you think you have a choice?" she retorted. "Think of it as a nice Mexican vacation."

She had a point, but he was still fuming over the glitch in his plans when the bus pulled up in front of the "best hotel in all of Platillo Volante." A collective groan arose from the captive guests. If the crumbling exterior of the once-grand building was any indication, they were in for a rough night.

Weary travelers dragged off the bus and stood around in dejected bunches, waiting for the driver to unload their luggage.

And in Rand's case, waiting some more. By the time all the others had picked up their bags and wandered into the hotel, he realized he had a little problem. When the driver would have gotten back on the bus, Rand stopped him.

"Wait a minute. My briefcase is missing."

All this got him was a blank look and a "*¿Señor?*"

"I said—"

"Let me try," Maxine suggested, launching into fluent Spanish.

The man's response was not encouraging. He shrugged, spread his arms wide, said a few words, climbed into the bus and drove away.

"He says—"

"Yeah, I figured it out. My briefcase is missing."

"I'm afraid so."

"Dammit!"

She looked genuinely distressed. "I hope there wasn't anything valuable inside."

"Just my life," he grumbled.

An exaggeration, but he was in no mood to worry about that. In addition to a few personal letters, a magazine or two, an address book and a bottle of water, all he could remember sticking in that briefcase was a safe-deposit key to a box in a bank in Boston—a nearly empty box, unfortunately. Nobody in Mexico was likely to figure that out.

"You can always contact the police," she interrupted his thoughts.

"Think so?" He glowered at her. "You may not have noticed, but I don't speak Spanish."

"Really? Even a little?" She appeared dubious. "I mean, you grew up in Texas, after all."

"What makes you think I grew up in Texas?" He looked around and realized everyone else had gone inside. "I spent most of my time at boarding schools or in Boston with my mother's side of the family." He lifted his remaining piece of luggage. "Summers I spent in Texas, but I only picked up enough Spanish to order *desayuno, comida* and *antojitos*—breakfast, lunch and something to go with the beer." He headed for the hotel door.

She hurried after him. "I still think—"

"I wish you wouldn't. I've got enough trouble without that." He strode through the hotel entrance. "The briefcase is spilled milk. There's no need crying about it."

"Okay, if you're sure."

"I'm sure." Stepping up to an ornately carved desk, he spoke to the grinning clerk. "Wipe that smirk off your face or I'll do it for you. The young lady and I would each like a single with bath. Tell 'im, Maxine."

The clerk's dark eyes flashed and the smile vanished. "Tell the gringo I caught that one," he replied in accents that could only be learned on the mean streets of Los Angeles. "You say you'd like two singles with bath, huh? Well, I'd like a trip to Europe, which is just about as likely." The clerk, José, according to his name tag, reached under the counter, pulled out an ornate key and slapped it down in front of Rand. "Room one."

Embarrassed but too tired and annoyed to apologize, Rand plunged ahead. "Room one—that sounds good. Best in the house, right?" He handed the key to Maxine. "That'll do for the lady. Now, how about me?"

"I told you, room number one. That's all we got left. It's downstairs next to an air conditioner. We don't usually rent it, but since you ask so damn nice—" José's mouth curled up. He was really enjoying this.

Rand stared at the key, then at the clerk. "If I apologize and ask real nice, do you think you could find one more room?"

The man's slowly shaking head ended that line of questioning. "This is all we got. Take it or leave it."

Rand glanced at Maxine. "Do we take it?"

"Have we got a choice?"

"Apparently not." His stomach rumbled. "Any chance we can get something to eat?" he asked José.

The clerk seemed to relent a bit. "I guess I could send something to your room. Nothing fancy, though. A couple of burritos, maybe a quesadilla."

"That sounds great." Rand's mouth watered at the mere mention of food. He hadn't had anything since breakfast, if you didn't count a couple of cheese cubes and a package of pretzels. He looked around. "There wouldn't be anybody handy to show us the way?" José's expression made him add, "No, I suppose not."

"It's just me," the clerk said with a shrug. "I can take you to the room or bring food, your choice."

It really wasn't a choice at all.

RAND'S CLOSET in Boston was bigger than this room. His sister's childhood playhouse behind the Rocking T ranch house was bigger than this room. The desk clerk's *ego* was bigger than this room.

Maxine took the high road. "At least it looks reasonably clean," she said primly, dropping her suitcase at the foot of the bed.

"Reasonably." Rand sat down cautiously on the double bed. Other than that, the only furniture in the tiny room was a small chest of drawers and a night table with lamp.

"If you hadn't been such a jerk, this wouldn't have happened," she said, abandoning the high road.

"That's harsh." He gave her a reproving glance.

"Reality's harsh," she countered. "And the reality is, I'm stuck in this cubbyhole with a complete stranger. I don't deserve this."

"If it's any comfort, neither do I."

"No comfort at all." She opened the top drawer of the bureau and looked in curiously. "How are you going to explain this to your girlfriend?"

"What makes you think I have a girlfriend?"

"You do, don't you?"

"I sure as hell don't." But he wished he did, because then he wouldn't have to figure out how to get around his great-grandpa's will. He could just get married and be done with it. "How about you?" he added.

"How about me what?"

"Got a boyfriend?" As unlikely as that seemed.

Her eyes flashed behind the unattractive glasses. "As a matter of fact—"

A knock on the door interrupted. He pulled a bill from his pocket and handed it to her since she was nearer the door than he and the room wasn't big enough to get past without major maneuvering. She glanced at the bill and her eyes widened; then she passed it on before accepting a small metal tray from unseen hands.

Sitting on the foot of the bed, she put down the tray and lifted the light cloth covering. "On top of everything else, you're an overtipper."

"Hell," he said, "I can afford it." Or could once, but that was none of her damn business.

The heady aromas of spicy Mexican food floated up to him, and his mouth watered again in anticipation. "I'm starved." He reached for a burrito.

"Me, too." She chose a wedge of quesadilla oozing cheese. They ate in silence for a few moments, then opened the two bottles of water and drank.

Eventually she said out of the clear blue, "I wonder what will become of the hijackers."

"I hope whoever locks them up throws away the key." He selected another burrito. He could hardly believe she'd been thinking about those two jerks. "They sure played hell with my life," he went on. "I should be in Hells Bells, Texas, right about now, trying to—" He shut up, musing that he was probably better off stranded here than trying to fast-talk his father.

"Trying to what?"

"Did anyone ever tell you you're nosy?"

"Yes." She gave him that assessing look again. "Does it have anything to do with you giving all the credit for stopping those hijackers to that guy from Dubuque?''

''What if it does? I just don't want my name in the newspapers. What's so strange about that?'' One thing would lead to another. If anything got printed about his recent business reverses, he wouldn't have a snowball's chance in hell of convincing his judges that he was a changed man. ''Besides,'' he added, ''I didn't do all that much.''

''A guy saves an entire plane full of people and dodges credit for it. You don't consider that a bit peculiar?''

''No stranger than setting out for San Antonio and ending up lost in Baja California,'' he improvised. ''Besides, my mother would probably have a heart attack if she heard about this. I want to keep her in a good mood and this wouldn't do it.''

''Why?''

''Why what?''

''Why do you want to keep your mother in a good mood?''

''Because…'' Fed up with her questions, he glared—and gave in. ''Look, I'm on my way to Texas to claim an inheritance. I need my mom's co-operation.''

''That sounds simple enough.'' She brushed crumbs from her skirt.

''You'd think so.'' Shut up, Rand. ''Unfortunately there's nothing simple about it. I don't meet the conditions of the will because, for starters, I'm not married.'' Now, why had he said that? Maybe because he was sick and tired of keeping his problems to himself.

She was incredulous. "You've got to be married to get whatever this is?"

"It was my great-grandpa's bright idea. He left me his ranch and everything on it, which adds up to a small fortune. But to get it, I have to not only be *married* but be *happily* married before I turn thirty."

"Which is—?"

"September 30...less than two weeks."

"Gee, you *are* in trouble." She took a swig from her water bottle. "Look at the bright side. The key word is *married,* because once you've done that, who's to judge what *happily* means?"

"That's easy—my parents and two sets of aunts and uncles. The final say is theirs. But since I'm not married, happily or otherwise, it's a moot point."

"What is it you're trying to get out of them, exactly?"

"I want to break my great-grandpa's will. The only way I can do that is with their help."

"And your chances of pulling that off are...?"

"Only slightly less than slim and none." He was desperate enough to give it a try, however. Cocking his head, he considered. Now that he'd had a little food, he felt worlds better. But he was talking way too much, so he changed the subject. "How about you? How important is that job in San Antonio?"

"You mean the one with the interview set for tomorrow morning at ten—make that *this* morning at ten?" She sighed a bit dramatically. "Not that important, I suppose, since it's out the window now."

"Surely they'll reschedule when they learn what happened."

"I doubt it. I only got the interview as a favor to my sister, who used to date—oh, never mind." She shook her head wearily. "My life's a mess, so what difference will it make if this job doesn't pan out?"

He felt a pang of sympathy. "You're young. You have skills. You can find something. Hell, I'll help you."

"You? But you said you don't even have a job yourself. You're just some rich guy who—"

"Hold on there!" Incensed, he glared at her. "I'm *not* just some rich guy. I have…business interests." Yeah, *failed* business interests. But the situation might improve if he could get his hands on Bill Overton for five minutes. "I also have a certain amount of influence here and there—and even if I didn't, I could get you a job. How hard can it be?"

"Have you ever done it? Gotten anybody a job, I mean."

He had very little experience with gainful employment.

"Your hesitation speaks volumes," she said. "What do your business interests include?"

"Nothing that concerns you." Damn, that sounded hostile.

"I see. You're clamming up on me again."

"Not really. I'm a dull boy."

"Sure you are." She gave him a disgusted glance and rose, still cold. "Thanks so much for your offer of help, but I think I'll find my own job. Now, if you'll excuse me, I'm going to hunt down the bathroom.''

"Okay." He also rose, disconcerted by her attitude. "Don't wake me when you come back in.''

She looked him in the eye, which was easy enough at her height, although he himself was a good six-foot-plus. "That brings up something else. I'm here because I have no choice—here sharing this room with you, I mean.''

"I know that," he said, annoyed.

"I'll stay on my side of the bed and you stay on yours. If you so much as *touch* me, I'll…I'll make you regret it.''

He rolled his eyes, tempted to say that if he touched her it would only be because he was asleep or delirious. "I have no intention of touching you.''

She didn't appear to believe him, despite the nod. "I'm going to sleep fully clothed and I suggest you do the same.''

"Dressed? I can't sleep in my clothes.''

"Under the circumstances, I insist. Your other option is to bed down in the lobby.''

He sighed. "Okay, Maxine. We'll do it your way…this time ''

But never again. If there was one thing she didn't need, it was protection against Rand Taggart.

PLATILLO VOLANTE LOOKED even drearier by the light of day. Dirt roads and adobe buildings were the norm, with a few dilapidated hotels and more gracious dwellings perched on the surrounding hills. But the air was sweet and clear. Rand drew in a deep breath, squared his shoulders for the inevitable crises to come and walked back inside to join Maxine in the crowded dining room for breakfast.

José, the expatriate Los Angeleno, appeared with menus.

Maxine spoke to him in Spanish.

As usual, José answered in English. "I recommend the *huevos rancheros*."

"Works for me." Rand closed his menu.

Maxine nodded. "Me, too."

"Can I ask a question?"

They both looked at Rand as if he were a nuisance.

"What does Platillo Volante mean?" he asked.

José grinned. "It means flying saucer. They say one visited here in the late forties. Everybody thought it would come back, which is why they changed the town's name and built that *campo de aviación*—the flying field that saved your lives. Several fancy hotels went up—" He gestured to the spacious if shabby room. "Rich American tourists came in droves for a while, but when no more flying saucers dropped by, they got mad and went home. By the mid-fifties, the boom was all over." He shook his head in wonder. "Flying saucers—do you believe it? Some people will fall for anything."

Rand didn't need anybody telling him *that*.

THE TWO-LANE PAVED ROAD wound its way through some of the most beautiful country in Mexico or anywhere else. On the left lay the ocean, miles and miles of unspoiled beaches; on the right a range of low mountains shimmered green in the distance.

Rand and Maxine sat near the front of the rattle-trap bus, sweltering in noonday heat. Rand's thoughts were not pleasant.

The hijacking had turned out all right, but unfortunately the Mexican detour had given him time he didn't need, or want, to brood, to question his plan—and to arrive at the unwelcome conclusion that he was on a fool's errand.

He would never gain his family's support in challenging Thom T.'s will. Hell, he'd have a better shot at that inheritance if he hired some bimbo to play his wife and—

An explosion rocked the bus. The driver dragged hard on the wheel, bumping to a stop on the shoulder. Rand let out the breath he'd been holding. That had been a close one.

Maxine stared at him, eyes wide and a hand over her heart. "What happened?"

"Flat tire, I think."

"Do you suppose he has a spare?"

"Who the hell knows?"

There was indeed a spare tire, but it was even balder than the one with the big old nail sticking out of it. While the driver grunted and cussed and toiled, passengers spilled out of the stifling bus and spread out in a vain attempt to find anything cool or shady. Maxine and a few others wandered across the narrow road to stand on the bluff overlooking the ocean.

Finishing the job, the driver wiped sweat from his forehead and lowered the jack. As if sensing imminent departure, Maxine turned from the sea.

Rand caught his breath. For just an instant she

stood there framed against a pristine blue sky. Tendrils of hair blew around her face and the dowdy dress molded a figure he'd never imagined. Just for that moment, she looked…fantastic.

But then she walked toward him and it was the same old Maxine who asked, "Are we ready to go?"

He blinked, figuring he was in worse shape than he'd realized if he saw something that couldn't possibly be there. "Yeah. Get in."

When everyone was aboard, the driver ground the gearshift into first and once more they were under way.

Maxine said suddenly, "What if the bus driver keeled over with a heart attack or decided he'd had enough of this nonsense? Do you know how to drive a standard transmission?"

"Maxine, don't we have enough to worry about without that?"

"Just answer the question."

"Yes, I know how to drive a standard transmission. My great-grandpa taught me out in the pasture in the middle of a bunch of longhorns."

"That's a relief. The way things are going…" She relaxed back against the tattered seat cover. "Is that the same great-grandpa with the kooky will?"

"The very same."

"He must have been a real character," she said. "If you want that inheritance so much, I'm surprised you don't just get married."

"You think that's so easy?" he shot back.

She shrugged. "Piece of cake. I'll bet you've got girls lusting after you from coast to coast."

"Aren't you funny." He gave her a disapproving glance.

"I notice you don't deny it."

"Would it do any good?"

"Probably not." She folded her hands primly in her lap. "Maybe there's one special girlfriend and you'd marry her, but she's...I don't know, unavailable or something."

"Why wouldn't she be available?"

"Lots of reasons. She could be out of the country. Or...in jail?"

Rand laughed incredulously. "You've got the damnedest imagination of any woman I've ever met. Do I look like the kind of guy who'd hang with some babe who'd get thrown into jail? I don't think so."

"I didn't mean to insult you," she said stiffly. "If you don't really care that much about your inheritance, I don't suppose—"

"I *do* care. I care a helluva lot. But I can't go waltzing in with some bimbo and expect my family to fall into line." He grimaced.

"I don't care for the word *bimbo*," she said. "Just what does it cover?"

"You want a definition? It means... Okay, how about this. A bimbo is a woman who goes to bed with a guy on the first date."

"You mean like me?"

He was so shocked he nearly choked. "You didn't—" But she had. She'd gone to bed with him and lain next to him all night, even though they were both fully clothed and wrapped in individual blanket cocoons.

Embarrassed, he tried to turn aside her wrath. "Lighten up, Maxine. Don't take it personal." Uncomfortably aware that he'd blasted her pretty good without meaning to, he added, "You know what you are."

"Yes, but *you* don't." She sounded completely exasperated. "Inside, I could be...Madonna." She glared at him.

"Maybe so, but outside, where the rest of the world can see it, you're...you're..."

"I'm what, Rand Taggart?"

"You're..." Inspiration hit him right between the eyes. "You're *not* a bimbo. In fact, you're just the kind of woman I need to get my family to approve my inheritance."

CHAPTER THREE

"I'M *WHAT?*"

"Take it easy, Maxine. You're just the kind of woman I need to get my family to—"

"I heard that part. What I want to know is what you *meant.*"

"Just that you're smart," he said quickly, wondering why she didn't calm down. "Did we work great together to foil those hijackers or what?"

"Yes, well—"

"And you're *serious.* I mean, you're a serious person. You work for a living."

"You *don't.* Does that mean you're *not* a serious person?"

That stung. "I'm getting serious, okay? It's just a little case of arrested development."

"Oh, really."

Despite her scorn, the idea uttered in jest was seeping deeper into his consciousness. Maxine was an ideal candidate for a make-believe bride. Surely he could get her to see that.

The bus rattled on down the road. After another ten miles or so she said, "I can't imagine you're talking about a real marriage."

"No way." He shuddered. "I could just call my

folks and *tell* them I'm married, let them speak to you, you back me up. *Voilà!* Inheritance released."

"*Voilà!* You've got to be joking. They'd fall for that?"

"I don't know. I never tried to scam my own family before."

"But you have scammed others?"

"I didn't say that." He gave her an annoyed glance. "Hell, at this point, anything's worth a shot."

"Desperate times…"

"You got that right."

The bus passed the turnoff to Ensenada. Eventually a highway sign indicated that Tijuana was just up the road.

She said, as if curiosity had gotten the best of her, "So give me details."

"No details. I'll just tell my mom I'm married. In a perfect world, she'll swoon with delight and declare the terms of the will fulfilled."

Maxine looked pained. "Rand, that will never work."

"I can at least feel her out on the subject." Traffic was increasing, cutting into his concentration. The old junker of a bus rumbled from lane to lane, the driver ignoring the indignant honking of many horns.

Maxine shook her head. "That's crazy."

"Not as crazy as letting a multimillion-dollar inheritance slip through my fingers without even taking a shot at it. What's the worst thing that can happen? Even if they turn me down, I'll be no worse off than I am now."

She pursed her lips disapprovingly. "Why did you wait until the last minute to do this?"

Her question produced silence. He couldn't tell her that he'd never expected to need the Rocking T.

Finally he said, "Something…happened. I don't have access to the majority of my funds at the moment, plus the time just got away from me. Now I'm at the point where I've got to do something even if I do it wrong."

"I see." Strangely enough, she looked as if she really did.

Another long silence ensued and then he said, "It wouldn't hurt you to help me out a little here."

"Probably not."

He frowned. "Maxine, you're not getting into the spirit of this thing. After all, my great-grandpa wanted me to have the ranch or he wouldn't have left it to me, right?"

"He wanted you to have it under certain conditions as specified by *him*."

"Sure, but that's because he was such an old busy-body." Rand couldn't help smiling, remembering Thom T. Taggart. "He was a real character, Maxine. He loved taking credit for getting my folks together, and both my uncles and their wives, too. He was quite the Cupid."

"I've never had a grandpa myself, great or otherwise, but you sound vaguely disrespectful to me."

"I would never disrespect Thom T.," Rand said indignantly. "Neither would anyone else who knew him. He was just about the finest man ever to walk this earth, but he liked playing games. This is one of them. He couldn't hang around long enough to get me and my sister and my cousins married, so he's pulling strings from the grave.''

''Rand!'' She gave him a scandalized glance. ''You can't believe that.''

''I sure as hell do.'' The streets had narrowed and traffic kept increasing. The bus slowed almost to a crawl. ''Looks like the main business district is right up there,'' he said. ''What say we dump this buggy?''

''I'm not sure they'll let us.''

''Why not? We're just innocent victims.''

''I suppose you could try.''

''Got to. The battery's dead on my cell phone and I need to put through that call. You wouldn't happen to have…?''

''Sorry. I don't believe in the things.''

''In that case, we've got to make our break and find a phone. You're with me on this, right?''

''Up to a point. I'm not promising anything, though.''

''If worst comes to worst, I'll let my mom speak to my blushing bride. That'll be you.''

She grimaced and said, ''All right,'' again.

Being nobody's fool, he didn't push it.

MEG TAGGART ANSWERED the telephone on the second ring, her arms overflowing with flowers freshly picked from the garden she cultivated outside the back door of the Hells Bells ranch house. Fresh flowers helped her deceive herself into believing that this rustic existence held a candle to life in her hometown of Boston.

She'd been battling such natural inclinations ever since she'd met Jesse James Taggart, the love of her life. A rodeo cowboy and a Boston socialite were an uneasy mix at best, but somehow they'd managed to work everything out—obviously, since they'd been married thirty-plus years and had two children to show for it.

She supposed one of those children would be on the other end of the line—Clementime, probably, who called at least once a week from her job at Taggart Oil in Houston. Meg said a cheery, "Hello," then buried her nose in the shaggy bouquet of daisies.

"Mom? It's me, Rand."

Meg straightened in surprise and pleasure. "Randy? Honey, it's been so long since we've heard from you." She dropped the flowers on the kitchen counter, instantly alert. Unlike his sister, her only son called rarely. When he did, you could bet he'd slip some bombshell into the conversation. Once, it had been the announcement that he was dropping out of college; another time, that he was moving to Europe.

Still another call was to explain that they shouldn't believe everything they read in the newspapers. That call had occurred just before photos hit the newspapers of him attending the Academy Awards with some actress—"Taylor Thompson and her fiancé, wealthy Texas playboy Rand Taggart..."

"Sorry about that, Mom. I've been...busy."

His voice crackled on the line as if he was a very long way away. Bracing herself for the worst, she said, "Where are you, Randy? This connection is terrible."

"Uh, I'm in Mexico."

"Mexico! What in the world are you doing there?" She'd probably regret asking that.

"Actually…I was hijacked."

"This is a terrible connection. It sounded as if you said you were hijacked."

"I did. I was. Have you heard about the hijack yesterday of a flight from Chicago to some village in Mexico?"

Meg's heart fluttered painfully in her breast and she pressed a hand to her chest. "You mean those two prison escapees who—Randy, you were on *that* plane?"

"Uh-huh, but don't worry. I'm fine. In fact, no one was hurt, just inconvenienced."

"This is terrible," she wailed. "From what I hear, if it hadn't been for that brave man from Iowa—"

"Yeah, old Larry was something, all right." His tone was dry. "That's not why I'm calling, though."

Here it came, the bombshell. Meg sat down heavily on a chrome chair at the breakfast table. "I'm almost afraid to hear this."

"No, Mom, this is good." A long pause; she could picture him taking a deep breath. Then he blurted, "I'm married."

"You're…married?" She repeated the word stupidly, too shocked to censor her disbelief. "Randy!"

His laughter sounded anxious. "Don't have a stroke, Mom. She's exactly the kind of girl you and Dad and Great-granddad always told me I needed."

Images of actresses and models flashed across her mind, not the sensible types she'd longed for her son to find. At almost thirty, he was certainly old enough for marriage, although his maturity was still in doubt.

She was relieved when he filled the silence.

"We were on that plane—me 'n' Maxine, that's her name. We were on our way to tell you and Dad the good news, that we were going to—"

"You mean you're not already married?"

"We are *now*. We ended up in Mexico, where it's easy to get married. It…it seemed like a sign. I mean, why wait?"

"Married…exactly when, Randall?" Oh, she shouldn't have called him by his formal name. She had no right to be angry at his marriage, a marriage she'd yearned for.

Did he hesitate? "This morning, actually. We got married this morning."

She didn't believe him.

Meg Taggart, who took her son's side in all things, who defended him against his father's criticisms, who believed everything he ever said to her, simply didn't believe this. "That's pretty far-fetched, dear," was the best she could come up with. "Tell me the truth. Why so sudden?"

"Well, because…I want to start the legal wheels turning to get my inheritance from Thom T."

"I see."

Only, she didn't. She didn't see at all and he'd said very little to clarify matters. Why would she care about Thom T.'s Rocking T Ranch all of a sudden?

Unless…maybe this Maxine was a ranch girl. Maybe she would be a good influence on Randy.

Meg got hold of herself. "May I speak to her, Randy?"

"Who?"

"Your wife, of course. Maxine, you said?"

"That's right. Maxine. Sure, Mom, you can speak to her."

A brief pause and then another voice came over the line, a woman's voice that was low and cautious. "Mrs. Taggart? It's nice to meet you, so to speak."

"Maxine?" Meg's mouth had gone dry. "Please call me 'Mom,' if you'd like, or 'Mama.' Even 'Meg' would be fine, but no 'Mrs. Taggart,' okay?"

"Of course."

"My son tells me you're married."

Light, perhaps nervous laughter. Then Maxine said, "I warned him it would be a terrible shock, but he said he'd been remiss in not keeping in touch with you in the past. He wants to remedy that, Mrs.— Meg."

"That's good to hear." At a loss, Meg stumbled over her words. "So h-how did the two of you meet, dear?"

"In an airplane. Planes seem to be good luck for us, even when we're being hijacked."

"Oh, don't joke about it! It could have been a tragedy."

"But it wasn't. In fact, it gave Rand and me a chance to…really get to know each other so much better than we did when it all started. I guess you could say we truly…bonded."

Jesse barged through the back door, took one look at his wife and stopped short, his gray eyes narrowing. "What the hell?" he demanded. "Bad news?"

Meg covered the mouthpiece with one hand and shook her head furiously. Licking her lips, she spoke into the phone again. "Well...that's really...uh, it's been nice chatting with you, Maxine. Will you put Randy on again?"

Randy said, "Isn't she great? I told you you'd like her. Uh, Mom, can you start the ball rolling with the lawyers on that inheritance? I'd like to get that taken care of as quick as possible."

"It may not be that easy, dear."

"Why not?"

"They'll want to see your marriage license and then we'll all have to meet her—your father and me, Trey and Rachel and Boone and Kit."

A long silence greeted this explanation. Then her only son said, "You don't believe me."

"That's not it," she protested. "Exactly. I mean, this is awfully sudden. I'm sure when we get to meet her... When *will* we, dear?"

"Soon. Uh, Maxine's schedule is tough, actually. She has obligations in Chicago."

"But—"

"You'll meet her in good time," he cut in defensively.

"That time had better be before September 30," Meg retorted, "because that's the deadline if you really truly want that ranch. And I have my doubts about that."

"Thanks for your support, Mom. I thought of all people you were the one I could count on."

"No, darling. You thought of all people I was the one most easily snowed—and you're right. I hope everything is *exactly* as you say, that you and this girl are madly in love and will live happily ever after. But forgive me if I need more proof than a quickie telephone call from Mexico."

She hung up with a hand that trembled. Automatically she turned to her handsome husband for the support he never failed to offer. "Oh, Jesse! What have I done?"

He threw back his head and laughed. When he straightened, dark hair with only a few strands of gray fell over his forehead. Dressed in the clothing of a working cowboy, he carried a coiled lariat in one hand and a halter in the other. Fearless and frank, Jesse was also solid and unyielding and stubborn as the day was long.

And he loved her. He dropped the halter and the lariat on the floor and took his trembling wife in his arms. "What the hell's that boy done now—gone and got himself married?"

"He says so, but there's something fishy about his story."

He surprised her by saying, "I hope to hell it's true." At her astonished glance, he grinned and added, "Nothing like a little responsibility to make a man grow up fast. Ask me how I know?"

And he kissed her, just as he'd kissed her the first time.

MAXINE SAID, "She didn't believe us."

"Didn't seem to."

"Well, I tried." She walked across the hotel room to look down on the bustling streets of Tijuana.

Rand had gotten the room so they'd have a place to make their calls in peace and quiet—not that it'd done much good. "It wasn't you," he said honestly. "You were great. In fact, you were so great that I've just realized I'm gonna have to watch you in the future. You managed to imply all kinds of stuff without telling a single lie."

"Lying comes easier to some people than to others." She kept her face turned toward the window. "Okay, we tried and it didn't work. We may as well go to the airport and get out of here."

"Uh-uh. Not yet." He picked up the telephone handset. "We've got two more shots. Just stand by...."

"YOUR NEPHEW'S on the phone, Mr. Mayor."

In the mayor's office in Showdown, Texas, attorney Boone Taggart put down the stack of city ordinances he'd been studying and picked up the handset. "Randy, is that you?"

"Sure is, Uncle Boone."

"Bad connection." Boone switched the receiver to the other ear. "What's up, lad?"

"What makes you think something's up?"

"Experience. The last time I heard from you was about 1995 and you wanted me to smooth over one thing or another with your parents."

"Okay, I stand corrected. I'll level with you. I just

got off the phone with Mom and I need help with her.''

"Meg's okay, isn't she?''

"She's fine. Here's the deal. I want to claim my inheritance from Great-grandpa.''

"You'll never break that will,'' Boone said. "Guaranteed.''

"I don't want to break it—I want to comply with it.''

Boone, an expert at reading between the lines, put two and two together in a flash. "You called Meg to tell her you're married. I'd have expected her to be pleased.''

"If she believed me, which I don't think she did. Do me a favor and convince her, okay? I got married this morning in Mexico and...''

As the boy explained, Boone could hardly keep from chuckling. He didn't blame Meg for being dubious and said so first chance he got, ending with, "If you want my help, bring your wife here and give us all a chance to meet her and decide for ourselves if you've fulfilled the conditions of that will. It's the only way.''

A sigh. Then Rand said, "Yeah, I guess I'll have to do that. You can't blame me for hoping, though. Give my love to Aunt Kit, okay?''

"Will do.''

"I was sorry to hear about her cancer surgery.''

"That was three years ago.'' Boone hated to be reminded of the toughest ordeal his wife—or he—had ever faced. "We had a happy ending, anyway.''

"That's what Mom said. The kids okay?''

"Yeah, they are." Travis was eighteen and had just entered his senior year at Showdown High School; Cherish was an adorable eleven-year-old and still Daddy's girl.

"That's good. Okay, Uncle Boone, I'll be in touch soon."

Boone doubted it. He really did. For some reason, Randy wanted the ranch he'd ignored for nearly ten years and was willing to hustle his own family to get it.

What the hell. Taggart family life had been way too tame since Thom T. had died.

THE TELEPHONE was ringing when Trey Smith finally got the door open to his ranch house in the San Fernando Valley. This was Rachel's day to work at the free clinic and the kids were in school, so his footsteps made lonely echoes across the hardwood floors.

"Yeah," he said into the phone, "I'm here."

"Uncle Trey, it's Rand."

"Rand who?" Trey looked down at the mail on a small silver plate next to the phone, then began sifting idly through it.

"Ha, ha, very funny. Randy, your favorite nephew, who else?"

"Oh, *that* Rand. What's up, kid?"

"Nothing much. I was hijacked to Mexico and I got married. You're the next stop on the family gauntlet."

"Married?" Trey straightened. "What took you so long?"

"That's the spirit." The kid sounded relieved. "Mom and Uncle Boone were less enthusiastic."

"Any particular reason?"

"Who knows?" Rand sounded disgusted. "The deal is, I want to claim that inheritance Great-grandpa left me and I've only got something less than two weeks to do it in. I thought Mom or Uncle Boone could start the ball rolling, but they seem to have a problem with this marriage."

"There's an easy way out of that."

"Name it!"

Ah, such eagerness. No wonder Meg and Boone weren't buying the boy's story. "Take your blushing bride on the grand family tour. Where are you calling from, by the way?"

"Mexico."

"Oh, yeah, the hijacking."

"How did you—?"

"It figures, that's all. Anyway, bring your bride here to meet your dear old Uncle Trey and Aunt Rachel—we're closest and easiest to convince. Then you can tackle the rest of 'em."

"Time is of the essence here."

"Time's *been* of the essence for damn near ten years. Now all of a sudden you're in a hurry?"

"Good point," Rand said. "Okay. Gotta go, but you'll be hearing from me."

"Wanna bet?" Trey asked nobody in particular. He hung up the phone. Wait until he told Rachel about this. That kid was up to something, sure as the world. Trey wished him luck but knew it would take more than that to get anything past Daniel Boone and

Jesse James Taggart, even if their wives tended to be soft touches.

"WELL, HELL." Rand gave Maxine a dour look. "I must have been nuts to think that would work."

"I told you so." She picked up another tortilla chip from the basket on the tray delivered earlier by room service, painfully aware of the trembling of her hand. "I guess that's that, then."

"Not so fast. I haven't given up yet."

She waited, her heart in her throat.

Suddenly his eyes widened. "Why didn't I see this before? We have to *really* get married. That should be easy in Mexico, and equally easy to get *un*married once we've achieved our ends."

Maxine gasped. "You can't be serious. When I get married it will be once and for all."

"This won't count against that," he argued, "because this will be a business arrangement."

"You just said—"

"It will be *legal* but not *real*, in that we won't really be husband and wife."

"Meaning no sex and I wouldn't have to live with you?" Blunt but precise.

"Meaning no sex but you would have to make what Trey called the 'grand family tour' to convince everyone concerned that we're married and madly in love. Then you can do anything you want to do, with my blessings."

She regarded him for a moment in silence, her heart throbbing erratically. She had never expected anything like this, even in her wildest imaginings. Finally she said, "Isn't that kind of a dirty trick?"

He obviously didn't want to consider that aspect, but she'd forced the issue. "I guess it might look that way," he said slowly, "but…my back's to the wall, Maxine. There are complications you know nothing about."

"Go on."

"Not now. Look." He hauled out his checkbook. "Let's be businesslike about this. I want to hire you for a maximum of…say, one month? That should be enough time to do what I have to."

"Hire me?" She couldn't believe what she was hearing.

"That's right. I'll pay you ten thousand dollars now and another twenty if we pull this off and I get my inheritance."

She gasped. "What makes you think I can be bought?"

"You're out of a job, right? Besides, I don't want to buy you. I just want to rent you for a little while. What do you say?"

"Give me a minute to think." She pressed her palms to her temples. "If I do this—and I'm not saying I will—there will be absolutely *no sex.*"

His expression said he had absolutely no interest in her *that* way. "No sex. Agreed."

"Put it in writing."

"Sorry, no can do. You'll have to trust me on that."

"Why should I? Why should you trust me?"

He eyed her solemnly. "Maxine," he said slowly,

"I always go with my first impressions. My first impression of you is that you're a woman who *can* be trusted. I liked the way you handled yourself on that airplane and the way you stood up for yourself when we had to share that room. As Great-grandpa Taggart would say, 'Girl, you got spunk!'"

She couldn't return that smile. "I suppose your first impressions are always right."

"I wish. Sometimes you just have to go on faith." He put out his hand. "Is it a deal?"

She looked at that hand in panic. She'd never bargained for anything like this, but maybe it was a golden opportunity. Squaring her shoulders, she took a deep breath and slipped her hand into his for the briefest of shakes.

"Rand Taggart," she said, "you're out of your mind—but okay, I'll go along for the ride. We'll have to do some homework. I'll have to know everything there is to know about you."

"We'll worry about that later. First we have to get married. It's supposed to be easy in Mexico, right? Where should we go to?"

"Rosarito Beach," she said promptly, a plan popping into her head full-blown. "It's just a few miles south and there's a wonderful old hotel I...I've visited before."

He shrugged as if it didn't much matter so long as they did the deed. "Works for me. I'll rent a car and tell the authorities we won't be flying out this afternoon with the rest of the hijackees."

"I'll call the hotel. I can make reservations and see what's involved in arranging a wedding."

Rand nodded, his expression a blank. Was he as shocked as she was to be involved in such a scheme?

WHEN IT ACTUALLY HAPPENED, events proceeded with such smoothness that he never did get his bearings.

The drive south on a paved and well-maintained highway passed in a blur. After being welcomed with smiles and champagne at the stately old beachfront hotel, they were escorted upstairs to a lavish suite overseeing a pool, the beach and the ocean. An official-looking gentleman waited for them there. He declared himself to be from the Oficina del Registro Civil, whatever the hell that was, and launched into some long explanation in Spanish.

Maxine translated: "He'd like to see our driver's licenses…sign here, it means you've never been married before—you haven't, have you?"

"Are you kidding?" Rand signed in his usual slashing letters: *Thomas Randall Taggart.*

"He's waiving the blood test," she translated.

"Blood test!"

"Relax." She listened, nodded. "He's arranged for witnesses. We need two apiece."

"I thought getting married in Mexico was simple," Rand grumbled. "Sure, anything. Let's just get this over as fast as we can."

The preliminaries took longer than the ceremony. Rand didn't know what he was saying *sí* to, but he said it just the same. He took some comfort in Maxine's fluent Spanish; at least one of them would know what the hell had happened.

There was a moment's confusion when neither could produce a ring, but with shrugs all around, the ceremony proceeded to its logical conclusion...at which point Maxine looked at Rand expectantly.

"What?"

"You can kiss the bride." She offered her cheek.

He'd be damned if he was going to get married and kiss his bride on the cheek. Grabbing her, he planted his mouth squarely on hers.

And got the shock of his life. Her lips were soft and warm and...dammit, exciting. He jerked back as if stung.

The Mexican official and the four witnesses applauded. Embarrassed because he was such a fraud, Rand belatedly realized that Maxine appeared downright exasperated. She did, however, manage an unconvincing smile.

"Now we have to sign on the dotted line," she said through clenched teeth.

"No problem." Hell, no. The deed had been done. He was willing to sign anything they put in front of him.

The official offered a copy of the marriage certificate along with a smile and another burst of incomprehensible Spanish.

"Now what?" Rand automatically turned to Maxine.

"Now you escort everyone to the door, hand the gentleman who performed the ceremony a few hundred dollars and each witness a hundred, say 'Thank you' in your barbarous tongue and close the door."

He could do that.

RAND GREASED the palm of each person passing through the doorway with nods and farewells and congratulations. When everyone was gone, he shut the door, gave Maxine a thumbs-up and crossed to the bottle of champagne chilling in a silver bucket.

At which point Maxine aimed a forefinger at his sleek back, cocked her thumb and silently mouthed a single word: *Gotcha!*

CHAPTER FOUR

SOME WEDDING NIGHT.

Maxi stole a glance at her handsome "husband." He leaned against the wrought-iron balcony just beyond the open French doors, staring across moonlit water as if he could see forever.

When in actual fact he couldn't see *anything*. Otherwise he wouldn't be here with the one woman in the world devoted to bringing him down.

"More champagne?"

He turned so unexpectedly that she jumped in surprise. "Sure." She held out her empty crystal flute. "Why not? After all, I don't get married every day."

"You're mad at me." He crossed with a natural grace to the hammered-silver ice bucket. For a big man—more than six feet tall and broad-shouldered—he moved with surprising ease. He picked up the bottle and examined the label. "Why?"

She should keep her mouth shut but decided against it. After all, she'd be "living" with this guy for the foreseeable future and the "Meek Minnie" act was hard to maintain. "Because you kissed me," she said. "You had no right to do that, especially after we agreed there'd be no sex."

He laughed and started toward her. "That wasn't sex. That wasn't even *close* to sex."

Then why had she been thunderstruck the instant his lips touched hers? Why had she felt all kinds of unwelcome physical sensations?

With unfriendly eyes, she accepted the glass of wine he offered. Fortified by a drink, she said, "You had no right to touch me."

"You're wrong." He sat down on a white brocaded ottoman, so close his knees nearly brushed hers. "Get used to it, Maxine."

"I will not!" She took a defiant sip of champagne. "Why should I?"

"Because we made a deal. If we're going to convince anyone that this is real, I'll have to touch you once in a while." His broad mobile mouth curved up at the corners in a devilish grin. "We just got married. If I never lay a hand on you, what will everyone think?"

"Probably the truth—that we're faking it."

"In which case I won't get my inheritance and you won't get your money."

She wanted to tell him that she wasn't doing this for the money but couldn't without tipping him off. "Okay," she conceded, her tone cross. "Just don't forget we're talking *public*. In private, touch me and you die."

He looked at her as if she were a deluded child. "No problem," he said much too cheerfully. "You're not my type." He yawned, lending emphasis to what was essentially an insult.

Giving her knee a friendly pat, he rose and wandered back outside onto the balcony, leaving her to seethe alone. Of *course* she wasn't his type. In this getup, she wasn't *anybody's* type, which was the point of it for a woman who made her living as a model for Violet's Advantage, the fast-rising Los Angeles lingerie company. No way would she be able to do what had to be done if she had to spend every moment fighting him off.

For the truth was, Maxi didn't get on that airplane and settle into the seat next to Rand Taggart's by accident. There was no job in San Antonio. She'd simply been wishing to strike up a conversation with him in the hope of hearing something—anything— she could use against him. She'd even stolen his briefcase in the hope of finding something incriminating.

What she'd found was a few personal items: some kind of funny key, a few magazines—nothing to help her cause. She'd felt guilty dumping them all in a handy trash bin at the Platillo Volante airport, but not guilty enough to be deterred. Maxi was on a mission.

Staring at his silhouette, she brooded over her champagne. This man had turned her life upside down when he'd involved her older sister, Helen, in an embezzlement and money-laundering scheme. Because of him, Helen was incarcerated in a Chicago jail. Maxi wouldn't rest until her sister was vindicated and justice had triumphed.

Helen's arrest had been an awful shock. Maxi had immediately walked out on a modeling assignment

to fly from L.A. to Chicago and her sister's side.
There Helen had told her tale of woe:

She'd already been working for several years as
executive secretary to Bill Overton, president and
CEO of Coconutty, manufacturer of health concoc-
tions and suntan products based on coconut oil, when
he'd set out to raise money to take his company into
Internet marketing. That was when his old college
roommate, Rand Taggart, had arrived on the scene
as a potential investor.

Rand seemed like a terrific guy, Helen had said
darkly, until you got to know him. In truth, he was
a rich and ruthless playboy with no concern for anybody else.

Maxi's suspicions were immediately aroused.
"Was there something going on between you and
this Rand Taggart?" she'd asked.

Helen paled. "No! How can you even suggest
such a thing?"

"Because I know you, Helen. There's always a
man. Did he sweep you off your feet, use you and
leave you holding the bag?"

Helen looked evasive. "I don't have to answer
that. Please, Maxi, just stay out of this. I don't need
or want your help."

"I can't stay out of it. You're my sister and I love
you. First, I'm going to pay your bail. Then we can
decide what to do next."

Helen shook her head. "No! Go back to L.A. and
don't get involved. Bill—Mr. Overton will take care
of me."

"But hasn't he disappeared? Aren't the police hunting for him, not Rand Taggart?"

"Only because the police are in cahoots with Rand Taggart. He's done everything in his power to make us appear guilty, but Mr. Overton and I are *innocent*. Rand is the real crook—you wouldn't believe all the schemes and scams he's involved in! Mr. Overton has to be free to gather evidence to clear us because nobody else is going to."

"What specifically are you accused of?" Maxi asked.

Helen looked disgusted. "They say I couriered stolen money to the Caribbean. Do you believe it? Sure, I've vacationed in the islands a few times, but so have thousands of other Chicagoans. That doesn't prove a thing."

"I believe you, Helen, but maybe your boss isn't as honest."

"Isn't it proof of his innocence that he's retained his own lawyer, R. Renwood Keever, to defend me? He sent word, Maxi. I'm to sit tight until he can clear me or raise bail."

"But—but—" Maxi stammered. "I can't leave you in here and just go on with my life."

"You've got to." Helen's mouth tightened. "You're out of your depth, Maxi. Mr. Overton is my only hope and I'm going to do exactly what he says."

"Then maybe there's some way I can find out what this Taggart person is up to, or at least—"

"For the last time, stay out of it!" Helen's eyes

flashed and her mantle of persecution fell away. "The best thing you can do for me is *nothing*."

Helen had asked for the only thing Maxi couldn't give. If she couldn't bail her sister out, maybe she could help clear her. But how?

A meeting with Helen's attorney had provided an unexpected answer. R. Renwood Keever had waved a leather passport case beneath her nose while reporting that Rand Taggart was about to flee the scene of his perfidy.

"The man thinks of nothing but himself," Keever had declared indignantly. "He came here to my office, looking for trouble and making all kinds of threats against my client, Mr. Overton. Then he announced he was leaving town, but he'd be back, which I took as a threat. When I mentioned your sister, he said, 'And your point is?' If professional ethics didn't demand that I return these documents to him..."

Maxi's pulse quickened. "Is his passport in there?"

"Yes, and an airline ticket—apparently fell out of his pocket when he stomped out of here. Like I have time to do him favors—"

"Let me. Do you know where he's staying?"

"Yes, but—"

She snatched the case from his wavering hand, her heart pounding so she thought he might hear it. "Consider it done."

Her opinion of Attorney Keever was not high, but at least he was on the correct side in this matter. "Don't worry," she assured him, "I'll take care of everything. Goodbye, and thank you for all you're doing for my sister...."

Outside on the sidewalk, she'd opened the passport case with trembling hands. An incredibly handsome man stared back at her from a cheap passport photo. Poor Helen! No wonder she'd gone gaga over this guy.

Then Maxi had turned to the ticket: an Alar Airlines direct flight to San Antonio.

She'd booked the seat next to his out of pure desperation. She wanted to see, in the flesh, the man who'd wreaked havoc with Helen's life. Maybe she could strike up a conversation, even uncover some clue. If he thought she was just a fellow traveler, he might give something away—mightn't he?

Unfortunately, she had no practice or even talent for ferreting out information from someone who chose not to be ferreted. Nevertheless she must try. Certain that Maxi Rafferty wouldn't get anything out of Rand Taggart beyond the usual pass, she'd decided to call upon her alter ego, plain Maxine Rafferty.

But first she had to call her agent, Ron Walters, who freaked when she told him she was flying to Texas. She'd already missed one modeling date and if she wasn't back by Monday—

Like she cared. Modeling was a job, not her life, and she was getting tired of all the hassle anyway. She'd saved practically every penny she'd ever made, so if the gravy train ran off the tracks tomorrow, as she fully expected it would, she'd shed not a single tear.

She *did* care that Rand Taggart was so damn
cagey. All that time together on the plane, all that
stress, and he'd never uttered a word about Coconutty or anything connected to it. All he'd said was
that he "didn't have access to the majority of his
funds at the moment." Yeah, like he'd stolen his
own money and that of many others, but all those
lovely tax-free dollars were hidden away because the
heat was on and would be for who knew how long.

Of course he needed his great-grandfather's be-
quest!

It took a cool customer to sit back calmly while
armed hijackers spread fear and panic. If that little
girl hadn't been in danger, Maxi doubted he would
ever have acted. Even then, he'd gone to great
lengths to avoid attention. This was distinctly unguy-
like, in her experience.

He wanted to avoid the spotlight for nefarious reasons, she was sure of it. But should she have gone
this far to find out what they might be?

He interrupted her thoughts by turning back inside,
all rumpled male beauty with unbuttoned collar and
shirttail hanging out of his trousers. For an instant
she almost wished they'd met under other circumstances...

She cut off *that* line of thought double-quick. She
wasn't here to sleep with the enemy or even to get
friendly; she was here to clear her sister's name. To
do that, she'd somehow wound up in this place she'd
so enjoyed during a photo shoot a couple of years
ago.

Lingerie modeled on beautiful sandy beaches...

everyone fawning over the models, while margaritas flowed like water...

Rand Taggart yawned and stretched, the soft blue shirt stretching tight across his chest.

"I'm whipped," he sighed. "I don't think I've had a decent minute's rest since we left Chicago."

She just looked at him, thinking, *Why are you telling me this?*

"You're sitting on my bed," he elaborated.

She glanced at the pale-gray goose-down sofa on which she sat.

He nodded. "I'm giving you the bedroom."

"You take it," she decided. "I'm not ready to go to bed yet. I'll sleep out here."

"Are you sure?" Another prodigious yawn overtook him.

"I'm sure."

She watched him wander off toward the bedroom, footsteps dragging. Sighing, she settled back on the sofa with her champagne.

This wasn't even close to the way she'd dreamed of spending her wedding night, but at least the setting was right. This suite was fabulous, not new, but so classy and sophisticated with its green-and-white decor that she just wanted to sink into it and not come up. The champagne was right; the gentle breeze ruffling sheer balcony curtains was right.

Everything else was wrong. Rand Taggart was not the man of her dreams, wouldn't have been even if she didn't know what she knew about him. When the time was right, she would set her sights on a sensible, hardworking, professional man: doctor, lawyer, merchant chief, something along those lines.

Meanwhile she'd turned her attention to earning a living, leaving little time for romance. Strike that, she corrected herself. Rising, she walked outside onto the balcony, wanting to see what he'd seen. In her type of work, guys didn't romance her—they hit on her. Just because they could view her whenever they wanted to in her underwear—make that Violet's Advantage lingerie—they seemed to think she owed them something.

At least Rand hadn't come on to her, which both pleased and annoyed her. She didn't want him to see through her deception, but she didn't enjoy being overlooked like some wallflower, either. She'd fallen into modeling without ever expecting it to last, since, as her mother had always taught her, "Pretty is as pretty does."

But that didn't mean she didn't enjoy occasional male appreciation. How would Rand react if she did masterful things with hair and makeup, put on something clingy and revealing—

Forget it. Finishing the last drops of champagne, she leaned her elbows on the iron railing with a sigh. She was an honest person involved in a dishonest undertaking. She was in over her head, but she had no choice but to go forward.

She owed her sister too much to take the easy way out.

MAXINE LOOKED different in her sleep.

Softer. Prettier. Sweeter. Somehow almost…desirable.

Rand shook his head in amazement. He was seeing things that weren't there. This was Maxine Rafferty—make that Taggart, Maxine Taggart—not some sex kitten.

A soft knock brought him swinging toward the door. He'd phoned for coffee and breakfast from the bedroom and didn't want the waiter to awaken her. Too late. She sat up abruptly, obviously groggy, and shoved a hand through her tousled hair.

She had slept fully dressed. What the hell?

"What is it?" She glanced around in drowsy confusion.

"Breakfast."

"Oh, Lord, don't open that door until I get out of here!" Leaping from the bed, she fled toward the second bathroom, where she'd undoubtedly stashed her things.

Feeling like a jerk for sleeping so well and so long in the bed while she struggled with the couch, he tipped the waiter and pulled the cart inside himself. By the time she reappeared, he had everything set up and waiting on the balcony.

He gestured. *"Desayuno,"* he said grandly.

She laughed. With her hair combed back and her glasses firmly in place, she resembled her sensible self again. "You really should learn a little more Spanish."

"Why, when I have you to translate?" He held a chair for her.

She sat down and reached for the coffeepot.

"Mmm, this smells heavenly. A lot of my friends are tea drinkers but nothing beats a good cup of coffee in the morning."

"That's how all us Taggarts feel. You'll fit right in." He took his own place. "Thom T. used to say tea drinkers were a bunch of sissies."

"Your great-grandpa sounds like quite a man."

Rand smiled. "He was. The old guy was doing his damnedest to reach a hundred, but he missed it by ten days. I couldn't believe it." He shook his head at the memory of his father's phone call. He'd never heard Jesse Taggart so broken up. "I thought he'd live forever," he added softly.

"I wish I'd known him."

The sincerity in her tone earned her a sharp glance. That had sounded almost...wifely. "You won't be able to meet him, but you'll get to see him in action."

Her eyebrows rose above the glasses. "Are we talking séance?" She lifted the silver lid from her plate and looked down with approval at a steaming plate of shredded beef with chopped onions, peppers and tomatoes mixed with scrambled eggs and topped with melting cheese and a red sauce.

"We're talking film," he said. "Thom T. videotaped his will. I've never seen it myself, but maybe I'm ready to do that now. Enough years have passed..." He trailed off. It had been cowardly of him to skip the "reading" of Thom T.'s will, but at the time, he didn't think he could have handled it.

"I see." She plucked a hot tortilla from the basket. "So what's our next move?"

"I've been thinking about that. I've decided to do this the easy way, if there is such a thing."

"Meaning?"

"As much as I hate to, I've got to trot you and the marriage license out for inspection. We'll start with my uncle Trey and aunt Rachel. They'll be infinitely easier to convince than my parents or Uncle Boone and Aunt Kit."

"You have funny names in your family." She tore off a piece of tortilla. "Jesse, Boone—"

"Funnier than you realize. My dad's full name is Jesse James Taggart and his brother is Daniel Boone Taggart. Thom T. used to get all bent out of shape when people called attention to their names. Said they were all named for grand-uncles and great-great-grandpas and who knows who all."

"You believe that? Sounds to me like someone just had a sense of humor."

"Could be." He picked up his fork. "But I believed him."

"How about this uncle Trey? Someone in your family was named 'three'?"

He grinned. "You're close. Trey represents a long-lost branch of the family. His full name is Thomas Trenton Taggart Smith—three Ts, get it? He grew up in foster homes and on the streets and didn't even know he *was* a Taggart until Thom T. hunted him down and dragged him kicking and screaming to Texas."

"I sense a story there."

"Quite a story. Trey was a movie stuntman back then. Today he's a second-unit director in Hollywood, and handles action sequences for some really big flicks. He's led a different kind of life and he's a lot more laid-back than my dad or Boone.''

''What about his wife?''

''Aunt Rachel was the Showdown town librarian—Showdown's a little old Texas burg near the Rocking T Ranch. She already had a son when Trey came to town. Now they've got sixteen-year-old twin boys, too.''

Maxine groaned. ''How will I ever keep everyone straight?''

''Don't worry about it,'' he advised. ''When you meet them, it'll all straighten out for you.''

''Do Uncle Trey and Aunt Rachel live in Hollywood?''

''In the Valley. We'll fly to L.A. and rent a car.''

''Today?'' She looked almost frightened, as if this were all happening too fast.

Which, of course, it was. ''If we can get out,'' he said. ''We'll drive to the Tijuana airport and see what it takes to get past the authorities.'' He made a face. ''Nobody was too crazy about us taking this little side trip instead of flying out yesterday with everybody else.''

Her forehead creased in a disapproving frown. ''You didn't tell me that.''

He shrugged. ''I didn't want to worry you. Who cares whether they approve of our plans or not. It's none of their damn business what we do.''

She didn't look convinced but let the subject drop. ''I need to do some shopping.''

''I assumed you would.''

She frowned. "What's that supposed to mean?"

"You're a woman. Women always need to do some shopping. I learned that at my mother's knee."

"If that's how you feel about it—"

"Maxine, lighten up!" He leaned forward to pat her arm, which she quickly pulled away. She was tense, way too tense. "This is never going to work if we examine every word we say in case some offense was intended. We'll stop on our way out of town, okay?"

"Okay." She had the good grace to look ashamed of herself.

"We'll ask at the desk if there's a place—"

"I know a place," she said. At his incredulous glance, she added, "Well, I do. I've been to Rosarito before on a sort of...a working vacation, I guess you could call it."

"Maybe someday you'll come back just for the fun of it," he said. "I've been to Cancún and Acapulco, but I've got to say, this place appeals to me more. It's quieter and more...real."

She nodded. "The funny thing is, when I came here before, I thought what a wonderful place this would be for a honeymoon. I never dreamed that someday..."

Their glances met and something clicked, some unspoken acknowledgment that life really *was* what happened while you were busy making other plans.

"YOU'RE NOT GOING to get *that* one."

Maxi continued to admire the white cotton nightie

frosted with lace at the high neckline and the wrists. "I certainly am. I love it."

"It looks like something a nun would wear." Rand held out a long, tiered and brightly embroidered dress. "I like this one."

"To sleep in?" Maxi carried her choice to the cash register at one end of the overflowing counter.

"Of course not, but—"

"I need a nightgown, Rand." Desperately. She'd slept in her clothing last night because the nightgown in her bag had come from Violet's collection and left absolutely *nothing* to the imagination. She might not be Rand's type, but that nightgown sure would be.

"You need this, too." He tossed the dress on top of her selections and smiled broadly at the curious dark-eyed teenager waiting for their money. "You take Visa, I hope?"

"*Sí, señor.*"

"I can pay—" Maxi stopped short. He *should* pay for these things, of course. She added a belated, "Thank you."

"And this." Rand held out a small silver circle. "I'm sorry it's not diamonds, but under the circumstances…"

Her heart gave a funny little lurch when she heard that cliché about diamonds. Glancing up, she caught an almost tender expression on his face. "I don't need a ring," she said, her voice husky.

"Of course you do. We should have had it for the ceremony, but better late than never. Put out your hand so we can see if it fits."

She could hardly bring herself to comply with his

very reasonable request. So far this all seemed like a dream, but a ring, even a cheap little silver band from a hole-in-the-wall shop in Mexico, carried with it a certain reality she couldn't ignore.

"Please, Maxine."

Holding her breath, she extended her left hand slowly. He slipped the ring over the third finger, halting at the knuckle. "With this ring," he murmured, then slid it into place.

She'd been blindsided. What an awful thing to say! He had no right to joke about something as important as marriage and its symbols. For two cents, she'd give him a tongue-lashing he wouldn't soon forget—

If he hadn't already turned back to the counter to offer his credit card. She was stuck with this ring. She glared down at it, such a perfect fit that it might have been made for her.

She pressed her lips together. Someday she'd have the pleasure of snatching this ring off and flinging it in his face.

But not today. Today they had a lot of territory to cover.

Unfortunately they hit a snag at Tijuana International Airport. As the last passengers from the ill-fated Alar Airlines plane to leave Mexico, they had "a lot of 'splainin' to do," as the scowling policeman pointed out. Although their stories never varied, he still didn't seem convinced until Maxine burst into tears and declared herself mortified to be spending her first full day of married life in an airport being grilled by the *policía*.

"That was a stroke of genius," Rand commended her fifteen minutes later while he buckled himself into his seat for the short flight north.

She grinned. "Since it worked, I agree. Once he saw our marriage license he was a different man."

"You hang on to that license," he ordered. "We'll have to show it around a lot in the next couple of weeks."

"Aye, aye, sir."

"Wise guy." But he gave her a friendly smile, gratified that she was smart enough to see a loophole and grab it. Leaning back in his seat, he sighed. "We're getting out of Mexico a lot later than I expected. We'd better spend the night in a hotel in Los Angeles and call Trey and Rachel in the morning."

"All right." She looked thoughtful. "I've been thinking about what you mentioned earlier today. They really sound like the odd couple."

"How so?"

"You said he was a movie stuntman and she was a librarian. If that's not odd, I don't know what is."

"I never thought of it that way," he admitted. "They've just always been part of my family. I was about six or seven when they got married, so I never questioned it. Still…"

She perked up. "Still what?"

"Mom told me once that Trey and Rachel had a hard time getting together. Rachel thought he was a conniving con man, and fought tooth and nail to keep Thom T. away from him and vice versa."

Maxine smiled. "I'll bet Trey figured Rachel was a small-town prude."

"Lucky guess." He returned her dazzling smile.

"They say opposites attract. In their case, opposites fell in love and it lasted."

"Lucky them," Rand said, but he was thinking *Go figure* and eyeing Maxine with considerable doubt about the "opposites attract" theory.

CHAPTER FIVE

MAXI THOUGHT they would *never* get away from LAX. Once they did—in an extravagant red convertible instead of the cheap compact she'd have chosen—she sighed and leaned back against the soft leather upholstery. A million stars glittered and gleamed overhead.

Maybe a convertible wasn't such a bad idea after all. It was *his* money—or Coconutty's, as the case might be.

He hit the freeway as if he'd been driving one all his life. "Where'll we stay?" he asked. It was obviously a courtesy question. "I know of several nice hotels. They're a little out of our way, but—"

"How about the nearest Motel Six?"

His laughter was incredulous. "You're kidding, right?"

She should be. "Wrong. Look, it's already late and all we're going to do is sleep," she pointed out. "Why pay a fortune for some fancy hotel when we'll only be in it for a few hours? Just stop at the first decent place you see."

"Maxine Taggart, you're cheap!" he accused.

"I'm thrifty. There's a difference." She hoped.

"I told my mother she'd love you. If she finds out

you're trying to put me on a budget, she'll worship you.''

''I hope not. I won't be around long enough for her to get attached to me.'' Or vice versa. She must keep her distance from these people he was trotting her around to meet. *They* must like her, but *she* mustn't like them…not too much, anyway.

''Are you hungry?'' he asked suddenly. ''It's kind of late to find anything but fast food, I'm afraid.''

''I could handle a hamburger.'' She sat up suddenly, alerted by neon on the frontage road paralleling the freeway. ''Get off at the next ramp and circle back! There're a bunch of fast-food places and several motels.''

''I really thought you were joking,'' he said. ''You want to stay in some sleazy motel instead of a nice four- or five-star hotel?''

''Not sleazy,'' she said firmly. ''Inexpensive. There's a difference.''

''If you say so.'' He maneuvered off the freeway and onto the frontage road leading to the cluster of restaurants and motels. ''But remember, this is your idea.''

AND NOT A BAD ONE, as it turned out. Even Rand had to admit the room was clean and neat, with two double beds to simplify their sleeping arrangements. While Maxine showered and prepared for bed, he flipped through the television channels and wondered why he suddenly felt very married indeed.

He had the name, but he sure didn't have the game.

He grinned, remembering how mention of a convertible and fancy hotels had horrified her. Something had happened to her along the line, something he couldn't as yet comprehend. Idly he watched a man demonstrate a knife that could apparently slash through anything, up to and including a truck tire.

Sometimes Rand felt as if he was on the verge of slashing through her defenses and finding the real Maxine. But the feeling quickly dissipated. She played everything too close to the vest, remaining incredibly self-contained and lacking in spontaneity.

He leaned back on one of the beds, hands cupping his head on the pillow. Tomorrow would be a real test for both him and her. He would be trying to convince a very savvy man and an equally intelligent woman that not only was he married, he was in love.

With a woman named Maxine?

Not very damned likely! When she walked out of the bathroom covered from chin to toe in virginal white, he said, "Maxine, there's something we have to get straight."

She looked startled. "This sounds ominous."

"Not really. It's…your name."

She frowned and reached for a hairbrush. "What's wrong with it?"

Besides the fact that it was butt ugly? He couldn't say *that*.

"It's too formal," he announced. "Maxxxx-*eene*." He drew it out. "No Taggart would ever call his wife Maxxx-*eene*."

A smile tugged at those full lips. "In that case, what *would* a Taggart call her?"

"Max," he announced promptly. "Does that work for you?"

She appeared amused. "I've been called worse."

"Then Max it is." He crawled off the bed. "How's the shower?"

"Limp. Not much water pressure, but I persevered."

He had a feeling that perseverance was probably one of her strongest suits.

RAND CALLED Trey and Rachel after breakfast—English muffins with hard-cooked egg and plastic cheese. Not half-bad. Coffee stunk, though.

This time Rachel answered.

"Hi, Aunt Rachel. It's Rand. I thought I might bring Max by to meet you later today, if that's not inconvenient."

"Max?"

"Maxine—my wife. I call her 'Max.'" He winked at said wife. "Trey told you I'm married, right?"

"Of course." Her voice soared. "This is wonderful! Trey's home, too—he doesn't start the new picture for a couple of weeks so he's underfoot a lot." The warmth of her voice told him she didn't much mind that. "The boys will be at school—that is, depending on where you're calling from."

"We're in Inglewood…Westchester—somewhere in there. We flew into LAX last night."

"Randall Taggart, why didn't you come here?" She sounded hurt. "We have plenty of room. Now, you get right in your car and drive straight over, you understand?"

"Yes, Aunt Rachel."

"You remember the way, don't you?"

"Yes, Aunt Rachel."

She laughed. "Randy, that's what you always said and then you went out and did exactly what you pleased. You come on along, hear?"

He hung up grinning. Rachel was a Texan born and bred and he purely loved her for it.

"What did she say?" Maxine wanted to know.

"She said to hurry."

"Not too fast. I need to stop off at a shopping center and pick up a few things. I only packed enough for a few days."

"No problem." He glanced around the room. "All ready to go?"

She nodded. She wore loose-fitting green knit pants this morning with a white blouse loose around her hips. Her hair, as always, was slicked back into a knot at her nape. She didn't look bad, he decided, just…incredibly boring.

She started for the door.

"One more thing." His words stopped her in her tracks. "I'm pretty sure Rachel will insist we spend the night there."

"You mean at their house?" She seemed alarmed.

He nodded. "You know what that will mean."

The corners of her pale mouth turned down. "Then you just have to insist that we go to a motel," she decided. "No problem."

He wanted to say, *You sure don't know Rachel!* but instead he simply shrugged. He'd worry about that bridge when he came to it, as he surely would. At least Max was warned.

TREY AND RACHEL and their sixteen-year-old twin boys lived on a ranch. It was reached by freeway winding through golden hills, which Max proclaimed to be brown.

"Don't say that in front of a Californian," Rand warned, turning off the wide highway onto a smaller paved road. "Brown, golden—it all depends on your point of view."

The Smith ranch nestled among those hills, the buildings shaded by pepper trees and eucalyptus. Corrals and outbuildings surrounded the sprawling ranch house and Rand caught a flash of sunlight off the water of the swimming pool out back. Several horses switched lazily at flies from the safety of a corral. A long-horned steer, no doubt an import from the Rocking T, peered curiously over a tall barbed-wire fence as they passed.

The spread was pretty much the way he remembered it. Rand parked between a pickup truck and a silver minivan. Turning to Max, he found her staring, openmouthed.

She saw him looking, pulled herself together and smiled sheepishly. "I'm sorry. I'm simply overwhelmed. I've never seen a place like this before, but it strikes me as totally right."

"Yeah, I'd say it is. Trey and Rachel have lived here since just after the twins were born. They've traveled a lot for his work, but they always come back here. It's home to them."

As the Rocking T was home to the rest of the Taggarts?

Rand pushed that thought aside. The Rocking T had not been home to a Taggart since Thom T.'s death. Rachel's brother, Lee, managed the place, but nobody else had indicated any undue interest in it.

Max said in a faint voice, "I never had this kind of home. I hate to say I'm envious, but...I'm envious."

"Damn, Max, I think it's about time you tell me a little more about—"

"Randy!"

The screen door flew open and Rachel stepped out, waving. She crossed the yard with a spring in her step, as trim as a teenager in jeans and a bright orange T-shirt. But a few wisps of gray touched the dark curls now, and a few more creases etched the corners of her hazel eyes.

Rand stepped out of the car and she hugged him with all her might. "I'm so glad to see you!" she exclaimed. "It's been *years!*"

With a guilty start, he realized she was right about that. Holding her back, he said, "I want you to meet my wife, Aunt Rachel. This is Max. Honey—" He looked at her, and caught the flare of surprise in her eyes at the endearment, hoped his aunt hadn't. "This is my aunt Rachel."

"Darlin'!" Rachel let go of Rand and hugged the considerably taller Maxine just as hard. "It was a shock when this rascal phoned to say he was married, but that doesn't mean we weren't happy to hear it."

Max returned the smile. "I was kind of shocked

myself," she said, "but you know how Rand is." She gave him a slanted, teasing glance. "Once he gets an idea in his head, there's no stopping him."

Rachel laughed uproariously. "Does she know you or what?" she challenged her nephew. "You two come on in the house and—"

"Hold on." Attracted by the pounding of horse's hooves, Rand turned toward the lane leading around the house. "If I'm not mistaken, Uncle Trey's about to make a grand entrance."

"Oh, Lord," Rachel groaned. "You don't suppose that man—"

At that moment, a big red horse charged around the side of the house, with a tall man in the saddle. Max gasped and jumped back—just as the horse stumbled and went down, throwing the rider face-down in the dirt.

"OH, MY GOD! He's hurt!"

Maxi darted forward, unable to believe what she'd just witnessed. She'd never touched a horse in her life and had never wanted to, instinctively certain they were all killers or worse.

Now she'd been proven right. Dropping to her knees, she struggled to roll the man over onto his back.

Whereupon she gazed into laughing blue-gray eyes in a handsome, deeply carved face.

"You must be Maxine, the newest member of the Taggart clan," a rich voice drawled. "I'm your uncle Trey. Glad to meet you."

Maxi sat down hard in the dirt, shocked speechless. Hearing laughter, she swiveled around to find Rachel and Rand convulsed with mirth. Outrage swept over her, but then she looked back down at the man on the ground and couldn't help a sheepish smile.

"Rand told me you were a movie stuntman," she said, "but I thought that was only on company time."

Trey sat up. "Rachel won't let me get into fights anymore, so I have to fall off a horse or down the stairs once in a while to keep my hand in," he said. "Hope you're not mad at my little joke, Maxine."

"Trey…Uncle Trey, why would a person want to make a living getting beat up and thrown off horses?"

"Because it's there—sorry, that's why men climb mountains." He stood up and dusted himself off before offering her a hand. The horse, grazing peacefully nearby, gave him a disinterested glance and went back to cropping grass.

A phrase she'd heard to describe an irresistible type of man leaped into Maxi's mind: bad boy. Trey Smith must have been the baddest of the bad boys in his prime. Poor Rachel the librarian didn't stand a chance.

Trey cocked his head. "Now, what are *you* grinning at?" he inquired.

"You," she said. "I'm grinning at you—and I'll never again believe anything you say or do after that little exhibition."

"Aw," he said, "I was just having a little fun. There wasn't a chance in the world of anybody getting hurt. See this?'' He scuffed the toe of his boot in the soft earth. ''I dug up the dirt a little to soften the fall and kept old Red down to a slow canter. In my prime, I used to bail off at a dead run into anything—rock, cactus, the sides of boxcars. I'm too old for that stuff now, but I still like doing the baby stunts.''

''Uncle Trey,'' she said, slipping an arm around a whipcord-taut waist, ''I can't imagine you're too old for *anything.*''

Together they turned toward the house and walked arm in arm past Rachel and Rand, each looking more amused than the other.

''I can see,'' Trey said to Maxi, ''that you and me are gonna be great friends.''

He let the screen door slam closed in Rand's face.

RAND FIGURED this was going to be a piece of cake. Max had Trey eating out of her hand in the first five minutes. He'd assumed she'd do all right. He *hadn't* assumed she'd conquer with little more than a glance.

Rachel liked her, too. Rand looked across the lunch table at the two women cleaning up the kitchen and loading the dishwasher. They chattered away like old friends.

Trey slid his chair away from the table. ''Hey, kid, let's you and me go for a little walk.''

''Sure.'' Rand's heart took a dip. He'd been expecting this but was hardly looking forward to it.

He rose and followed his uncle out the back door, onto the wooden deck surrounding the swimming pool. Max and Rachel spared a single curious glance before returning to their own conversation.

Trey walked over to a long-handled pool strainer leaning against the small utility building set unobtrusively against the back wall of the house. After returning to the edge of the free-form pool, he skimmed out a few leaves and tossed them onto the grass.

His look was sharp and cautious. "Nice girl," he said. "How'd you meet her?"

"On an airplane." They'd decided to stick as close to the truth as possible.

"How long have you known her?"

"Not long." Rand stuck his hands into the pockets of his khaki trousers and rocked back on his heels. "Long enough."

"She doesn't seem like your type."

Rand felt a flare of temper, which he tamped down. Was this a knock on Max? "Watch it, Trey. That's my wife we're talking about."

For a moment their eyes met. Then Trey nodded.

"Good, that's good," he said. "Love should be blind."

The casual use of the word *love* rocked Rand. "Yeah, well—" He glowered. "What are you getting at?"

"Your motives." That was Trey, straightforward as always. "You've got to admit, this is all pretty sudden. Nobody in the family had a clue you were serious about anybody."

"Nobody in the family has a clue about anything I'm thinking or doing."

"Whose fault is that, do you suppose?" Trey ambled over to a patio table and chairs set beneath an umbrella on the edge of the deck. He sat down, then leaned back with a contemplative expression on his face. "Just seems a little funny is all. You getting married only a couple of weeks before your thirtieth birthday…"

"You want to hear me say I'm after my inheritance from Great-grandpa?" Rand pulled out a chair and joined his uncle at the table. "Okay, I *do* want to fulfill the conditions of his will and take over the Rocking T. You got a problem with that?"

"Not me. I kinda expect Boone and Jesse may, especially if they think you just want to get the money and run." He cocked his head, his eyes narrowing. "Do you?"

"I…I'm not sure. There's a lot to consider. Maybe…" Hemming and hawing, but the best Rand could manage.

"Jesse especially's been stewing over this. That ranch means a lot to him. He doesn't want to see it overrun by naked sun worshipers and tree huggers."

That brought a reluctant grin from Rand. "Neither do I. But would it be so bad if the place were in the hands of somebody who'd use it and value it the way Thom T. did?"

"Not at all—as long as his name's Taggart," Trey shot back. "Or her name. Can't afford to be sexist these days."

That lightened the atmosphere until Trey added, "Nobody knows where you're coming from, Rand. Hell, nobody even knows where you *are* half the time. Meg's been praying you'd find a nice girl and settle down to that productive life old Thom T. was so dead set on you leading.''

"Then Mom should be happy to meet Max."

"She will be, if this is the real thing. If you're pulling a scam…'' Trey let the warning stretch out. Then he said, ''What the hell. Maxine's obviously too good for you. Maybe she won't *let* you sell your heritage.''

His *heritage?* That throwaway word hit Rand hard. He'd never thought of it as selling his heritage, it was simply a way to raise badly needed cash. He needed money to honor his commitments and continue the lifestyle he'd led since his twenty-first birthday. Why should anyone care what he did with the ranch? At least it wouldn't be turned into a nudist colony.

He had nothing to be ashamed of and yet…

As the day wore on, he found himself withdrawing more and more into the kind of self-questioning in which he rarely indulged. When the sixteen-year-old twins came home from school, he welcomed the distraction. Thom and Tag, they were called. Fraternal instead of identical, they still resembled each other a great deal.

It soon became apparent that they were not two peas from the same pod, however. Thom, a good-looking kid with his mom's hazel eyes, was quarterback of his high-school football team and apparently a devil with the girls. Tag, blue-eyed and thoughtful, was the long-distance star of the local swim team, and even held the state high-school record for the mile.

They greeted Rand like a long-lost brother, pounding on his arms and offering the usual unintelligible teenage-boy greetings. They shook Max's hand with solemn good manners, but neither of them appeared to be very impressed.

Rachel smiled on her offspring and ordered them to do their chores before dinner, which turned out to be a cookout beside the pool. Rand joined the boys in the water, but Max declined.

She'd grown much quieter, for some reason. She watched the three males frolic in the crystal-blue water without expressing either approval or disapproval.

For his part, Rand found watery horseplay just what he needed: a chance to work off some of the tension and restless energy that plagued him. When he finally launched himself onto the side of the pool to dry off before dinner, Max offered him a colorful beach towel.

"Thanks," he said. Noticing Rachel observing, he added a quick, "Honey." Max was wearing the brightly colored Mexican dress he'd insisted on buying her, which pleased him. He scrubbed at his wet hair. "Sure you don't want a quick dip?" he inquired. "It'd do you a world of good."

"Probably, but I'll pass."

"Suit yourself." Leaping to his feet, he dropped his towel and caught her arms when she would have turned away.

Her startled glance flew to his face and he smiled.

"Easy," he said, leaning close and speaking under his breath. "We're newlyweds, remember?"

"Like I could forget!"

He nuzzled her ear and was gratified by her shiver. "Trey's got his suspicions, I'm afraid."

"So does Rachel, although she seemed impressed when I showed her the marriage license." She touched his bare wet waist, the pads of her fingers pressing. "They're nice people."

"They think you're nice, too. They're just not sure we're the happily married couple we purport to be."

"Gosh, I can't imagine what makes them so suspicious." Her lips twitched with suppressed humor. "What else can we do to convince them, Rand?"

"Oh, a little of this...a little of that..." He kissed her cheek, his lips cool against her warm skin. Her mouth—that full and generous mouth, which was her best feature—was very near his own now. She didn't pull away and he knew she wouldn't, but if he took that kind of advantage—

"Hey!" The roar of disapproval came from Thom. "Cut that out, Rand! There are kids present!"

Laughing, Tag joined in. "If you guys knew what we see and hear in school, you wouldn't listen to this big goof. They're newlyweds, you jerk. Leave 'em alone."

"Make me!"

"Think I can't?"

"Boys! Stop that this instant!" But Rachel didn't sound angry, more resigned. "These steaks are just about ready. You two set the table out here, okay?"

"Ah, Mom—"

"Do as your mother says, kid," Rand told the boy.

Throughout the entire exchange, Rand and Max faced each other, almost touching. Now she smiled and stroked the side of his face. "Boys will be boys," she said. "Shall we lend a hand?"

The only hand he wanted to lend wouldn't have anything to do with setting the table.

DINNER ENDED and the boys took off to do their homework—which, judging from raised voices inside, was yet another bone of contention between them. The adults lingered at the table near the pool, sharing a bottle of good California wine…and memories.

Except for Maxi, of course; she had to settle for the wine without the memories. Nevertheless she enjoyed the give-and-take between members of the kind of family with which she had no personal experience.

Rand said, "Honey?" and it took her a couple of moments to realize he was speaking to her. When he had her startled attention, he asked, "Did I ever tell you about the summer I spent here with Aunt Rachel and Uncle Trey?"

"I believe you overlooked that one," she answered with a smile. She knew quite a lot about him, actually, but not that. She knew more than he imagined and none of it was good.

But based on his family…could Helen have been mistaken in her charges? Maybe Rand wasn't the one with the secret accounts in Caribbean banks. Maybe—

"I was twelve," he said, interrupting her thoughts. "Trey was working on a movie and he got me a job as a stuntkid."

"*You* worked in a *movie?*"

His broad grin revealed his pleasure at the memory. "I doubled for this kid actor. I had to ride a horse—which of course I already knew how to do—and fall off—which wasn't all that hard to learn. But climbing around on a mountain and getting tossed off a cliff—"

"You got tossed off a cliff?"

"Relax!" He laughed. "It was into water and Trey was waiting to drag me out."

Rachel pursed her lips. "Frankly I was surprised Meg allowed you to do that," she said.

"She didn't know anything about it. Still doesn't." Rand could barely keep back the laughter.

Rachel's eyes flew wide. "But you said—"

"I lied." He cracked up over that. "No way would Mom have let her baby get thrown off a cliff."

They laughed together. Then Trey said, "I kinda suspected something like that, but I figured gettin' roughed up a little would be good for you. Besides, Thom T. was egging me on."

Rand nodded. "Grandpa told me once he worried because I was danged near a sissy."

"That's exactly the way he talked," Rachel said. She added to Maxi, "Thom T. was actually Randy's great-grandpa, but he was known simply as 'Grandpa' to just about everybody. He was the dearest, the kindest old man. I can't begin to tell you how much he did for me."

"Sometime I'd like to hear." Maxi realized she meant it and frowned. She wasn't going to be around long enough to get to know these people.

"Thom T. did a lot for all of us." Trey's usually cynical tone was completely absent. "He was especially fond of you, Rand—his first great-grandchild."

Rand sighed. "Yeah. I disappointed him and he didn't even know the half of it."

The atmosphere had undergone a lightning-like transition. Trey and Rachel exchanged guarded glances and he said, "Care to elaborate on that?"

Rand shook his head. "You've got a pretty good idea the kind of life I've been leading."

"Not really," Trey drawled. "For example... where were you last week?"

"Chicago."

"The week before that?"

"Florida."

"The week before that?"

"The Caribbean."

A shiver shot through Maxi. Helen had vacationed in the Caribbean; had it been with Rand? Even Maxi knew banks were discreet there, and money could disappear from official eyes. One business partner could defraud the other and come out smelling like a rose.

Rachel persisted. "But where do you *live,* Rand?"

"I still own Grandpa Randall's place in Boston, but it's...currently leased. Other than that, I visit friends...stay in hotels...rent villas..."

"God," Rachel said, "what a lousy existence."

She turned her sharp gaze on Maxi. "I hope you're planning to put a stop to his gypsy wanderings."

"I...can try." Maxi's stomach muscles clenched painfully. Why was Rand so determined to throw away his heritage? He should be on his knees giving thanks for a family like this.

Trey said, "Maybe Randy and Maxine will settle down on the Rocking T. That's where Taggart roots are."

Rand rose abruptly, his expression darkening. "Okay, folks, stop planning my life. Max, it's time we get out of here so these people can—"

"Out of here!" Rachel rose, too, her eyes flashing. "Do you honestly think I'm going to let you stay in a hotel, Randall Taggart, when I have a perfectly good guest room?"

"I don't want you to go to any trouble, Aunt Rachel. We'd already made up outs minds to—"

"Forget it." Trey's lazy grin ended the debate. "If Rachel says you're staying, you may as well give in gracefully, because *you're staying.*"

Trey looked at Maxi, who shrugged helplessly. No way did she want to spend the night here in these close family confines. But what could she do?

They were trapped.

CHAPTER SIX

RAND WOKE UP SLOWLY...or rather, his body woke up and his mind eventually had to follow. If he kept his eyes tightly closed, maybe he could go right on believing he was in some silken harem with the sultan's favorite wrapped around him like lights on a Christmas tree.

His hands seemed to move of their own accord, stroking down the curved length of the woman in his arms. He reveled in the feel of firm female flesh. She sighed and rubbed her breasts against his chest until he felt her nipples peak. As unerring as a magnet heading toward iron, he curved one hand around her breast—and caught his breath.

Maybe he'd died and gone to heaven, because he sure hadn't crawled into bed with this sensuous creature last night. In fact, when he'd slipped gingerly between the silky sheets, Maxine had been lying on top of the bedspread as stiff as the proverbial poker, with only a crocheted afghan—

Maxine! Rand's eyes flew open and he stared down at the face resting on his shoulder. Incredibly long lashes lay upon high cheekbones and a rosy flush covered her cheeks. She was gorgeous, all warm and tousled and—

Suddenly awake, staring at him with drowsy amber-brown eyes. He should stop kneading her breast, stop pressing the top of his thigh between her spread legs, stop staring at her mouth. None of these things, however, was he able to accomplish.

She, on the other hand, stiffened, and her eyes went wide with shock. Then, very slowly and very deliberately, she pushed herself out of his arms and sat up. Licking her lips, she glanced at him over her shoulder.

He said, "Good morning?"

She said, "You're joking."

Without hurrying, she slid to the side of the bed and rose. Not looking back, she walked with unhurried steps to the bathroom, went inside and closed the door very softly.

Rand stared after her, his passion ebbing, gradually. She wasn't his type…but without the dowdy hairstyles and the glasses, without the funny clothes and the Minnie Mouse shoes, she was quite… attractive. At least, she attracted the hell out of *him*.

In his defense, he'd been asleep. He'd had no idea who he'd been groping…had he? This could turn into a serious complication if he let it. Fortunately she didn't appear to be affected in the slightest.

Under other circumstances, that would hurt. Now it was a blessing.

SAFE IN THE BATHROOM, Maxi collapsed against the sink in dismay.

If she'd "slept" for another three minutes, it

would have been too late. She'd have been spread beneath him like a picnic lunch and he'd have been—

Don't even go there! Although every inch of her throbbed with frustration, her mind was in a worse whirl.

This was not the way it was supposed to go. The man might be charming—okay, he *was* charming—but he was still a crook and responsible for her sister's incarceration. Hell, he was even willing to deceive his own family for financial gain.

Get a grip!

She whipped off the cotton nightgown and dropped it on the floor, then stared in the mirror at her body, aroused and unsatisfied as never before. Her nipples were tight pink points on breasts rising and falling rapidly with the force of her breathing.

What had happened—almost happened, anyway—was as much her fault as his. They'd come together in their sleep and awakened just in time. The difference was, he'd seen who he held and recoiled; she'd seen who held her and wanted to show him once and for all that she wasn't what she seemed. An honest mistake, one she'd nurtured, but a mistake nonetheless. She wasn't the hopeless little match girl he took her for. She was a woman whose fortune was her body, dammit!

Beneath the stinging spray of a cold shower, she tried to calm herself. How long had it been since she'd slept with a man? She'd been working so hard, been so involved in other things, that she'd almost stopped even thinking about men and romance.

Which wasn't as hard as it might have been, actually. Her father had seen to that.

She and Helen had taken their father's defection some fifteen years ago in completely different ways, she reflected, patting herself dry with a fluffy towel. Helen hungered for love to the point of throwing herself at every unsuitable man who came her way—and Rand Taggart wasn't the first who'd misled her, either. There had been others, too many others.

Maxi, on the other hand, had relegated men to a subordinate position in her life. She'd had a boyfriend in high school because she needed one to take her to the dances and parties, but never, not once, had she mistaken that relationship for love. After graduation she'd found a job as a photographer's assistant and, with so much to learn, had gone for more than a year without a single date.

Her boss had seen her potential and sent photos to a friend, a photographer who worked for Violet's Advantage; the rest, as they say, is history. At twenty-two, Maxi had found it difficult to pose in her underwear for the camera, and even more difficult to see the resulting photographs in Violet's famous catalog. She, who had been poor all her life, had done it for the money.

Period. Her only regret was that her mother hadn't lived long enough to enjoy it, too.

When the adulation had begun, Maxi had let it go to her head, at least for a little while. She'd dated a couple of movie stars, a professional football player, a rock star. After the initial excitement, she'd found them all boring and interested in only one thing—one thing that didn't include her mind.

Now she'd run afoul of Rand Taggart, who was not only sinfully sexy but a man with the kind of family Maxi used to dream about. Too bad he was who he was. Too bad he was going to hurt a lot of people when the truth came out, including, but not limited to, Trey and Rachel and their boys.

Not Maxi, though. She was doing an honorable thing, fighting for her sister's future. Rand would be brought to justice; he had to be. When he was, Helen would be cleared.

But before that happened… Maxi took a deep breath and visualized his reaction if she were ever to let him see who she really was. Then, with a sigh, she pulled her hair back into a tight twist, planted the glasses firmly in front of naked eyes, squared her shoulders and went out to rejoin the fray.

"DO YOU REALLY have to leave so soon?"

Rachel's plaintive tone made Rand smile. "Yeah, we do. When I called Mom and told her I'd brought Max here first, she was…let's just say she wasn't pleased."

Rachel wrinkled her nose. "I suppose I can't blame her. If Jason got married and went to see Meg before me, I probably wouldn't like it, either."

"How is Jason?"

"*Who* is Jason?" Maxine looked from one to the other.

"My grown son," Rachel said. "I had him before I met Trey. He's a few years older than Rand." To whom she added, "He's a minister with a church in Showdown. Did you know that?"

He didn't. He'd expected studious Jason to become a teacher or a librarian like his mother, not a minister. Rand was really out of the family loop to have missed this.

"Jason's a good kid." Trey rose from his chair at the kitchen table. "If you're determined to go, Rand, we might as well get the luggage loaded."

Here comes another lecture, Rand thought as he followed his uncle from the kitchen.

"Do Trey and your son get along well, Rachel?" Maxi asked when they were alone.

"Very well. Trey loves Jason and it's mutual." Rachel leaned forward, her elbows on the table. "Jason's father died before he was born, so Trey's the only father he ever knew." She cocked her head. "Trey and I have a good marriage, Maxine. I hope you and Rand will be as happy."

Maxi felt a twinge of shame. "Thank you."

"I don't want you to think it's been easy for us, though. Marriage never is."

"I suppose not."

"How much do you know about small southern towns, hon?"

"Hardly anything. I grew up in Chicago and lived there most of my life."

"Well, I grew up in a little Texas town, the daughter of the town drunk."

Maxi felt a jolt of recognition. "My mother was

an alcoholic,'' she blurted, then wished she'd kept her mouth shut.

''That's a tough thing to have in common.'' Rachel sighed. ''When I was sixteen, I had a child out of wedlock, as they used to say. That was Jason.''

''When I was sixteen, my mother died.'' Maxi threw caution to the wind, figuring she'd already said too much.

''Poor Maxine.'' Rachel's smile was warm and sympathetic. ''I hope you were as lucky as I was. You see, I had Thom T. Taggart. He made it possible for me to attend college and become a librarian. Then Trey came to town and I was sure he was out to bilk that kind old gentleman for every cent he had. ''

There had been no Thom T. in Maxi's life. ''I can see how it must have been hard for you and Trey to get together,'' she said.

''Hard and then some.'' Rachel nodded for emphasis. ''Trey breezed in from California, took one look at 'that trashy Cox girl,' which is what they called me, and moved in on me as well as on Thom T. I was struggling to overcome my lurid reputation and protect Thom T. at the same time. The last thing I needed was some fast-talking damnyankee blasting away at every single preconceived idea I ever had about myself.''

''But you found a happy ending, right?''

''Oh, yes.'' Rachel's smile sparkled. ''God, I love that man. He's given me the most exciting and wonderful life you can imagine. I guess what I want you to know is that marriage isn't easy, but if there's enough love, you'll make it—and it's worth the effort, believe me. Rand's parents have been there, too.''

"His parents?''

"They've had their problems. He hasn't mentioned it?''

"There's hardly been time.''

"In that case, I'll shut up. It's really not my place to get into details, but the details are important to understanding Randy. Then there're Boone and Kit. Nothing's come easily for them, either. At one point, Boone was actually determined to sell the Rocking T right out from under Thom T. and Jesse. It took Kit to stop him.''

She raised her eyebrows and smiled. "We're pretty much your average rootin' tootin' Texas family. It's only fair for you to know what you've married into.''

"Thank you.'' Maxi smiled back, thinking that she'd really like to belong to a family like this if it didn't take marriage to a crook to get in.

"You do love Rand, don't you?''

Maxi's smile faltered. "I married him,'' she said.

"People get married for all kinds of reasons.''

"Are you talking about money?''

"I didn't say that.''

"Trust me,'' Maxi said with finality, "I did *not* marry him for his money.''

Rachel traced the veined pattern on the glossy tabletop with a blunt fingernail. "I don't mean to offend you, but...I don't get the feeling that this is really a love match.'' She looked up quickly. "*Are* you offended?''

"No." Maxi met the other woman's gaze, her own level. "Rand is one of the most complicated and intriguing men I've ever met." That was certainly true. He was also one of the biggest liars. "I guess you could say I married him because I was swept away." By hijackers, all the way to Mexico.

Rachel seemed reassured. "The Taggart men tend to do that. I take it you know about Thom T.'s will."

"Yes, but I didn't marry Rand for that, either."

And then Maxi realized with a start that Rachel might be worried about *Rand's* motives, not hers. Could Rachel believe Maxi was an innocent victim of Rand's Johnny-come-lately determination to get his inheritance?

"Whatever," Rachel said. "I'm too nosy and I apologize. You're both adults. I wouldn't be so concerned if Thom T. hadn't appointed me one of the judges of Rand's marital happiness. Let's forget all that for the moment."

"Good idea." *Now,* Maxi thought. "Uh, I wonder if I could ask *you* something."

"Of course."

"I...understand Rand had a college friend n-named Bill Overton. You wouldn't happen to know anything about that, would you?"

Rachel frowned. "That was a long time ago."

"Yes, but now Bill Overton is in a...bit of trouble." Maxi crossed her fingers beneath the table. "If Rand should want to help him—"

"Don't let him!" Rachel stood up. "I haven't heard that guy's name in years. Now that I have, it brings back all the reasons nobody in the family liked him. He was a con man, plain and simple. The farther you both stay away from him, the better.''

Rachel peered at Maxi. ''Not to change the subject, but I have the funniest feeling we've met before. Have you spent much time in California?''

So much for that line of inquiry. At least Rachel didn't seen to suspect Maxi's motives.

WITH THE LUGGAGE stowed in the trunk, Trey leaned against the side of the rental car and nailed Rand with a level gaze.

''Okay, spit it out,'' Rand said. ''What's on your mind, Trey?''

''This so-called marriage of yours.''

''It's not so-called. You saw the marriage certificate.''

''Certificates are a dime a dozen. Unfortunately.'' Straightening, Trey started for the house.

Rand fell in beside his uncle. ''We're married. You can see we're happy.''

''I don't see any such thing.''

Rand stopped short. ''We're not fighting, are we? We're not yelling at each other. We're together.''

''That's the rub. You're *not* together.''

Rand frowned. ''I don't get it.''

''When I met Rachel, I could hardly keep my hands off her. Once I got that ring on her finger…'' Trey's wolfish expression finished the sentence. ''But you and Maxine—'' He shook his head slowly. ''You treat each other like strangers, polite but not very interested.''

''That's your official opinion?'' Rand asked

stiffly, visions of dollar bills fluttering away through the still air.

"Not my *official* opinion, at least not yet. I'm trying to keep an open mind, but it's damn hard."

"I thought you liked Max."

"Hell, I do. I like you, too, partner." Trey banged a fist on Rand's shoulder. "But Thom T. was specific about what he wanted—you not only married but *happily* married and a contributing member of society." Trey cocked his head. "You contributed anything to society lately?"

"I haven't rescued any little old ladies from burning buildings, if that's what you mean."

"It's not, but let it go." Trey turned back toward the house. "Look, I want you to get what's coming to you. I want you and Maxine to settle down on the Rocking T and have a whole passel of little cowboys. Somehow I don't think that's what's going on here, though." He stopped at the door, reaching for the screen. "If it was another kind of girl, then I'd understand. But *this* girl doesn't fit the scenario I've got in mind."

Irritated, Rand followed his uncle into the house. Clearly he had his work cut out for him before he tried to do a similar number on his parents.

But at least Trey hadn't laughed in their faces, so there was hope.

TREY AND RACHEL STOOD in the front yard waving goodbye to the newlyweds. When the car was out of sight, they turned back to the house, arm in arm.

She sighed and he squeezed her tighter against his side. "What's that supposed to mean?"

"That I'm really confused about what just happened here."

"For instance?"

"I can't figure out why Randy married that girl."

"I think it's fairly obvious he did it to get the ranch. It's equally obvious he doesn't have any intention of living there and running it."

"Oh, God, Trey, everybody's just been waiting for him to come to his senses and return to the family fold. If he really intends to sell the Rocking T to the highest bidder, it'll break a lot of hearts."

"Including yours." He turned her in his arms and touched his lips lightly to hers. Even after all these years, he felt that familiar spark of desire and almost laughed at the pleasure of it.

"I'm not the only one," she said as they entered the house. "What about Jesse and Boone and Kit? Meg...well, she's never really understood the pull of the land, but she loves Jesse enough to keep on trying."

"But you don't think Maxine loves Rand that way." He led her into the house.

"Good Lord, no. I don't think she loves him at all, or he her, although they seem attracted to each other. I think she's in this for a completely different reason, but I have no idea what that might be." She frowned. "Something funny happened when you and Randy left us alone, though."

"Such as?" He pulled out a kitchen chair and sat.

"She brought up Bill Overton. Don't you think

that's kind of...strange? So far as I know, Rand hasn't seen him in years.''

"You think her maiden name was Overton?''

Rachel laughed. "No way! He was a sleaze and she's very straightforward. I like her a lot. Whatever she is, I *don't* think she's a gold digger.''

"Me, either.'' Trey watched her move around, preparing iced tea. "If Randy's marriage is a scam, I wonder why he picked someone so...plain,'' he mused.

"Plain!'' She faced him with a tall glass in each hand. "She isn't plain. She's...reserved.''

"You used to be reserved.'' He was flirting with her, teasing her, as he'd enjoyed doing ever since they met all those years ago. "You were just a small-town Texas librarian trying to be oh-so-proper.''

"And you were a sophisticated damnyankee,'' she teased him right back. She placed the glasses on the table, then sat down on his lap and slid an arm around his neck.

He put one hand on her thigh and the other on her breast. "Those were the good old days,'' he said softly. "Rachel, do you remember that night your brother stole the pickup and the sheriff came out to the Rocking T looking for him?''

"Lee didn't steal Dub Partridge's pickup. I've explained that to you a million times.'' She covered his hand with hers, pressing it closer against her breast. "But yes, I remember.''

"After the sheriff left, you really lit into me. I can still see it.... You were standing a couple of steps above me on the front stairs, wearing a nightgown so thin that it looked like gauze...."

She'd been so beautiful in the silvery moonlight, so beautiful and so uptight. She'd wavered beneath his hungry gaze, crossing her arms over her breasts as if that would protect her from him. Yeah, as if.

"I'm not even vaguely interested in your opinion," she'd said in that prissy voice.

And he'd lost his head. "If you're not interested in anything I have to say, maybe you'll be interested in what I plan to do," he'd said.

The words had rolled out, full and soft with promise, without any of the half-joking quality that had so often marked his dealings with her to that point. She stood as still and straight as a statue, not softening even when he drew her to the edge of the step—but not running from him, either. He reached beneath her nightgown with both hands and stroked up the fullness of her bare calves, at the same time pressing the side of his face to her abdomen beneath her folded arms.

Then, with a provocative slowness, he lowered her to the next step, the top of his head nudging aside her arms. His seeking mouth fumbled against her, then closed over one straining nipple.

Perhaps she was remembering, too, for now she stirred restlessly on his lap. "What happened that night...I wanted it to happen," she whispered. She rubbed her lips lightly against his cheek. "But I still shocked myself. I'd never done such a thing...let anyone do such a thing to me."

"I knew that." He pressed his hand to the vee

between her denim-covered thighs. "I couldn't help myself, sweetheart. I still can't."

"I couldn't help *my*self, either...."

She'd been adrift on a cloud of sensual feeling. When she found herself straddling his thighs, she'd instinctively held on to his shoulders and arched her back. Spreading her thighs, she'd lifted her breasts toward his clever, seeking tongue.

She wanted to do things with him she couldn't even name. Mindless with wanting, she felt the shattering of her vaunted self-control and the blossoming of passion she'd ruthlessly suppressed for a very long time.

He caught one nipple between his teeth and tugged, setting off another series of deep, quivering contractions that made her groan. His hands roamed over her as they did now, kneading and molding her buttocks, touching her with intimate understanding.

His nimble fingers inserted themselves between his flesh and hers. The white heat of desire shuddered through her and she shifted ever so slightly to give him better access. He molded his palm to her contours while little, wordless gasps and tremors shook her. For a moment, she wasn't sure if this was now or then.

"Trey." It was a weak gasp. "You really began to set me free that night."

"I know," he said in a raspy voice. "It cost me plenty, but it was worth it."

She began unbuttoning her shirt. "If it can happen for us, different as we are, it can happen for Randy and Maxine."

"Forget them." He stood up with her in his arms. "I love you, woman."

"Then take me to bed and show me how lucky we both are," she murmured, grateful that Randy and his unlikely bride had reminded her of things she never wanted to take for granted.

CHAPTER SEVEN

RAND AND MAXI MADE IT onto the airplane, but just barely; they were the last to board. Maxi didn't even like to *think* about how much he'd paid for the two last-minute first-class tickets. She was beginning to suspect that his lifestyle required all those never-again-to-be-taxed illegal dollars he'd squirreled away in some Caribbean bank.

With that likelihood very much on her mind, she couldn't help remarking as she settled into the comfortable seat, "You sure do throw money around."

"That's what it's for."

"Only if there's plenty of it."

He shrugged as if money were no object. "You don't have time to worry about that with everything else that's going to hell around us," he said.

Startled, she frowned. He'd barely spoken in the car on the trip to the airport. "What's that supposed to mean?"

"Trey and Rachel didn't buy it—us, I mean."

"Oh, I don't know about that." She relaxed back in her seat. "Rachel seemed willing to give us the benefit of the doubt."

"Trey's a harder sell. He pretty much said that

since we weren't constantly all over each other, I must be faking it."

"There is that." A smile tugged at her lips. "I'll bet Trey and Rachel have an active sex life."

"Jeez!" He gave her a horrified glance. "You're speculating on the sex life of my aunt and uncle?"

"Sorry. It's just that if this so-called marriage we have was real, we could do worse than to take them as shining examples of what's possible."

"That sounded a tad cynical."

"Maybe it was. I've never seen a good marriage close up. Until them, I mean."

He looked thoughtful. "My parents have a pretty good marriage, too. But if we're gonna get them on our side, we've got to put on a better act than we did in California."

"Meaning what, exactly?"

"A little physical affection is in order, Max."

She'd been dreading this. "What comes under the heading of 'a little physical affection'? I'm not going to sleep with you just to earn a few bucks, if that's what you mean. There are names for women like that."

"Yes, and nobody's calling you by any of them, so relax. It's just that when we're around other people, we need to…at least…you know, touch each other once in a while, act like lovers." He seemed uneasy even suggesting it.

"That's all it'll take?" She rolled her eyes, thinking that this was the most ridiculous situation she'd ever got herself into.

"Damn, I hope so." He shut up then, settling into

a brooding silence, which she didn't break until they were airborne. Then she said, "Rachel implied your parents have their own story illustrating the rocky road to love."

"What the hell were you two talking about?"

"Things. What *is* the story on your parents?"

"It's not much…or actually, maybe it was. They got married impulsively."

"Unlike their son, who always thinks things through."

"Right." His smile was rueful. "He was a professional rodeo cowboy and she was a spoiled little heiress from Boston. They managed to stay together long enough to have me and then she split."

"She left him?"

He nodded. "She took me back to Boston. We lived there with my great-grandpa Randall until I was five or six."

When he didn't immediately go on, she said, "And then what happened?"

"The way I hear it is, the two grandpas got together—Randall and Taggart. They didn't like each other much, but they did it for…" He grimaced. "They did it for me. I must have been a total brat to bring those two old warriors together. Anyway, they decided to blackmail their respective grandchildren into—well, as Thom T. related it, 'We decided to just lock 'em in a room like a couple of wildcats and let the fur fly till they worked it out.'"

"I'd have loved that man," Maxi declared, remembering what he'd done for Rachel. "I'm so sorry I never got to meet—" She stopped short. She was out to bring down that fine old gentleman's great-grandson. She should be grateful Thom T. wouldn't be around to see it.

"He was a corker, all right," Rand said, completely unaware. "Somehow they finagled to get Mom and Dad back to the old family homestead on Handbasket Creek near Hells Bells, Texas, where they'd spent their honeymoon. When they came out a week or two later, we were a family again." His smile was bittersweet.

"You have problems with your father," she guessed.

He gave her a sharp glance. "Those years we were separated put a distance between us that we've never been able to completely get past. He's a great guy— I admire the hell out of him. But I've never felt able to…" He laughed ruefully. "To live up to him, if you know what I mean."

She didn't, not through personal experience anyway. But strangely enough, she felt his pain as sharply as if it were her own. "There's still time," she said. "Maybe—"

"Max, have you forgotten why we're going there?" he cut her off. "Basically I'm out to deceive him. No matter how I try to tap-dance around it, once I get my hands on that ranch I'm selling it."

Why should she feel such shock? She'd known all along why he wanted this inheritance. He just hadn't stated it so baldly.

He made an incoherent little growl deep in his throat. "Don't look at me like I just kicked your cow dog."

A burst of nervous laughter escaped her. "What does that mean, kicked my cow dog?"

"Hell, a cow dog's the most loyal and faithful animal on God's green earth. Anybody who'd kick one would be the worst kind of lowlife."

"I see." She met his gaze squarely. "How do you justify what you're about to do? Or maybe I should say rationalize…"

He got a stubborn expression on his face, one she hadn't seen before. "Thom T. left the place to me," he said. "He wanted me to have it, right?"

"Under certain circumstances."

"Well, sure, but he was just hoping. He's trying to manipulate me from the grave and it ain't gonna happen. Besides, would the Rocking T be better off in the hands of some rancher who'd take care of it, or overrun with herds of naked people? Because if I don't get it, it goes to some nudist colony, and *then* hear everybody holler."

She looked at him with a mixture of admiration for his nimble mind and disgust for his conclusions. "Is there anything you *can't* rationalize?"

He pretended to give her question serious consideration. "If there is, I haven't run into it yet." After lowering the back of his seat, he crossed his arms over his chest and closed his eyes. Only then did he add, "Just don't forget."

"Forget what?"

"Forget and slap my face when I make a grab for you."

She didn't answer because there was no answer.

She didn't know *what* she'd do if he started groping her.

Nor was she eager to find out.

ANOTHER AIRPORT, another rental car, another drive through the countryside. Only this time, instead of Southern California's bare golden hills, their route took them through the fall colors of the rolling Texas Hill Country.

The drive gave him plenty of time to think and he did, mostly about his rapidly diminishing bank account. He wasn't exactly ready for the poor farm yet, but Maxine was right; he should show a little more financial constraint. Would flying tourist have killed him? If he didn't gain access to his inheritance in a hurry, he was going to have to think about liquidating a few assets—and he only *had* a few.

Nearing Hells Bells, Max suddenly stirred. He looked at her in surprise and she said, "I was wondering…"

He slowed the car, glad to have her interrupt his gloomy thoughts. "About what?"

"You." She gave an unconvincing little laugh.

"What about me?"

"Oh, you know…" She appeared uneasy. "About your childhood, about your education, about the way you spend your time. For example, why were you flying from Chicago to San Antonio when we met? Had you been visiting friends or…or…what?"

"Definitely not visiting friends." Her questions put him off; he didn't intend to spend the next few weeks dodging her curiosity. Might as well get that straight here and now. "Max, quit pumping me."

She drew herself up. "I wasn't asking for state secrets. If we're going to be spending time together trying to convince people we've got a marriage going, you could at least—"

"I *couldn't*. I don't *want* to. You're going to hear way too much about me from my family without me saying a thing."

"If that's the way you feel—"

"I do."

"Fine." The word emerged between clenched lips.

While she pouted, he found a distraction in the increasing familiarity of his surroundings. Hells Bells wasn't his home and never had been, not really. But he'd spent good times and bad here; he'd learned about horses and cows and girls. He'd never gone to school a day in Texas, but he *felt* like a Texan every time he came back.

Max read aloud from the city limits sign: Hells Bells, Texas, 2,113 Nice Folks And A Few Old Grouches. She laughed, apparently over her snit.

"Corny," Rand agreed. "My mom loves that sign—always cracks her up."

"This must have been a neat place to grow up."

"I wouldn't know."

He made the turn down Main Street and drove slowly past the Hells Bells Low Life Saloon, the Lone Star Texasburger Drive-In and on out of town. Max seemed enchanted with the entire dusty little burg.

Go figure.

The Taggart place lay in a bend of Handbasket Creek, seven miles southwest of town. To get there, they had to drive past a sign hanging over a gated entrance that read Hell-on-the-Handbasket Dude Ranch, Joe Bob Brooks, Prop.

Max laughed with delight. "You mean Texans really do have names like Joe Bob?"

"Oh, yeah. And Joe Bill and Billy Bob and all the other combinations you've ever heard. That particular Joe Bob is a good friend of my mom and dad. You'll probably meet him."

"I expect your parents know everybody around here, and everybody knows them."

"Pretty much. It comes with the territory in a small town." He glanced at her and was surprised to see how pensive she looked. "You've only lived in the city?"

"Yes. I always thought I'd like a small town, though."

"You know what *I* like?"

She gave him a curious glance. "What?"

"You." He turned down the road leading to the ranch. "That's why I said what I did earlier. I like *you,* Max, and I want to keep it there. You've been a great sport. You don't whine, you don't make demands, you don't back off from anything. I hope when this is over, we can part friends."

"That seems unlikely, Rand."

"I don't see why."

"Think about it. We're talking different worlds." She gave a short sharp laugh. "I'm working-class Chicago and you're upper-crust Boston. I'm thrifty and you're extravagant. We have absolutely nothing in common and never will.''

"Maybe, but there's something kinda special going on here. I've never been friends with a woman before—just friends, no sex, you know? Feels weird, in a nice kinda way.''

"It's only possible," she said sarcastically, "because I'm not your type.''

"Not for a quick romance," he admitted. "For the long haul, friendship might be better. Who the hell knows?''

He pointed suddenly toward a log cabin nestled in an oak grove well back from the road. A stone chimney indicated a fireplace, and a porch wrapped around one end and half the front. "That's the original ranch building," he said. "That's where my folks honeymooned and that's where they made up. On up ahead—''

They drove out of the trees. Before them sprawled the new ranch house—new only in the sense that it had been constructed long after the original cabin, which continued to be used as a vacation destination for Taggarts. Jesse built the new house for Meg shortly after he left the professional rodeo circuit, not long after they'd patched up their marriage.

Outbuildings and log corrals circled the house, giving it an air of permanency. Sleek horses ran in fenced pastures alongside the road, and when they drove up to the hitching racks at the side of the house, a black Border collie leaped off the porch and bounded toward them.

Max pointed. "Is that a cow dog?''

Rand grinned. "Around here he's more like a horse dog, if there is such a critter." He touched her hand where it rested at the edge of her bucket seat. "Are you ready?"

She took a deep breath, her smile fading. "As ready as I'll ever be."

"In that case..." Leaning forward, he pressed his mouth lightly to hers. Or at least that was what he'd intended. But her lips felt so surprisingly soft and inviting that he wrapped his arms around her shoulders and deepened the kiss into something entirely different.

For a moment she was docile and unprotesting in his embrace. Then she wrapped her arms around his neck and let her lips part, let him slide his tongue inside her mouth—

A pounding on the window brought them springing apart guiltily. Made dim-witted by the unexpected potency of that kiss, Rand fumbled to open the door.

His mother stood there, alternately frowning and smiling. *Get it together,* Rand warned himself. *Get it together or you can write off the Rocking T.*

NUMBLY MAXI WATCHED Rand fold his arms around the beautiful blond woman who'd interrupted the most passionate kiss she'd ever received. For a shocked instant, she thought this must be an old girlfriend. Then the woman leaned down to smile through the open door and Maxi realized this was his *mother.*

Meg Taggart was gorgeous, with her unlined face

and melting brown eyes. Trim and toned as a model, she had a pampered and expensive air about her.

It was easy to see where Rand got his good looks—or was until his father stepped off the porch.

Jesse James Taggart radiated power the way a stove radiated heat. Broad-shouldered and narrow-hipped, he ambled forward with that easy Western walk. Shoving his hat back on his head, he revealed hair so dark as to be nearly black, with only a hint of distinguished gray.

Maxi saw welcome on his face, but he didn't embrace his son. Instead he extended a hand, which Rand took in the fast shake he'd give a stranger. Then he turned immediately back to the car.

"Folks," he said, "I'd like you to meet my wife, Maxine." He opened her door and helped her out.

Feeling awkward and out of place, Maxi wished she were here as herself, not this dowdy impostor. But it was far too late for second thoughts, so she squared her shoulders and braced for the worst.

Meg stepped closer with a smile. "Maxine, dear. Welcome to our family." She embraced the taller woman.

"Th-thank you." It had been much easier to play games with Rand's aunt and uncle than with his parents, Maxi was quickly realizing.

Jesse said, "Maxine," and dipped his head.

He offered nothing more, just looked her over with a narrow-eyed glance that made her want to squirm.

"It's been so long," Meg went on. "Come inside, darlings. The cook's made up a batch of those pecan cookies you like so much, Randy, and we've got a fresh pitcher of iced tea.''

Rand fell in beside his mother, leaving Maxi to walk with his father. Jesse gave her an overly casual glance and asked, ''You ride?''

''You mean horses?''

He sounded astonished. ''What else is there to ride?''

She laughed. ''Where I come from, bikes and buses would be more likely. But in answer to your question, no, I don't ride. I've never been on a horse in my life.''

''That's a downright cryin' shame.'' He appeared almost comically sorry for her.

''I suspect there's someone around here who can rectify that sad situation.''

''You got that right!'' His grin carried almost as much wattage as his son's.

OVER A PLATE of cookies and tall glasses of iced tea, the older generation and the younger fenced cautiously.

Or so it seemed to Rand, who grew more and more tense with every passing minute. He could handle his mother; he always had. His father was another story. He never knew what Jesse was thinking or what he'd do next. It had been that way for nearly thirty years and Rand had no particular hope that this would change any time soon.

Meg, who'd been chattering on about her latest trip to Boston, turned to Max. ''Clementine will be here later," she said. "Randy did tell you he has a sister, I hope."

"Oh, yes. I'm looking forward to meeting her."

"She's about your age, I suspect. Twenty-one?"

Rand didn't groan, but he wanted to. Talk about obvious!

"I'm twenty-five," Max said calmly. "Close enough, I guess."

"Absolutely." Meg looked relieved. "I was twenty-one when I got married myself. Believe me, it was much too young."

Jesse laughed. "I robbed the cradle. Then I had to wait for her to grow up."

"Oh, you." Meg made a face. "It's just better not to jump into marriage so young, don't you agree? Fortunately Clemmie's busy with her career. She works in Houston for Taggart Oil—did Rand tell you?"

"He mentioned it."

"Enough about family." Meg rose, slender and graceful in matching silk trousers and shirt. "Randy, please put your suitcases in the guest suite."

"Ah, Mom, I thought we could stay at the cabin." Had *counted* on staying at the cabin, in fact.

"Absolutely not. We want you closer than that—both of you."

"But—"

"Jesse, speak to your son."

"Kid, your mother says—"

"I heard her, Dad. I'm not deaf."

"Did I say you're deaf?" Jesse rose abruptly. "Good meeting you, Maxine. Now I've got to get back to work with that three-year-old. Danged horse is just about halfway broke. See you at supper.''

He strode from the room. Glancing at Rand, Maxi saw a look of naked longing on his face—longing for his father's approval but total denial of that desire.

Meg apparently saw nothing she hadn't seen a thousand times. She patted her son's shoulder and turned to his new wife. ''Let's go into my sitting room. We can have a nice talk while Randy carries in your suitcases. There's so much I'm *dying* to know....''

RAND WAS ALONE on the broad porch when Clemmie drove into the yard in a silver Porsche. She leaped out and rushed to throw her arms around her brother.

He held her close, recognizing a faithful and badly needed ally.

She pushed back, her gray Taggart eyes laughing. It occurred to him then that his kid sister had grown up to be a real knockout.

''Where is she?'' Clemmie demanded. ''When Mom told me you were married, I almost drove off the road.''

''Never relay important news to a person on a cell phone.''

''You got that right. So fess up. Are you just trying to get your inheritance or are you crazy in love with her?''

''Both,'' he said, knowing he couldn't tell a barefaced lie to his sister and get away with it. Despite the difference in their ages, she'd always seen right through him.

"Really?" The gray eyes narrowed. "You're crazy in love with her?"

Be careful, he warned himself. "Okay, I'll level with you, but you've got to keep your mouth shut. I guess you could say I'm crazy in like with her."

"Are you kidding?"

"Not a bit. Max is just about the smartest, bravest—"

"When was there occasion to test her bravery?" Clemmie looked appalled.

"I'll explain that later. She's the smartest, bravest, most interesting, most honest—"

"I'm not hearing beautiful, sexy or sophisticated in there," Clementine broke in.

"She's beautiful inside."

His sister stared at him as if he'd lost his marbles. "You, of all people, have married a woman who's beautiful inside? Holy cow, Rand, this *must* be love! So where is this woman who's done the impossible by snagging my elusive brother?"

"With Mom in her sitting room."

"Then she's in dire need of rescuing." Clemmie hesitated. "But before I go, how's…everything else? The camp, Laura and the kids…?"

"Getting by." Why had he ever told her?

"Oh, you!" Clementine touched her fingertips to her lips, then planted the kiss on his cheek. "Big brother, you'll be a mystery to me until the day I die. Most people—" She frowned, shrugged. "Forget most people. We'll talk more later, okay? In the meantime, try not to start World War III with Daddy.''

And she was gone.

Rand was alone again, not an unusual circumstance at the Hells Bells Ranch.

MAXI DIDN'T KNOW what the third degree was until Meg Taggart got hold of her. Fortunately Meg's questions were usually followed up by her own answers, or speculations, or guesses, or elaborations. Even so, by the time Clementine dashed in, Maxi was in a cold sweat.

Clementine was adorable: long blond hair and long-lashed gray eyes in a perfect oval face, a neat figure like her mother's, clothing that Maxi instinctively recognized as designer quality.

She was definitely her mother's daughter, but with her father's down-home manner about her. Bending, she kissed her mother's cheek, giving Maxi a conspiratorial wink.

''Hi, Mama. I take it this is the newest member of the clan.''

''Hello, darling. This is Maxine, your brother's wife.''

Clementine smiled. ''Welcome to the Taggart family, Max. If you can survive us, you can survive anything.''

''Thank you. Everyone's been wonderful.''

''When did you and my handsome brother get married?''

''A few days ago.''

''How long have you known each other?''

"Long enough."

"What are your plans?"

"You'll have to ask him."

Clementine burst out laughing. "Okay, those are the necessary questions." She dropped her shoulder bag onto a chair. "Would you like a tour before dinner, Max? I hope you don't mind me calling you 'Max,' but that's what Randy called you. Mama, want to come along?"

"Maxine's tired, Clemmie," Meg objected. "Why don't you entertain your brother while Maxine and I continue with our nice chat."

"Being grilled by your new mother-in-law is definitely not in the 'nice chat' category. Let's go, Max!"

Maxi shrugged helplessly to indicate that this wasn't her idea, then followed Clementine from the room. Once the door closed behind them, she turned to Rand's sister and said, "If you were a guy, I'd kiss you for that."

"If I were a guy, I'd let you. Come on before she comes after us."

"WHAT DO YOU think of her?" Meg demanded of Jesse hours later, pausing with the brush poised for another stroke.

He shrugged broad bare shoulders. The rest of him was bare, too. Jesse refused to wear anything to bed and always had. It was one of many things Meg had come to appreciate about him.

"No, really," she insisted. "Tell me."

"She seems okay."

"Jesse!" Meg threw down the brush and stood up, shoving the dressing-table bench aside. "She's not the girl for him."

"That's not for us to judge."

"She's all wrong for him. I can see what's in this for him—the Rocking T, although why he wants it now I don't know. But what's in this for her?"

"You think it's so far-fetched that she might love him?"

"No," Meg said slowly, "but..."

She went on about it at great length while Jesse tuned her out as he'd been doing for years. He didn't know what Randy was up to and didn't intend to lose any more sleep over it. Jesse didn't understand his son and didn't expect he ever would. He'd liked Maxine from the get-go, but considering how riled up Meg was, that wasn't going to pack a whole hell-uva lot of weight.

Fortunately it was Randy's problem, not his father's.

CHAPTER EIGHT

CLEMENTINE'S DEPARTURE Sunday afternoon was a real downer for Maxi. Clemmie was her only support in this place, friendly and fun and willing to take everything at face value.

Meg took nothing at face value, while Jesse seemed more interested in avoiding Rand than in anything else. He was rarely around and when he was seemed preoccupied.

The week would be a long one, Maxi thought.

The nights weren't going all that well, either. Maxi and Rand shared a king-size bed in the guest suite Saturday night and it should have been fine, a piece of cake. After all, she'd argued with herself, it wasn't as if this were the first time. But for some reason, this felt different. Maxi wondered if that kiss in the car was to blame.

Kissing Rand Taggart was obviously not something she could do with impunity. Maybe this was true because her love life had been so nonexistent for so long, or maybe it was because Rand was just too damn attractive. Whatever the reason, she felt a new and nerve-jangling awareness, especially when they were alone.

Luckily she saw no indication that he felt anything at all.

When he announced Sunday night that he'd be sleeping on the couch in the small sitting-dressing room, he took her by complete surprise. He didn't look at her when he said it, just pulled an extra blanket and pillow from the closet and ambled out of the bedroom.

She glared after him, furious. Sleeping next to him wasn't easy on *her,* either, but did she go slinking away like a coward? The more she thought about it, the more annoyed she became. It wasn't that she considered herself irresistible or anything, although plenty of men had told her she was, after seeing her in her underwear in the Violet's Advantage catalog. But she had never expected to find herself cooped up with a man who barely even saw her.

To hell with that!

The next morning she waited until he went into the bathroom and then, in a fit of pique, proceeded to half undress while waiting for him to reappear. He walked out of the bathroom wearing jeans and a towel, with which he then vigorously rubbed his wet hair. His glance touched her and screeched to a halt, his eyes widening in disbelief.

She grabbed her dress off the bed and held it haphazardly in front of her plain white cotton bra and equally plain panties. "Oh, dear!" she exclaimed. "You—you startled me!"

"Sorry about that." Head down, he almost ran across the room and out the door.

She finished dressing, allowing herself a smug

smile, which slipped when she reminded herself that she was playing a dangerous game. She mustn't do that again. After retrieving the phone, she dialed the Chicago number of R. Renwood Keever.

"IS THAT YOU, Mr. Keever? This is Helen Reed's sister, Maxine Rafferty. I didn't expect you to answer."

Woody Keever gripped the receiver, his eyes bulging in a most unattractive manner that mocked him from the ornate gold-framed mirror opposite his mahogany-and-leather-tooled desk. Although he'd managed to hang on to his luxurious offices in an upscale Chicago suburb, he'd been forced to let all the help go. That was what happened when you put all your eggs in the wrong basket. After Coconutty, his few remaining clients had departed in droves.

Which was why he'd picked up the telephone himself. That he'd had to was humiliating, but he controlled his ire. "Yes, Ms. Rafferty. My secretary just stepped away from her desk. What can I do for you?"

"You can tell me how my sister is."

"Fine, she's doing fine. Or at least as fine as possible while incarcerated."

"I wanted to bail her out, Mr. Keever. She wouldn't let me."

No, because the silly bitch was waiting for her boyfriend to ride to her rescue. Like Bill Overton cared. "She doesn't want you to become involved in her troubles," he said sanctimoniously. "She was quite adamant about that."

"Yes, but I had to do something so…" Long silence and then she said, "I'm in Texas with Rand Taggart. I'm…trying to get the goods on him so I can help Helen."

At mention of the Taggart name, a shiver shot down Woody's back and he sat up straighter. "Rand Taggart? My God, that's dangerous! Whatever possessed you—"

"*He's* not dangerous," she interrupted quickly. "Being around him tends to be, though. Did you hear about that Chicago plane hijacked to Mexico a few days ago? We were on it."

"You were—" Woody sucked in a disbelieving breath.

"In fact," she went on, "he's the one who overpowered the hijackers, but he lied and another guy took the credit." She gave a disgusted grunt. "He lies when the truth would serve him better."

"Maybe he has good reason to keep his name out of the newspapers," Woody suggested, thinking fast. "You're still with him?"

"Yes, but he has no idea that I have any connection to Helen or any of that. And please don't tell her what I'm doing, either. It would break her heart to think he can go on with his life without giving her a single thought."

"I won't mention it." Unless it suited his purpose. "Have you come up with anything?" Jeez, he hoped not.

She sighed. "I've been through his wallet and briefcase and luggage, and there's nothing. He hasn't said anything helpful, either."

Good! "Take care, Ms. Rafferty," Renwood said dutifully. "Taggart is a dangerous man playing a dangerous game."

"He's shifty—I'll give you that. But dangerous?" She didn't sound as confident as she had earlier. "Don't worry. I'll be careful. Is there anything I should know? Anything I should be looking for, specifically?"

"I've heard talk of a safe-deposit key." He didn't think Taggart had it, but who knew?

Long silence, then she said, "Oh my God. A safe-deposit key?"

"You know something about that?"

"No, no, just thinking out loud."

"Oh. All right. In that case, merely keeping me posted as to his whereabouts would be beneficial." Yeah, if Taggart got close to Overton before Woody got his money, knowing could be *real* beneficial. "I'd also urge you to avoid the police at all costs. They're only interested in pinning the rap on your sister and Mr. Overton."

"That's what Helen said." She sighed. "I really wish I were better at this. I'll never make a detective, but I'll do my best."

"You wouldn't want to tell me how you ingratiated yourself with him so quickly."

"Don't even ask. Just watch out for my sister."

Woody's telephone hadn't even cooled before it rang again. Picking up, he heard the unmistakable tones of the man responsible for his current predicament.

"Hey, Woody," Bill Overton said with hearty

good humor, "stop making all those strangling noises and say you're glad to hear from me."

"Glad? Glad!" More strangling noises; Woody caught himself up short. "Where are you? When are you coming back?"

"None of your business and never."

"Dammit, Bill, you left me in a serious bind."

"Which I intend to get you out of, old pal," Bill said soothingly. "Just not quite yet."

Woody groaned. "The law is on your tail and they're harassing *me*. Your secretary's still in jail and—"

"That's why I called, about Helen. I want you to bail her out."

"With what? I'm on the verge of bankruptcy. Even if I had the money, I can think of a lot better uses for it."

"Take it easy." Bill leaned heavily on his fabled charm. "Did you figure I'd leave you out on that limb all alone? Not a chance, pal. I'll get the money to you somehow."

"How and how much? Don't forget, you owe me more than you do your silly secretary."

"Can't tell you *how* because I don't know yet, but trust me. There'll be a nice little bonus for you, too."

Somewhat mollified, Woody said, "Well, okay, but there better be. I don't know why you're bothering with her, though. At least when she's in jail we can keep track of her."

"She's got something of mine that I need back. Just bail her out when you get the money, and tell her I'll be in touch."

Woody let out a hissing breath. "Once out of jail, the woman will be a loose cannon."

"Yeah, but she's nuts about me. She'll take orders. Just tell her I'm raising the money and she should sit tight. Anything else going on?"

Woody's tone became conspiratorial. "It might interest you to know Taggart's...not on your trail, at least not at the moment. He's gone home to Texas."

Bill let out a surprised whistle. "That's good news. How did you—"

"I have my contacts. Give my best to your wife."

Bill Overton hung up the telephone, his thoughts all over the place. It might behoove him to find out what Keever knew about Rand Taggart and how he knew it. Bill was sorry about fleecing Rand along with the rest of the suckers, but he didn't feel guilty enough to regret it. His business had been headed down the tubes and he'd had no choice.

Especially if he wanted to keep the affections of his beautiful blond showgirl wife, at whom he now glanced.

Kristi saw him look at her and gave him a seductive smile. She was gorgeous in the tiny red bikini that barely covered the essential points of her voluptuous anatomy. Framed by gently waving palms and sparkling blue sky, she looked like what she was: high maintenance. She probably suspected he wasn't as innocent in the Coconutty case as he maintained, but she never pressed him on the subject and went along with anything he said.

He figured she was as crazy about him as his secretary was—and just as dumb. He liked that in a woman....

"WHAT KEPT YOU?"

Maxi started guiltily. She hadn't known Rand waited right outside the bedroom door. Had he heard anything? "I needed to make a phone call," she said defensively. "Is that all right with you?"

"Of course. I was just waiting to have breakfast with you."

"Oh." Now she felt guilty for snapping at him. "Okay. Rand—"

"What?" He indicated that she should lead the way down the hall.

"I think I've lost my safe-deposit key. You haven't seen it, have you?"

"No." He gave her a curious glance. "That's quite a coincidence."

"What is?"

"I had a safe-deposit key in that briefcase that disappeared in Mexico."

"You—" she swallowed hard before adding "—did?"

"It was no great loss. I've got another someplace." He stopped outside the kitchen door, putting his hand on her arm. "Let's go riding today."

"As in horseback?"

"You got it."

"I don't think so. You go and I'll just curl up somewhere out of the way with a book."

"You can't do that, Max." Stepping close to her,

he slid an arm around her waist. "We're newlyweds, remember?"

"Yes, but—"

"But me no buts. We're going riding. After breakfast, you can put on some jeans—you have jeans, don't you?"

"Well, yes."

"Okay, you can put 'em on while I saddle up." He laughed into her anxious face. "It'll be fun, Max, and it'll make you a bunch of points with my dad. That's why we're here, remember?"

"I remember."

His hand dug into her waist. "Good. Now, let's go show my folks what happy newlyweds really look like."

"Within reason," she said quickly, giving in too easily to the pressure of his arm because she was still stunned by his easy admission about the safe-deposit key, which she'd so blithely tossed away in her ignorance. "But *only* within reason."

SADDLING UP, Rand felt his spirits rise. He'd always liked this part of life in Texas: the horses, the ranch work, being out-of-doors. What he hadn't liked was dealing with his father on a day-to-day basis. He loved his dad and he was fairly confident his dad loved him, but there was no understanding between them at all.

After leading the little roan mare to the hitching rack, he tossed the reins over the wooden bars and turned to find Max walking toward him with what could only be called a reluctant gait. She'd put on jeans as he'd directed, along with white sneakers and a plain white shirt that hung loosely around her hips.

He'd had a glimpse of those hips this morning when he'd caught her in the process of dressing. That tantalizing glimpse haunted him; it also made him wonder if he was going nuts, because it didn't jibe with her usual appearance at all.

She stopped in front of him and planted her hands on her hips. "This is not a good idea," she announced.

"It's a great idea. Max, meet Lady." He stroked the mare's forelock, smoothing it over the headband.

Max frowned. "She has big brown eyes," she said accusingly.

"She also has a big heart and she's gentle."

"She's too tall."

"Look at my horse." He indicated the bay standing hipshot on the other side of the hitching rack. "He's way bigger."

"Well...I suppose." She reached out tentatively to lay her hand on the mare's neck. "Do I really have to do this?"

"You really do." But not just to impress his father; she had to do it for herself, Rand thought. Poor kid had missed out on a lot, growing up in a city. "Hey, if you don't like it, we won't go far. I promise. But I think you *will* like it, and then you'll have discovered something new."

"I don't need anything new." But her expression softened as she stroked the gleaming neck. "Okay, if I've got to, let's get it over with."

"Then put your foot in the stirrup and..."

THE FIRST TIME the horses broke into a trot, Maxi laughed so hard she nearly bounced off. Hanging on to the saddle horn with both hands, she threw back her head and shouted with delight, her heels flopping.

Rand stayed alongside her on the trail leading through the trees, coaching her but not getting very far with it. She was having too good a time to pay much attention to the words of someone who rode like a centaur. Finally he reached over to catch the mare's rein and pull her to a stop.

"Hey!" Maxi tried to glare at him but knew she wasn't doing too good a job with it. "Why'd you do that? I was on a roll!"

"Yeah, but you were also about to end up in a pile on the ground. You wouldn't like that so much."

"Probably not, since I couldn't do it as well as your uncle Trey did." Her grin was impish. "Really, how am I doing?"

"Great," he said, meaning it. "Have you changed your mind about horses, then?"

She patted the mare's sleek neck. "Maybe."

"Why so cautious?"

"I hate to admit I was wrong." She shoved her glasses, which had slid down her nose, back in place. "I'm sorry. I just don't have much experience with animals. Like none."

"Horses I can understand. There's not much room to put one up in the city. But no cats? No dogs?"

She shook her head emphatically.

"That's tough." He couldn't imagine not knowing and liking animals. He'd always had dogs and cats around, even in Boston; in Texas, there'd also been horses and cattle. "Didn't you ever want a pet?"

"Of course I did." She gave him an annoyed glance. "You have no idea how I grew up, Rand, you with your rich Boston grandpa and another rich grandpa in Texas and rich parents someplace in between."

"You're right. I don't." He tossed the reins over the big red horse's head and stepped out of the saddle. Then he put his hands on Maxi's waist. "Let's remedy that."

She covered his hands with hers. "What are you *doing?*"

"Pulling you off that horse so we can sit over there beside Handbasket Creek while you tell me the story of your life." Without further ado, he lifted her out of the saddle and set her on the ground in front of him.

Her chin jutted out. "You won't talk about you, so I won't talk about me." She turned away.

"Don't be like that." He followed her toward the banks of the creek. "*Everybody* talks about me. You must already know everything except my blood type."

"A positive." After selecting a large exposed tree root, she sat. Leafy shadows filtered down to make lacy patterns on her face. "But I don't know anything important. I don't know who your friends are, what you—"

"Cut it out, Max. It's your turn to do the talking." She bit her lower lip. "I don't like to whine...."

"I've never known a woman who whined less than

you do." Rand braced a booted foot on the root and leaned against the tree. "Start talking. You said you have a sister?"

"Yes."

"Older or younger?"

"Older."

"Parents?"

"Parents." She said the word with distaste, then seemed gripped by indecision. After a moment, she said, "My mother raised me."

"No father?"

"Obviously there was a sperm donor. But father? I haven't seen him since I was about ten." She shook her head. "My mom…drank a lot. She tried, but she couldn't hold a job. She'd go on benders." She grimaced. "I'm whining."

"You're telling me something I need to know. Please…."

SHE WONDERED if she could, but as the silence lengthened, a startling urge to share her story overcame her. She took a deep breath and looked into those clear blue-gray eyes. All she saw was encouragement.

"It's not an original story," she said at last. "We lived in a series of cheap apartments on the South Side of Chicago. When there wasn't money even for that, we lived out of the car or with my mother's… friends. My sister and I went to school when we could. I liked it and was good at it. She didn't and wasn't."

"Sounds tough."

"Yeah, well, Mom did the best she could," she said defensively. "We loved her and she loved us. She just couldn't handle the booze. I was sixteen when she passed out in a Chicago alley in January and froze to death."

"Oh, God." Squatting, he took her hands in his. "I wish I could make it better."

"You can't, Rand," she said calmly, although she didn't feel calm, even now. "Hel—my sister was on her own by then. She'd been after me for a couple of years to live with her, but I couldn't...I couldn't leave my mother."

Her voice dropped lower. "Mama needed someone to take care of her and there was only me. We lived on welfare, mostly. She—" Max stopped talking abruptly. After a pause, she said, "Mama did what she had to do to get the money to support her habit. After she'd pass out, I used to pour the dregs of the bottle—there was never anything left but the dregs—I used to flush them down the toilet." She gave a bitter little laugh. "When we had one."

"Ah, Max—"

"You asked, Rand," she reminded him sharply. "I used to take a shortcut to school through an alley, and one morning I found her there in the snow. She hadn't come home the night before, but that wasn't too unusual. I tried to wake her, although I think in my heart I knew she was dead. Then I tried to drag her inside, but...but—"

She choked, unable to go on. Rand leaned forward to slide an arm around her quivering shoulder. Gently he kissed her temple.

After a moment she lifted her head, eyes burning with tears she refused to shed. "My sister took me in following that, but it was tough. She was living with a guy who didn't like having me around. When he walked out on her, I almost felt as if I were caring for my mother all over again. Still, without her I'd probably have gone into foster care or run away."

"Poor Max."

"Don't pity me, Rand. I survived." She lifted her chin, but her lips trembled. "I don't talk about this because I don't want pity."

"How about sympathy?"

She sighed and her rigid shoulders slumped. "Okay, I guess I could handle a little sympathy. The point is, I don't want anyone to think I'm looking for a free ride because I had it a little rough."

"A *little* rough?"

"All right, a lot rough. That's all behind me now. At least, it is mostly. I'm cheap because I never had any money."

"Thrifty. You're thrifty." His mouth quirked up at the corners. "I could use a little of that."

"I'm suspicious. I'm always looking for hidden motives."

"Wary. You're just a little wary. There's nothing wrong with that."

"You don't think so?" She shrugged as if it didn't matter. "I'm also secretive and willing to do anything for my sister, who's the only person in the world I love."

"Now, *that* is really sad."

Her eyes widened. "That I'm loyal?"

"No, that there's only one person in the world you love."

Moving slowly and deliberately, he took her glasses off her nose, folded them carefully and slipped them into her shirt pocket. Then he reached behind her head to slide off the silky scarf holding her hair back. Using both hands, he fluffed the strands around her shoulders.

He rubbed a thumb across her sensitive lower lip. "Thanks for telling me that, Max," he said. "I almost think you're starting to trust me...a little." Cupping his hand around the back of her neck beneath her hair, he drew her forward.

She faced him again resolutely. "*Can* I trust you?"

"Absolutely." He kissed her temple, twining his fingers through hers. Then he lifted her hand to his mouth and kissed her knuckles, keeping his gaze locked with hers. "You'll think I'm crazy, but I'm grateful for the hijacking. Win, lose or draw, it changed my life."

Both their lives....

On the other side of the cottonwood grove, Jesse pulled up his horse at the sight of his son and daughter-in-law deep in what looked like serious conversation. He probably ought to ride over and say something, but if they were into anything important...

While he tried to make up his mind, Maxine slid her arms around Rand's neck and they came together in a kiss that sent guilty voyeuristic shivers down Jesse's back. The passion they shared could not be mistaken, and he turned his horse away, ashamed of himself, although he hadn't intended to spy on them.

Later he told Meg about the encounter, adding, "It makes me wonder if they really are a love match." He saw her stormy expression and conceded, "I know, the timing's too convenient. But if you'd seen them—"

"I don't believe this, Jesse," Meg cut in. "He obviously married her in an attempt to get his hands on his inheritance. He deliberately chose a woman he'd have no trouble walking away from after it's all over."

Jesse stared at his beautiful wife for several seconds in silence. Then he said, "That's cold, Meg."

"You think so?"

She walked to him and put her hands lightly on his chest. "I know a little bit about passion," she said, her eyes darkening. "Were they at that bend in Handbasket Creek where we saw the deer?"

"What deer?"

"Oh, Jesse! You know what deer. That day we went riding...when our grandfathers forced us to come back here together. Surely you remember."

He smiled. "I remember."

"I was lying there in the shade with my eyes closed, thinking...thinking that if you'd ever once say you needed me, everything would work out all right between us. I wanted you to tell me that you couldn't live without me."

"I couldn't, Meggie. You know that."

"I know it now. Then, I wanted to hear you say it. You knelt beside me and put your hand over my mouth, which nearly scared me to death. Then you pointed to a deer drinking on the other side of the creek. It was one of those magical moments that you never forget—at least, I never did.''

"I didn't, either.'' He kissed her eyelids.

"Th-then the deer saw us and ran away. And you kissed me—the first time you'd done that in five years.''

She'd tried to hold him off, but the magic of the moment had been too strong. She'd curled her fingers in his shirt, as she was doing now, and drew his head down.

Their lips met. The feelings rushing over her then were strong, but not as strong as they were today, after three decades of marriage. A melting languor flowed through her, into every extremity, leaving her weak and yearning yet again.

Then, he'd drawn back and said, ''Look, we're about to dive into some deep waters here. We need a time-out, some kind of distraction while we get our bearings. Want to go into Hells Bells for the big Fourth of July celebration?''

Now, neither one of them needed bearings to know they were exactly where they were meant to be. When Jesse scooped her into his arms, she clung to him, her rock and her love.

No way did Randy have this kind of passion with that strange girl.

CHAPTER NINE

CLEMENTINE RETURNED Thursday, just in time to join the rest of the family at a barbecue at Joe Bob Brooks's Hell-on-the-Handbasket Dude Ranch. After the tension-packed week she'd had thus far, Maxi was delighted to greet Rand's sister.

Maybe Clemmie could help her forget that she'd made an awful mistake telling Rand her life story. At the time, she'd rashly thought it might encourage him to be a bit more open to her questions. It hadn't, and now she felt more vulnerable than ever.

Nor did it help that Meg didn't like her new daughter-in-law. Not that Meg said or did anything overt; her manners were far too good for that. But Maxi could feel Rand's mother watching, always watching…. It was completely unnerving.

And Jesse… Maxi sighed. Jesse seemed to like her, all right, but he didn't believe in the marriage, either. Or maybe he simply didn't believe in his son. Rand and his father circled each other like a couple of big dogs, their expressions hostile and their mouths tight.

Clemmie's presence brought relief to everyone. Bright and pretty and ready for fun, she swept everyone along with her, including her father and brother.

As now, when they all stood gathered in the front yard for the short trip over to Joe Bob's. Clemmie took command.

"Rand, you and Max go in your rental car and I'll ride with Mama and Daddy. That'll give you time to warn her about ol' Joe Bob." Her smile wrinkled her nose.

"You could come with us if you want," Maxi invited.

"Max, don't argue," Clemmie said. "You and my big brother hardly have any time alone at all, except at night, I mean." She said it with perfect aplomb. "I'll ride back with you if the old folks decide to leave early."

Meg, who must be in her early fifties, laughed. She could afford to; she didn't look a day over thirty in her linen slacks and yellow silk blouse. "Who are you calling old folks, young lady?" she scolded, draping an arm over her daughter's shoulders and drawing her toward the sports-utility vehicle parked on the graveled driveway.

Jesse fell in beside them. "Speak for yourself, woman. I only go to these things because Joe Bob's an old friend. Leavin' early is the only thing I have to look forward to."

Smiling, Max climbed into the rented convertible next to Rand. When they were headed down the lane for the road, she said, "I have a question."

"Shoot."

"Why do you call your parents 'Mom' and 'Dad' while your sister calls them 'Mama' and 'Daddy'?"

He seemed to give that serious consideration. After

a couple of miles, he said, "*Mama* and *Daddy* are real Southern. I've known sixty-year-old men who still called their parents that."

"But you don't."

"Max, I'm not Southern. Or maybe I'm part Southern, but most of me is..."

"Is what, Rand?"

"I started to say *pure New England,* but that isn't true, either. If I was pushed, I'd have to say I don't really belong anywhere." He glanced at her, his expression guarded. "I'm a citizen of the world, I guess you could say."

She felt a twinge of sympathy for this man who'd grown up with everything she hadn't: wealth, of course, but also an extended family. "It doesn't have to be that way," she said.

"What way?"

"Estranged from your father."

"Estranged! I'm not—"

"You are, Rand. You and your father strike sparks, and your mother is constantly tense with the effort to keep peace. Only Clementine seems able to bring everybody together."

"You're wrong," he said flatly. "I'm not close to my father, I'll admit that, but it's nobody's fault. We don't know each other very well, but what he knows, he doesn't like."

He'll like it even less when he finds out you're on the wrong side of the law, she thought, but didn't say. How had a man with Rand's advantages got himself into such a mess?

For she'd just about come to the conclusion that

the Coconutty escapade *was* a mess, and he probably hadn't intended to do anything wrong. He had doubtless rationalized the whole thing long ago.

But he couldn't rationalize Helen, an innocent victim of his greed. Maxi must keep that firmly in mind. She couldn't get mixed up in his family problems.

So she said, "Let's change the subject. Tell me more about this Joe Bob."

Good choice; his stiff shoulders relaxed. "Joe Bob rodeoed with my dad—my daddy." He cast her a challenging glance. "When his first wife divorced him, he quit the circuit, bought the old Bar B and turned it into a dude ranch. I understand he recently remarried, but I don't know who."

"You like him," she guessed.

"He's a man's man, if you get my drift—a bit crude and occasionally rude, but a good ol' boy nonetheless. My mom, on the other hand, can barely stand him, though she tries to hide it."

"And this event tonight is…?"

"Just a big cookout and talent show for his current crop of dudes. He likes to include us Taggarts because he and Dad go back so far."

Ahead loomed the entrance to the dude ranch with the name emblazoned on a wooden sign suspended above the road, complete with the slogan: Punch A Cow With Old Joe Bob."

This, Maxi thought, should be interesting.

ONCE HE'D CLIMBED out of the convertible, Rand helped Max out and slid an arm around her waist in a friendly gesture. She must be getting used to it; she didn't jump or glare, just tensed ever so slightly.

"There's Joe Bob." Rand pointed toward a cluster of Western-dressed men and woman. "Come meet him, and then we can kick back and enjoy the proceedings."

Joe Bob turned from his dudes, saw Rand, grinned and waved. His belly sagged even farther over his ornate silver belt buckle than it had the last time Rand saw him, and his white Stetson was even bigger. The plaid shirt strained at the pearl snaps holding it over that massive expanse, making his hips and legs look downright spindly.

Rand stuck out his hand. "Joe Bob."

Joe Bob yanked and Rand found himself mashed against the big chest, fists pounding on his back. "Dang it, boy, that's no way to greet your daddy's oldest and best buddy," the man declared. Shoving Rand away, he grinned, then gave him another crushing hug.

Out of breath and disconcerted, Rand found his voice and regained his space at the same time. "Joe Bob, I want you to meet my wife, Maxine."

"I heard you got hitched. Mighty glad to make your acquaintance, little lady."

Joe Bob turned on Maxine, and darned if she didn't submit to his embrace with good grace. By the time he let her loose, she was gasping for breath, but apparently not unhappy about it.

Joe Bob beamed. "Now I gotta little surprise for *you.* You remember Donna, don't you?" He gestured for a slender dark-haired woman to join them. She did, smiling mischievously.

"Sure." Rand returned the smile. "Good to see you, Mrs. Dobbins."

"She ain't Miz Dobbins no more," Joe Bob crowed. "She's Miz Brooks. Her boy, Shane, is around here somewheres, too." He faced Maxine. "Your pa-in-law saved Shane's bacon when he was just a button. He—"

"A button?" Maxine inquired.

"Just a kid," Joe Bob explained. "Knee high to a grasshopper—you know." He cocked his head. "Where you from, Maxine?"

"Chicago."

"Well, that explains it." Joe Bob gave Rand a pitying glance. "Anyway, twenty years or better ago, J.J.—that's what I call Jesse James Taggart, knowin' him so long and all—J.J. bulldogged a horse rid by Little Billy Vaughn that was about to stomp Shane into the dirt. Happened on a Fourth of July. I'll never forget it if I live to be a hundred. There we were, havin' a good time, when—"

Donna clapped her hand over his mouth, cutting him off in midrant. "Joe Bob, don't go into one of your long tales. Let these kids get something to drink and meet a few young people. Honestly, they couldn't be less interested."

"I'm interested," Max said quickly. At their curious glances, she smiled. "I'm *very* interested. I have a lot to learn about the Taggarts and you seem to know all about them."

"See?" Joe Bob gave his wife a triumphant

glance. "Ol' Randy found himself a real smart gal, even if she is a damnyankee."

"Go," Donna said to Max and Randy. "Go before he gets started again."

They went, laughing, heading for the big washtub overflowing with ice and beer.

MAXI, Randy, Meg and Clementine loitered beneath the shadows of a cottonwood tree, watching the party flow around them.

"So," Clementine said to Maxi, "did you meet our host?"

Maxi rolled her eyes. "I sure did. He's a real character."

"And then some. Watch out for him, though. He's the worst practical joker in the world."

Meg sniffed. "Some of his jokes aren't all that funny." She glanced around almost accusingly at Jesse, standing across the ranch yard in conversation with several men. "Excuse me, I need a word with my husband."

Clementine watched her mother go, then looked at Maxi. "I'll bet you wonder what *that* was all about."

"I'm mildly curious."

"Randy, did you ever hear that story?"

"Apparently not, since I don't know what you're talking about."

Clementine's tone grew conspiratorial. "The way I've pieced it together, it happened while Mama and Daddy were tryin' to reconcile—you know, Randy, when you were five or six and I was just a gleam in

Daddy's eye? It was when the great-grandpas black-mailed them into coming back to the old cabin.''

"I know about *that*," Maxi assured her.

"But you don't know the whole story, I'll bet. See, Joe Bob never liked Mama much because she was a damnyankee and took Daddy away to boot. Apparently Joe Bob wasn't all that keen on a reconciliation, so he put a pair of black lace unmentionables in Daddy's pocket. Naturally Mama found them. I don't know exactly how it played out, but there was hell to pay.''

Maxi was horrified. "What a rotten trick!"

"I'll say.'' Rand shook his head in disbelief. "I'm surprised Joe Bob survived to tell about it.''

"I don't think he did—tell about it, I mean,'' Clementine said. "I picked up bits and pieces from Mama and Grandpa Thom T. or I wouldn't know myself. Anyway, he's paid for what he did big-time, so it's probably better off forgotten.''

She glanced around, waving at a handsome young cowboy loitering near the glowing barbecue, beer can in hand. "There's Shane Dobbins. Let's say hi.''

"Shane Dobbins.'' Maxi glanced at Rand. "Son of Donna Dobbins Brooks, saved from being horse-stomped by J. J. Taggart?''

"One and the same.'' His approval warmed her. "Let's go watch him moon over Clemmie for a while. I see Little Billy's joined him—''

"Little Billy Vaughn?'' Maxine stared at the huge man in cowboy gear. "*That's* Little Billy Vaughn?''

"He wasn't called little because he was *little,*'' Rand said. "He was called that because his father, who's about five-five, was already Big Billy. The son just naturally had to be—''

"Oh, Rand!" She squeezed his arm, laughing up at him. "It must be wonderful to be part of all this. You don't know how lucky you are."

And I never truly realized how un*lucky I was,* Maxi thought as they strolled toward the little group consisting of Clemmie and her admirers. *If this was real...if I was really about to become a part of all this—*

But she wasn't. It was stupid to think about it.

"HAVIN' A GOOD TIME, honey?" Joe Bob dropped a heavy, if friendly, arm around Max's shoulders and squeezed.

Rand frowned. He wasn't too crazy about seeing his wife manhandled, but she didn't seem to mind, judging by the way she smiled up at the bulky dude rancher.

"We're having a great time, aren't we, Rand?"

"Yeah, great."

"Wal," Joe Bob drawled, "it's about to get better. Maxine, I want you to come on over here and sample the world's greatest chili."

A chorus of groans from Clemmie and her admirers greeted this invitation.

"Don't do it," Clemmie cautioned. "Joe Bob's chili could peel the hide off a buffalo—if you could find one dumb enough to eat it."

"Ah, stop that," the chili cook complained. "I've reformed. By Texas standards, my chili's downright mild these days."

Max turned questioning eyes toward Rand, who shook his head.

"I wouldn't recommend it. Joe Bob's been feeding that stuff to unsuspecting tourists and dudes for decades. It's guaranteed to scorch your tonsils."

Max's eyes widened. "I'm sure you're exaggerating. A nice man like Mr. Joe Bob Brooks wouldn't do a thing like that."

Joe Bob looked alarmed. "Not on purpose," he blustered. "But if you thank it's too much for you—"

"Not at all. I'd love to try your chili."

"Maybe you better not. I wouldn't want to—"

"Relax, Joe Bob. It'll be fine." An almost-smile tickled the corners of her mouth. "Lead the way."

"If you're sure…" A bit wild-eyed, he glanced at Rand. "Is it okay with you, Randy?"

Rand laughed. "Max is a big girl. She's been warned. She wants chili, give her chili."

The small knot of people headed for the chuck wagon, set up at one edge of the broad meadow fronting the ranch house. Apparently intrigued by the procession, others began to tag along. By the time they reached the chuck wagon, just about everyone in attendance was with them.

Joe Bob picked up an apron cast over the wooden tailgate. Cinching it around his broad middle, he said defensively to Max, "You sure you're sure?"

"Very sure."

"Okay, but everybody remember—" He appealed to the audience. "She asked for it."

"Joe Bob Brooks, don't you dare give that girl

any of your awful chili!'' Meg Taggart thrust her way through the fringes of the crowd. "Make him stop, Jesse!''

Jesse, at her heels, laughed. "Lighten up, Meggie. Maxine's probably never eaten chili with rattlesnake meat and possum gizzards in it before.''

Finally Max looked shaken. "Do possums have gizzards?''

Joe Bob nodded. "They do in Texas. I also use special imported tomatoes and all kinds of larrupin' stuff. Here." He picked up a ladle and plunged it into the simmering pot of red. After filling a foam cup, he selected a plastic spoon and offered both to Max.

Who was looking something less than confident. With a tentative smile, she took the cup and spoon from the beaming cook.

Clemmie leaned close. "I wouldn't.''

Max eyed Rand. "Does this stuff really have rattlesnake and possum in it?''

"No." He chuckled. "That's just window dressing for dudes. But it does have more chili peppers than you'll ever want to meet up close and personal.'' He slipped an arm around her and kissed her cheek. "You don't have to do this, hon.''

"I want to." She dug into the cup, pulled out a heaping spoonful and stared at it for a moment. Inhaling deeply, she lifted the spoon to her mouth.

Rand held his breath and so did everyone else, it seemed. Max chewed thoughtfully, swallowed, picked up another bite and ate that, too.

They all let out their breath on a long, anticlimactic "Ahhhh...." Even Joe Bob, who stood to take a lot of flack if his chili did any real damage, appeared disappointed.

"So how is it?" he finally asked.

"Good. Really good." Max scraped the last big spoonful out of the cup. "Have a bite, darling." She lifted the spoon toward Rand.

Her casual use of the endearment sent a shiver shooting down his spine. Damn, he liked hearing it. He liked it when she treated him as what he technically was: her husband.

He had the name, but he sure as hell didn't have the game. In that instant, he admitted he *wanted* the game—and her. She might not be one of those glamorous creatures he was accustomed to, but what she had was infinitely more important: a caring heart and a beautiful soul. If he hadn't already realized that, the sad story of her early life would have convinced him.

Covering her hand with his, he guided the spoon to his mouth, taking what she offered. Even before he swallowed, he knew he'd made a mistake. Choking, he backed away, feeling as if flames were shooting from the top of his head. His face must be beet red; his mouth sure as hell was on fire.

"Rand!" Alarmed, Max grabbed his arm. "Are you all right?"

"Water!" he croaked. "Beer! Something!"

"Oh, gosh—"

He didn't know where she got the cup of water, but he downed it gratefully. Eyes tearing, he spotted Joe Bob on the sidelines, looking pleased.

"Doggone you, Joe Bob! What did you put in that stuff?"

"Just the usual. Possum gizzards, rattlesnake and imported tomatoes. Guess I didn't stir it well, though, 'cause all the chili peppers went to the bottom. Sorry, Randy, but at least the little lady didn't get bush-whacked." He raised his voice. "All right, folks, line up over there. We're about to start serving. Anyone wants to can sample the world's greatest chili, but I got another pot a' that stuff for the sissies."

He led the way around the end of the wagon toward the barbecue pits.

Rand, over the worst of it, sucked in a deep shuddering breath. He'd never tasted anything so hot in his entire life. How had Max done it?

She smiled. "That was nice of you."

"What was nice of me?"

"Giving Joe Bob and the dudes the reaction they wanted. I didn't realize until the second or third bite that I'd goofed up. If I'd been thinking—but you did great."

"Max, I wasn't being *nice*. I nearly did myself in with that one bite. How did you stand it? How could you shovel that stuff in without a quiver?"

"Because I liked it." She grinned impishly. "The chili peppers didn't worry me—it was the possum and rattlesnake. See, my mom's boyfriends used to, uh, come and go, and a couple of them were Mexicans who liked to cook. I can even chew those mean little peppers without blinking. That's also how I learned Spanish."

The ingenuous way she made her explanation

stunned him. So did the life she'd led. "Maxine Taggart," he said, "you're one in a million." When he linked her name with his, her eyes went wide, but she didn't say anything. "C'mon, let's go find something we can *both* eat."

With his arm around her waist, they strolled toward the barbecue pits. Her body felt firm, yet yielding, and somehow he found himself speculating on how it would look beyond the few brief and guilty glimpses he'd already had.

"ATTENTION! Attention, y'all!" Joe Bob waved his arms until everyone glanced up from their plates of ribs, coleslaw, tortillas and chili. "I gotta few announcements to make before we move on to the dancin'."

"Speak up, Joe Bob!" one of the dudes yelled from the back of the crowd. "We don't want to miss a word!"

"You won't, don't worry." Joe Bob's voice carried clearly. "First of all, I have a little announcement for my guests. The hayride will start at six tomorrow, not seven like we said before. The day after that will be dude day at the Hells Bells Low Life Saloon for y'all who want a taste of the Old West."

A smattering of applause greeted this announcement. Maxi thought that Joe Bob must be a great dude rancher, because all the dudes seemed to be crazy about the man.

"Guess that's about it—"

"Hold on, Joe Bob." Donna climbed up beside

him on the bench. "I've got an announcement myself."

Joe Bob blinked. "Okay, honey. Say your piece."

Donna grinned. "I just thought everybody would like to know that we have honeymooners with us tonight."

Maxi's stomach clenched into a hard knot of dismay. Donna was just about to enlarge the conspiracy.

"Randy and Maxine Taggart, come on up here."

Rand chuckled. Leaning forward, he whispered one word into her ear: "Sorry."

"It's not your fault." Licking her lips, Maxi rose, Rand with her. At the bench, she turned to face the crowd, clinging to his hand.

"Ladies and gentlemen," Donna said, "Randy's folks were pioneers in this area and a lot of us have watched him grow up. We've been waiting a long time for him to pick a bride. Now he has, and as we all saw, he didn't pick a sissy! Maxine may be from Chicago, but I think she must have been a Texan in another life, judging by the way she handled that chili."

Enthusiastic applause greeted this announcement. Even Jesse and Meg seemed to approve.

"Let's give the newlyweds a big round of applause. May they have as many years of happiness as Randy's folks have had."

Surrounded by smiling well-wishers, Rand turned Maxi to face him. His warm expression gave her a little start. Then he drew her into his arms, lowered his head and kissed her.

A gentle kiss that still managed to send shock

waves to buckle her knees. Leaning against his firm chest, she reveled in the possessiveness of his lips. The sounds of the crowd disappeared and she stood alone with Rand in an embrace that felt more like prologue than epilogue.

He lifted his head and she opened dazed eyes. Over his shoulder, she saw Joe Bob grinning like a Cheshire cat. Her cheeks burned with private embarrassment. She straightened her shoulders and lifted her chin, fighting the realization that the kiss hadn't been phony, as it should have been. It had been real.

Too real. What was happening here?

"LET'S GO HOME, Jesse."

He'd been talking to Joe Bob and one of the dudes, a dignified older gentleman who was a retired stockbroker from Chicago. He looked up with a quick smile for her.

"Sure, honey." He straightened away from the large rock where he'd leaned a booted foot. "How about Clemmie?"

"She'll come later with Randy and Maxine."

"That's good." He tipped his Stetson. "Thanks for the invite, Joe Bob. Good meetin' you, Chester."

"See you later, J.J."

"Do you mind?" Meg asked while they crossed the grassy meadow toward the graveled parking lot.

"If I did, I'd have said so." He slipped his hand beneath her elbow as if he wanted her as close as possible.

She gave him a grateful glance. "I love you,

Jesse," she said, the words coming from the very depths of her heart. "I've always loved you."

"I love you, too, honey." He held the door to the pickup truck for her. Once behind the steering wheel, he went on. "That guy Chester was telling me about this big scandal going on in Chicago. Seems Randy's old college roommate, Bill Overton, is mixed up in it. You remember Bill, don't you?"

"How could I forget? He was a natural-born con man. I never could understand why Rand put up with him."

"Yeah, well, apparently Bill bilked investors in that company he inherited out of millions. I'm just glad he and Randy didn't keep up their friendship."

"Not that we know of, anyway."

He gave her a sharp glance, his movement illuminated by moon glow. "Yeah. Randy's got enough problems without that."

"Meaning what?" She couldn't help the way her voice rose to a challenging note. Jesse had *always* been too hard on their son.

"Meaning that if he's really married to that girl—"

"You doubt even *that*? Jesse, she showed me the marriage license."

"Even so..." He drove for a few minutes in silence and then he burst out, "If he's really married, he'd better grow up and settle down. He wants the Rocking T, but what for?" He answered his own question. "To sell, that's what for. He wants the money, Meggie. That's all."

"I don't think so," she argued, although it wasn't

really true. "You said yourself that he seems to really care for Maxine." She laughed ruefully. "God, you're as ambivalent about this marriage as I am. I just have to hope Maxine likes the ranch, because if she does…"

His laughter sounded indulgent. "You've always made excuses for him. Give me one good reason to believe that a rich kid from Boston and a poor girl from Chicago have a prayer of making a go of marriage."

"Don't put me on the defensive," she said. She thought about that for a minute…and then she knew she had him. "Here's a good reason," she said. "Think back to a rich girl from Boston and a country boy from Texas. Jesse, the odds we faced were at least as long as theirs. You were living out the male fantasy of the cowboy—a self-sufficient loner pursued by crowds of women. I never actually believed that any woman would ever become indispensable to you…even me."

"And you wouldn't settle for anything less," he said softly. Pulling into the ranch yard, he killed the engine. "Remember another night when we came home from one of Joe Bob's dude barbecues?"

"Yes. Oh, yes. I tried to run away from you that night…."

"But not very far or fast. I caught you on the steps…picked you up and kissed you. What happened then was inevitable because I loved you so damn much. None of our problems meant a damn thing at that moment."

"I hope Randy and Maxine feel that way about each other."

"So do I, but I'm not holdin' my breath."

"I am. We made love that night, Jesse, for the first time in years. But even then, you never told me that you loved me. That was what I wanted to hear."

"I hurt you and I'm sorry. I was a stubborn cuss back then. Now I know better." Twisting in the seat, he cupped her chin. "Meggie, I love you and I'm about to show you how much."

"Promises, promises...."

Promises kept.

CHAPTER TEN

A SMILING MAXINE smoothed escaping tendrils of hair away from her flushed face. "I can't believe square dancing is so much fun!" she exclaimed. "You might have told me, Rand."

Clementine looked curiously from Maxine to her brother and back again. The two had danced every dance, undisturbed now that everyone knew they were newlyweds. They'd done the fast dances and the dreamy slow dances, completely satisfied with their own little world.

Clementine had danced, too, with Shane and several others. But she'd been here and done this many times and had never found the simple pleasure Maxine seemed to have discovered.

Still...

There was something funny about Maxine, funny-strange as opposed to funny-haha. And something vaguely familiar, if Clementine could only place it. Had they met before? But Maxine had said she'd never been in Texas, where Clementine had spent most of her life.

Enough with the speculation; she had a mission. "Rand," she said, "I hate to interrupt, but Joe Bob's lookin' to talk to you."

Rand frowned. "What for?"

"He didn't say. He's over there cleaning up the chuck wagon." Clementine pointed.

Rand turned to Maxine. "Do you mind?"

"Of course not." Her smile was warm.

"I'll be right back, then."

"I'll be waiting."

He walked away and Clementine seized the opportunity to say, "Maxine, this is going to sound silly but I have the strongest feeling we've met."

Instantly the dreamy expression on Maxine's face disappeared, to be replaced with…could that be caution?

"Really? I suppose anything is possible, but I don't think I'd have forgotten you, Clementine. Your name alone is unusual enough to stick with a person."

Clementine chuckled; she'd heard variations of that all her life. "I know, there's no real reason for me to feel this way, but I do—and very strongly."

"I guess I have a common face. Lots of people tell me that."

"Your face isn't common at all," Clementine protested. They'd begun to drift toward the chuck wagon on an oblique route. "In fact…" She narrowed her eyes and surveyed her new sister-in-law. "You've actually got a lot of assets, even if most of them are hidden."

Maxine gave a self-conscious shrug. "Thanks, but I am what I am."

A peal of laughter burst from Clementine's lips.

"That's ridiculous. No woman *is what she is*. We all invent and reinvent ourselves until we're satisfied."

"I'm satisfied." Maxine didn't look amused.

"Really? I don't want to offend you or anything…" Which under the circumstances, might be inevitable, but for her brother's sake Clemmie must go on. "With a little help you could be…really pretty." She added quickly, "Not that you're not pretty now. You are. But—"

"Oh, Clementine! I'm happy as I am."

"But you've got such great skin and wonderful cheekbones. Do you have to wear those glasses?"

"Only if I want to see."

"Contacts, then. Your eyes are beautiful. We could—"

"You're a wonderful sister-in-law," Maxine cut in, "and I love you for wanting to help me out. But really, I'm happy as I am and Rand isn't complaining, so could we just drop it?"

Rand wasn't complaining *yet,* Clementine thought dourly. Then a new possibility thrust itself upon her. What if Rand really did love Maxine just the way she was? After all the actresses and models and socialites he'd dated, that would be a miracle in itself.

"I'm sorry," she said. "I didn't mean to offend you, as I said when I lifted my foot in preparation for stuffing it in my mouth. You're right. If you and Rand are happy, I should butt out. So on that note of contrition, I will."

With a penitent smile, Clementine turned away. When was she going to learn to mind her own business?

THAT'S A RELIEF, Maxi thought, watching Clemmie walk away. *Violet's Advantage* was aimed right at women Clemmie's age—and men, of course, who liked looking at the pictures and buying overpriced little nothings for their wives and significant others. And Maxi's photos had been prominently featured in it for several years now.

No wonder Clementine was stricken with déjà vu. She'd probably seen Maxi's picture a hundred times.

Maxi turned back toward the chuck wagon just in time to see Joe Bob reach into his pocket and pull out a wad of bills. Without counting it, he handed the whole thing to Rand.

Rand, looking earnest, said something; Joe Bob shook his head vigorously and walked away. The entire exchange took only a few seconds.

What in the world?

Rand met her halfway. "Would you like something to drink?" he asked.

"I don't think so. Uh, what did Joe Bob want? Anything important?"

"No. We were just catching up on a few things since the last time I was here."

"I see."

The music began again, produced by three guys in cowboy clothes with guitar, violin and drums. Rand took her hand.

"Would you like to dance?"

All her pleasure in this event seemed to have evaporated; the combination of Rand and money tended to do that to her. "I think I'd like to leave," she said.

His face filled with quick concern. "You okay?"

"I'm fine. I...suppose I've just had enough fun for one night."

"Okay. Let's go find Clemmie."

"You go, Rand. I think I'd like a glass of water. I'll meet you at the car in a few minutes."

"All right." But his expression was no longer easy and relaxed.

After he'd gone, she made a beeline for the door through which Joe Bob had disappeared. It turned out to be the door to the kitchen, where he stood by a counter with a fork in his hand, eating coleslaw out of the serving bowl.

When Maxi entered, he jumped guiltily. "Lord, I thought it was Donna," he said with relief. "She'd kill me if she saw me eatin' this stuff. How's it goin', Max? You havin' a good time?"

"Wonderful." Until recently. "I wanted to thank you for inviting us."

"You're leavin'?" He put down his fork.

"Yes." She licked her lips. "I wonder if you could answer a question for me?"

"Shore 'nuff."

"Why did you just give Rand all that money?"

Joe Bob stared. "What're you talkin' about, darlin'? All what money?"

"All that money you just handed him over by the chuck wagon."

He shifted uneasily on his shiny snakeskin boots. His already-ruddy complexion turned even redder. "You're mistaken, you surely are."

"I know what I saw."

''What you *think* you saw, which you didn't. If you want to make points with old Joe Bob, you'll forget all about…what you didn't see—and you sure won't say a word to Donna.''

For a moment she considered the embarrassed and unhappy man. ''Joe Bob,'' she said, trying again, ''I'd really like to know—''

''There you are.''

The door swung open and Rand entered. He took one look at Joe Bob, then turned to Maxi with a frown. ''What's going on?''

''Joe Bob and I were just—''

''Nothin','' Joe Bob cut her off. ''She was just sayin' her goodbyes. Sorry you have to go, Randy. Hope to see you again before you pull outa town.'' He added hastily, ''You, too, Maxine. Now I gotta get back to the party.''

He was gone. There was nothing else to be done about the money exchange unless she wanted to ask Rand point-blank. But if he lied to her…

''Clemmie's waiting at the car,'' he said, taking her elbow. ''Anything wrong?''

''No. Nothing's wrong.''

That she could do anything about at the moment, anyway.

CLEMENTINE CHATTERED all the way back to the house. Rand was glad. Max was unnaturally quiet and he had no idea why.

She'd enjoyed the evening; he was sure of it. The food, the dudes, the dancing—she hadn't held back at all. *Especially* when they'd danced…

He could still feel the imprint of her body against his. It had almost been like making love on the dance floor.

Almost.

The thought of making love to his wife was not a new one, but it was becoming more persistent with every passing day. She'd seemed so attuned to him tonight. Maybe she felt the same way he did. Maybe tonight would be the night.

"...and I've got to leave tomorrow afternoon because I promised I'd go to that benefit concert Saturday, and there's so much going on at work..."

Rand groaned. "Clemmie, do you ever run down?" He pulled into the yard and killed the engine.

"I think I just did."

He could hear the pout in her voice.

Apparently so could Max, because she said, "Don't pay any attention to him, Clemmie. He's just jealous."

"*Rand,* jealous of *me?*" The very idea seemed to astonish his sister and she burst out laughing. "Now I've heard everything."

Not quite, Rand thought. Clemmie had no idea of his financial problems. If she did—

If she did, she'd want to help him, and he wouldn't accept anything from her. He'd made this mess all by himself and he'd get out the same way, with the exception of Max.

Joe Bob had helped out, too, although he had no idea how welcome that cash was. When Rand loaned him ten thousand dollars more than a year ago, he hadn't expected ever to collect—not because Joe Bob was a deadbeat but because he was glad to help a longtime family friend. When the man pulled those thousand-dollar bills out of his pocket earlier this evening, Rand had wanted to kiss him.

Cheek only, of course.

Gruffly he said, "You two women quit cuttin' me down. I'm an innocent bystander here."

Max said coolly, "Do you realize how thick your Texas accent has become since we got here?"

Clemmie said, "You can take the boy out of Texas, but you can't take Texas out of the boy."

Rand said, "Well, hell," and climbed out of the car.

THE MOMENT they were alone in their bedroom, he reached for her.

How could he want to kiss her when she was so furious with him? Maxi turned her head away and Rand's mouth grazed her cheek. She hadn't figured out any convincing reason for Joe Bob to be giving money to Rand Taggart that didn't reflect ill on the younger man: extortion, bribery, graft of some kind. Both men had looked too guilty for the exchange to have been on the up-and-up.

And now he wanted to kiss her?

"What's the matter?" he murmured, nuzzling her cheek, then her ear.

His warm breath sent tremors through her. "Nothing," she gasped. "I'm just not—not—" She intended to say *in the mood,* but couldn't get the words out.

He pressed his face into the curve of her shoulder. Standing in the darkness just inside the door to their suite, she couldn't see anything beyond a shaft of moonlight from the open window.

But she could feel…too much.

"I don't believe you." He sighed. "Did Joe Bob say something to upset you?" His warm breath touched her ear and then he clamped his teeth lightly on the lobe.

She nearly jumped out of her shoes. "He—he didn't—" Gasping, she clung to his shoulders, completely off balance.

"Did he tell you about the money? Is that what's upset you?"

"The money?" Only dimly did it enter her brain that Rand had actually brought up the topic she should have broached herself. "Yes, the money."

"I'm surprised he'd mention it. He's gone to great lengths to make sure nobody knows, because Donna would kill him." He ran his hands over her shoulders and down her arms to capture her wrists.

"W-why doesn't he want Donna to know?"

"Because it makes him look like a jerk. No guy wants to look like a jerk to his wife."

She turned her head, brushing her lips across his in the process. "I think you'd better tell me all of it."

"I thought *he* did. I gave him the money to save his bacon. I suppose you'll say I shouldn't have done it, but hell, he hasn't touched a card or a pair of dice since. I really didn't expect the money back so soon, but he's had a real good year, and under the circumstances—''

''He shouldn't lie to his wife.'' She gave in and went fully into his arms, feeling an enormous sense of relief. He felt wonderful against her, so strong and capable.

''You don't think he knows that? He's gone through hell trying to keep this quiet. He's learned his lesson, Max. I'm sure he has.''

''I hope so. And Rand... I'm glad you helped him.'' She wouldn't think about all those he hadn't helped, not right now. Not while she was in his embrace and he was lowering his head, not while his mouth was capturing hers in a kiss that seared its way straight to her heart.

Wrapped in his arms, pressed against him from shoulder to knee, she surrendered to passion at last. She wanted this man and she had to face that fact. And he wanted her, plain-Jane Maxine Rafferty—

He curved one hand around her bottom and hauled her up higher and tighter against his hips, so she couldn't avoid evidence of his desire. They could kiss their way across the floor and into the bedroom, where they could stretch out on that big bed and—

''Stop!'' She pushed away with her last ounce of strength. She dared not make love with him. If she did, she'd never find the strength to do what she had to do. He might be generous toward a friend, but he was ruthless toward a love-struck woman like Helen.

''What the hell?''

He switched on the light and they blinked at each other.

She licked her lips. "You promised you wouldn't do that."

"Kiss you?"

"You intended to do considerably more than kiss me."

"And you were ready to let me," he retorted. "What happened, Max? Don't you believe what I said about Joe Bob?"

"I believe you."

"Did you think…hell, I don't know, did you think I was holding out on you? It's true, I probably wouldn't have said anything if you hadn't seen the exchange of money. But that would have been to protect Joe Bob, not to deceive you."

"It doesn't matter." She edged toward the bedroom door.

He followed. "If it doesn't matter, then what does? Obviously something happened to make you—"

"I'll tell you what happened!" She faced him, blocking the door with her body. "I came to my senses. Rand Taggart, you're not an easy guy to resist. I could very easily sleep with you, but what then? I don't *want* to want you. I don't want to get…to get emotionally involved with you. And I especially don't want to be sorry when this is over and we go our separate ways."

He looked at her for a moment, the passion slowly fading from his expression. Then he said, "You're right, of course, but the thing is…I really like you, Max. Excuse me for wanting more of you than you're willing to share."

He reached down and fumbled at the button of his knit shirt. "That being the case, I'll just say good-night and..." His eyes narrowed. "Pleasant dreams."

As if.

CLEMENTINE LEFT her parents' ranch the next day more confused than ever by her brother's marriage. At the barbecue, she'd thought Rand and Maxine were just what they were supposed to be: happy newlyweds. This morning they'd been cool to each other, and by the time she drove away, they were treating each other like casual strangers.

Most of the time. When they realized anyone was watching, they warmed up considerably.

And why wasn't Maxine interested in looking as good as she could? She was deliberately playing down her attractiveness; Clemmie was sure of it. But what sense did that make?

By the time she hit city traffic, she was no nearer to an answer. Even after she'd parked her car and ridden up to her apartment in the elevator, she didn't have a clue.

She picked up mail strewn in her entryway via the slot in the door and carried it into the living room. Idly she flipped through the stack...bill, bill, flyer, catalog—

A copy of *Violet's Advantage* stopped her cold and she did a double take. Tossing everything else aside, she carried the glossy publication to the sliding doors opening onto a balcony and walked outside.

There, in the clear light of day, she confirmed what

she could hardly believe was true, even now: the
model on the cover of the brand-new *Violet's Advantage* was none other than Maxi Rafferty, currently
known as Maxine Taggart.

What in the world was going on? And what was
Clemmie going to do about it?

CLEMENTINE'S MOTHER faced a similar dilemma, but
with regard to Rand. It started with a call from one
of Meg's oldest and dearest friends in Boston.

Felicity Holliwell never phoned without a reason,
but she always took a while to get around to it. She
finally did, and said, "I drove past your grandfather's
town house the other day. Imagine my surprise when
I realized a very attractive young woman and two
small children are living there."

Meg frowned. "I have no idea what you're talking
about, Felicity."

"Really? I naturally assumed you'd know. Is
Randy up to something, Meg?"

"Of course not. You obviously misunderstood.
The woman you saw—she could have been a visitor
or...or an employee."

"Wearing a robe to pick up the newspaper? And
the children ran out the front door in their pajamas."
Felicity tsk-tsked. "No, I checked into this, Meg.
They're definitely living there."

"Checked how?"

"My butler, Sams, has a friend with the agency
that takes care of Rand's house when he's traveling.
He inquired, and this young woman and two children
have definitely moved in. Sams speculated that—"

"I don't want to hear your butler's speculations," Meg said tightly. "Randy will tell me anything I need to know."

"I've upset you. I'm so sorry, but I thought—"

"I know what you thought, and I'm not upset. Please don't give it further consideration."

Hanging up, Meg stood there with her heart banging. What was going on with Rand? And how was she going to find out before he and Maxine left for Showdown today?

"I'm sorry, Mom, I don't have time to talk now."

"But, Randy, this is important."

"Rand," Max said, "if your mother wants to talk to you—"

"All right, Mom, spill it. What have I done this time?"

Meg looked from her son to his wife. She couldn't blurt out her question and risk causing problems in the marriage, assuming it was a marriage. "I—" She couldn't go on. She couldn't say, *Why is a strange woman and two children living in your Boston town house? What is this woman to you? Are those children yours?*

Afraid of what his answers might be, she gave in. "You're right," she said. "This isn't the time."

Jesse, who'd been watching with shuttered eyes, let out a disbelieving grunt. "What's going on, Meg?"

"Nothing," she said, suddenly realizing that she should speak to her husband about this, anyway, before confronting her son. "Drive carefully. Remember, we'll all be there at the Rocking T on Sunday, the thirtieth, to consider the inheritance.''

"You mean everyone's coming?''

"Of course—Trey and Rachel, your father and me, and naturally Boone and Kit will already be there.''

"The Supreme Court, huh.''

Jesse gave a short laugh. "You got that right, kid.''

Meg said quickly, "We'll talk then, Randy. We have lots of things that need clarifying.''

"Care to give me a hint?''

"No, dear. We'll talk when I see you again.''

"Whatever you say.'' Rand looked annoyed. "You're holding all the cards.'' He kissed Meg's cheek, a cold peck. "I'll see you next weekend, Mom.'' He shook hands with his father. "Sir.''

Not Daddy, not even Dad: sir.

Meg's heart constricted with pain. How was she going to tell Jesse about the Boston town house? How was she going to tell the son she loved that she couldn't, in good conscience, support his bid for his inheritance?

"WELL, MAX,'' Rand said, "it's just you and me, kid. Here we go, off to the last stop on our 'we're in love' tour. And a miserable failure it's been to date, if I do say so myself.''

Maxi sighed. "What was your mother trying so hard not to say?'' she wondered aloud.

"I don't have a clue.'' He pulled into a combination gasoline station and convenience store at one end of the main street of Hells Bells.

Maxi lowered the window while he fumbled with the gasoline pump. "It was something specific, like she'd...like she'd heard something or learned something but didn't want to talk in front of me."

"Or in front of Dad. He's not exactly understanding where—"

"Hey, Randy!"

Both Rand and Maxi looked toward the speaker, a short blocky man in the tan uniform of a law enforcement officer. The man loped up, one hand on the leather holster on his hip. He was smiling.

Rand made the introductions. "Max, this is Mike Anderson, the town marshal. Mike, my wife, Maxine."

"Howdy." Mike tipped his Smoky the Bear hat. "Heard you was hitched. Congratulations." His jovial air disappeared and he added, "Randy, I thought you'd want to know somebody's been asking questions about you."

"Me?" Rand's eyes narrowed fractionally. "What kind of questions."

"Oh, the usual—if you've ever been in any trouble, how local folks feel about you in particular and the Taggarts in general...what your plans are."

Maxi, who by now was starting to know Rand, saw a dark tide of color rise into his face.

"Who's been asking these questions?"

"I got no idea. He called and talked to Pearl—she's girl Friday at the station. She swears she didn't tell him a thing, but knowing Pearl..." He shook his head regretfully. "She got the impression he was a fed—or wanted her to think so."

"That's it?" Rand sounded incredulous.

"I've told you all I know," Mike said defensively. "*I'd* want to find out, if it was me. And, Randy—"

"Yeah?"

"You might want to walk real careful. Someone's watchin' and you don't know why."

Mike walked away. Rand glanced at Maxi, who was holding her breath. None of this made any sense to her unless...unless the police had realized their error in suspecting Helen and her boss and were now on the trail of Rand Taggart.

CHAPTER ELEVEN

AFTER THEY HAD DRIVEN a good ten miles, Rand said, "Damn!" as if it had just occurred to him.

Maxi, brooding in the passenger seat, started. "What?"

"Why would anybody be asking questions about me?"

She felt a stab of uneasiness, which she ignored. She, too, wondered about that. "I have no idea," she said.

"Suppose it has anything to do with the hijacking?"

"Seems unlikely." She cast him an oblique glance. "Is there anything else you're interested in keeping quiet?" She held her breath, waiting for his response.

Did he look guilty, sound secretive when he answered, "Not a thing. My life is an open book"?

"Hardly. If it was, you wouldn't be trying to fool your family about our...deal."

"You got me there. I guess my life *isn't* an open book."

"The fact that you'd suggest it makes me wonder if there's anything else I should know." *Tell me now,* she silently willed him. *Explain everything. I might even believe you.*

He considered. "No," he said finally. "There's nothing. You're my only secret."

"Okay," she said, disappointed but not surprised. "I don't think we're fooling anyone about our so-called marriage, though."

"Maybe not, but if there's a shadow of a doubt they'll give it to me. I know them. They want to believe. It's our job to make it possible for them to do that with a clear conscience."

"In which case, I'll take off, never to be heard from again, and you'll sell the old family homestead right out from under them. Nice, Rand. Their conscience might be clear, but how will yours feel?"

"Jeez, Max." He gave her an annoyed glance. "Whose side are you on anyway?"

"I'm starting to wonder," she admitted, thinking about the welcome she'd received from Trey and Rachel, the affection she'd recognized between Rand and his mother, the friction with his father, the friendly acceptance from his sister.

With any luck, Boone and Kit would be grouches with chips on their shoulders. She needed someone in this family to reveal feet of clay and an attitude.

She could see she'd annoyed Rand, so she changed the subject. "Tell me about this final aunt and uncle we're trying to deceive."

He eyed her resentfully. "Boone's my father's younger brother. He was an attorney on the fast track, with offices in New York and London. Mom used to call him the man who had everything—before Kit got hold of him, of course.''

''And did what?''

''Kept him from selling the old home place, for one. Thom T. was getting on and Boone wanted him to sell the ranch and move to New York City with him. Which, now that I think of it, means I'm not the first member of the family with that idea.''

''But Boone didn't do it. Why?''

''It was Aunt Kit's doing. *Her* aunt was Thom T.'s housekeeper and Kit grew up on the ranch. She was as determined to save the Rocking T as Boone was to sell it.'' A sudden grin lightened the tension in his face. ''You can see who came out ahead on that one.''

''Apparently she came out ahead on everything, since they're living in Texas instead of New York.''

''Yes, but life hasn't exactly been kind to Kit. They lost their first child to SIDS—sudden infant death syndrome. That would be tough for anyone to get through.''

''Oh, God, how awful.''

''Yes, but Boone and Kit faced it together. A thing like that sometimes pulls a couple apart, but it seemed to make those two even stronger. Later Boone was elected to the United States Senate, but he resigned in the middle of his second term because Kit had breast cancer. He was with her every step of the way and she made a miraculous recovery.''

''Everybody has troubles, I guess.''

''Yeah. They're okay now, though. They've got a couple of kids and Boone practices law in Showdown. He's also the mayor and keeps an eye on doings at the ranch, which is managed by Rachel's brother, Lee Cox.''

''One great big happy family,'' Maxi murmured. She sighed. She hated to be the one about to throw sand in Taggart gears, but the fault would be Rand's, not hers. And *he* didn't seem to be worried about it.

RAND FELT great relief when Max finally quit asking questions. He had enough of them to worry about without her bringing up more.

Questions some strange guy was asking. Could be because of the hijacking, he supposed, but more likely it had to do with Bill's financial shenanigans. Follow the money. No money involved with the unexpected flight to Mexico but plenty in the other instance. And Rand wasn't the only victim.

What he resented most was that he no longer had a choice. He simply had to bull ahead and hope that what he'd told Max was correct; that he had a chance to pull this off.

Whizzing through the Texas Hill Country, he barely noticed the passing of miles. Boone was sharp, damn sharp. As a successful attorney, he was accustomed to looking beneath the surface. As for Kit, she'd always loved the Rocking T with an all-consuming passion. Could Rand dredge up any reasonable doubt there?

Something intruded upon his concentration and he jerked to alertness. A woman had been standing beside a car on the shoulder of the road. Something must be wrong. He'd ask Max to use the cell phone—

But no, that wasn't enough. He couldn't leave a woman standing forlornly on the shoulder while he continued blithely on his way. At the first wide spot in the highway, he hung a U-turn and headed back.

"What is it?" Max braced herself with a hand on the dashboard. "Is something wrong?"

"There was a car broken down. Maybe I can help out."

"What? I thought you were the guy who didn't like to get involved."

"That's me to a T."

He wished.

HE PARKED on the side of the road. Max got out with him, thinking that the woman beside the stalled car might be less alarmed by her presence.

At their approach, the elderly lady took a quick, alarmed step back. Rand smiled.

"May I be of some assistance, ma'am?" he drawled.

In a flash, her apprehension melted away. "My goodness, a nice Texas boy. What a relief." The woman stopped wringing her hands. "I have a flat tire and I can't seem to figure out where the jack might be."

"Let me take care of that for you." His smile was ingratiating. "You can just go on over and sit down in the shade of those trees with my wife while I change the tire. You'll be up and running in a few minutes...if you have a spare."

"Oh, I do. I believe it's with the jack. Thank you so much, young man. You're a credit to your bringin'-up."

Sitting on a rock beneath a clump of trees, Maxi learned that the lady had been on her way to visit grandkids, when she met with this adversity. Maxi had never had a grandma but thought it would be nice if she had. In fact, the woman's gentle soliloquy was making Maxi downright depressed.

When Rand closed the car trunk and waved, the two women rose and walked back to the now re-tired car.

"What do I owe you, young man?" the lady chirped.

"Not a thing, ma'am. Glad to do it."

"In that case…" As if prepared for the likelihood that a nice Texas boy would refuse payment, she opened the passenger door, leaned inside the car and emerged holding a large disposable plastic dish with a cover. She offered it to him with a smile. "With my compliments. Cookies, all homemade and all delicious, if I do say so myself."

"Homemade cookies?" Rand glanced at Maxi. "I don't think I can turn down homemade cookies."

"I wouldn't let you." Maxi took the dish. "I'll see he gets his share," she promised. "This is so kind of you."

"It's the least I can do," the lady averred. "Thanks again. If anybody criticizes young people to *me*, I'll set 'em straight."

With a farewell wave, she walked around to the driver's side, climbed inside, started the car and drove away. Only then did Rand turn to Maxi with a crooked smile. "I'll do anything for a homemade cookie."

"You didn't do it for cookies," she said. "You did it because you're a nice guy."

To herself she added, *Sometimes*.

THEY ATE COOKIES all the way to Showdown. By the time they passed the city limits, nothing but crumbs remained in the plastic container.

Rand slowed to a crawl through the sleepy Texas town, with its white picket fences and tall old trees. He patted his flat middle.

"That lady sure knows how to bake," he said with admiration. "I don't suppose you bake?" He cast her a teasing, hopeful glance.

She sniffed haughtily, but she didn't fool him; she was relaxed and enjoying herself as much as he was. "I certainly do," she announced. "I'm a great baker. If I get a chance, I'll prove it."

"I'll hold you to that." He pulled the rental car to the curb in front of a huge old Victorian mansion set well back from the street. Surrounded by a wrought-iron fence, it looked like a fairy-tale castle, with its soaring turrets and curving steamboat veranda.

Maxine gasped. "*That's* where they live?"

"Sure is."

"It's *wonderful!*"

"I guess so. Are you ready to face the music?"

"As ready as I'll ever be." Drawing in a deep breath, she opened the door and stepped out onto the sidewalk. Leaves crunched beneath her feet.

Rand joined her, taking her hand. By now she was used to that, and merely looked up at him with a faintly questioning smile.

She's beautiful, he thought suddenly. When he met her, he'd been deceived by her lack of gloss into judging her plain. He could see past that now. There were strength and symmetry in her face, humor and a quick wit. He could do worse—

Shake it off, Taggart! This was a business arrangement, nothing more. He was paying her to be here and he'd forget it at his peril.

Still holding her hand, he opened the unlocked iron gate and they walked together up the leaf-strewn sidewalk to the wide porch. He could tell she was impressed with the place and enjoying its eccentricities. At the ornate door, he rang the bell.

He could hear it echoing through the house and then, without warning, the door flew open. A redheaded freckle-faced twelve-year-old girl with a pretty, oval face stood there. She wore jeans, a striped T-shirt and a bored expression.

She said, "Oh, it's you."

"You were maybe expecting a rock star?" Rand grinned at his young cousin. "Good to see you, too, Cherish. Are your folks here?"

From somewhere inside the house, a feminine voice emerged. "Cherish, is that Randy? If it is, tell him to come on in!"

"Mom says come on in." Cherish opened the screen door wider. She added apologetically, "I thought it was Emily—she's my best friend." As

Max walked in, Cherish stuck out her hand and said, "And you would be…?"

Max laughed. "I would be Maxine—'Max' to my friends."

Rand put his arm around Max's shoulders. "This is my wife, short stuff. Didn't your folks tell you I got married?"

"Yeah, but I didn't believe it."

"I've got a marriage license to prove it," he said.

She shrugged. "I don't care about that stuff. I didn't get to go to the wedding so I can't be sure there was one. Simple as that." She lifted her hand in a kind of salute. "I gotta go find out what's keeping Emily. See you later."

When she was gone, Max shook her head, her expression admiring. "That's quite a kid," she said. "If she's anything like her mother—"

"She's *exactly* like her mother." The voice came from the hall leading deeper into the house. A woman stepped forward with a welcoming smile, a woman with red hair and freckles and a pretty, oval face. She, too, wore jeans, but her shirt was plaid and tucked in at the waistband. "Welcome, Randy," she said. "Welcome home."

ALL THIS HUGGING and family stuff were getting to Maxi big time. How could Rand—or anyone else, for that matter—not be completely in love with every single Taggart, whether by blood or marriage? Maxi would *kill* for a family like this.

Maxi would kill *Rand* if he persisted in his plan to deceive and betray them. But the man turning to her with a smile wouldn't, couldn't, do a thing like that.

"Aunt Kit, this is my wife, Maxine."

"Oh, honey, I'm so glad to meet you." Now it was Maxi's turn to get hugged. "Y'all come on back to the sunroom. I'll give you a big glass of iced tea and catch you up on everything that's goin' on. Boone should be along any minute. He's out puttin' the fear of God into Dwayne Partridge—you remember him, Rand? He's got a twin brother, Shayne?"

"Who could forget the Partridge brothers?"

"Exactly. Anyway, Dwayne got drunk the other day and ran his pickup into the side of the Dairy Domicile—that's the local drive-in restaurant, Maxine. Nobody was hurt, but there was considerable damage, which Dwayne swears he won't pay for. He claims he only had eight beers. It usually takes a dozen to get him drunk, so what happened must be an act of God."

She led them into a screened-in porch beautifully appointed with wicker furniture and an abundance of potted ferns. It could have been lifted intact from another century. "Iced tea?" She looked at Maxi, apparently knowing Rand's preferences.

"Yes, thank you."

"Sweetened?"

"No, thank you."

Kit poured the tea from a side table without a break in her monologue. "So how was the drive? I'll bet it was nice, with all the leaves changing and everything. Fall's my favorite season. I've always liked that drive between here and Hells Bells—takes just long enough to be interesting." She glanced up from her task with a smile. "If I'm not mistaken, Boone just came in."

Presenting the glasses, she gazed expectantly at the door.

A tall, broad-shouldered man in slacks and a sweater that appeared to be cashmere entered. Maxi would have known him anywhere, since he resembled Jesse so much. With a smile for the guests, he walked first to his wife and kissed her lightly on the lips. Then he turned toward Rand and Maxi, who sat side by side on a wicker settee.

"I see you made it, Randy. I take it this is your bride?"

"Yes, Uncle Boone. This is Maxine."

"I'm very pleased to meet you."

Outwardly friendly, inwardly shrewd. This was one savvy man, Maxi realized. It was going to take a lot to fool *him*.

She said, "I'm pleased to meet you, too. I've been pleased to meet all of Rand's family."

Boone seemed to pick up on the longing she couldn't keep out of her tone. Crossing to fix himself a glass of tea, he spoke over his shoulder. "Do you come from a large family, Maxine?"

"No." She must be very careful what she said to this man. "My mother died almost ten years ago. After that it was just my sister and me."

"That's too bad." Boone looked as if he meant it. He sat down on a wicker chair. "Kit didn't have much family, either."

Kit took the chair next to his. "I grew up with my

mother in California. She died when I was about twelve, so I came to live with my aunt at the Rocking T. She was Thom T.'s housekeeper and he became my surrogate...my surrogate everything. When my aunt retired to Florida, I stayed here because it was home.''

Maxi, trying to listen poker-faced, risked a glance at Rand. His expression revealed nothing.

Kit went on as if she hadn't noticed anything amiss. ''Thom T. sent me to nursing school and eventually I moved back to the ranch to take care of him after he broke a leg in a riding accident.'' Her laugher was merry. ''He was in his eighties at the time.''

Boone appeared pained. ''Can you blame me for thinking the old guy would be better off if he moved back East with me instead of trying to run a ranch at his age?''

Kit's face turned stubborn. ''He had help—me, for one.''

Rand laughed. ''Are you two still fighting that war? Give it up, Uncle Boone. Women always win those fights.''

Boone's grin held a mischievous edge. ''I hope so, because I predict that Maxine is purely gonna love that ranch. If she does, you'll have no choice but to keep it—live there, raise your kids there.''

Maxi smiled mechanically, thinking: live there, raise her kids there? Not a chance, and yet... The prospect held considerable charm.

Or would, if Rand were not the man he was.

''Speaking of the ranch...'' Kit stood up. ''Lee's

got everything ready for you, kids." She added in case Maxi didn't know, "Lee's my brother. He's been in charge out there since Thom T. passed away."

Rand said quickly, "What do you mean, *ready for us?*"

"Don't you want to look everything over? If I recall..." Her glance narrowed fractionally. "You haven't been there since Thom T. d-died."

Her mouth actually trembled when she said the word. Here was a woman who had truly loved the old man who had befriended her.

Rand looked stricken. "You mean now? You want us to go *now?*"

Boone caught Kit's forearm in a light grip. "You're rushing them, sweetheart. Give them a few minutes to catch their bearings. For that matter, give them lunch. You got anything to eat in the kitchen?"

Kit seemed dismayed. "What am I thinking? Of course we'll eat lunch first. It's just that I'm so sure once Rand and Maxine see the Rocking T they won't possibly be able to even consider—"

She stopped, biting her lower lip. "Not that I have any reason to believe you don't honor your heritage, Randy," she said. "No true Taggart would sell the Rocking T. Other members of this family may have their suspicions—" She glanced at her husband, leaving little doubt about who these "other members" included. "I won't believe such a terrible thing is possible until it happens, which I'm confident it never will."

Everybody eyed Rand, who was sitting there tight

jawed. "Whatever," he said. "If you want me to go look at the place, I'll go look at the place."

"Uh-uh," Boone said.

"Uh-uh?"

"It isn't a question of looking at the place. It's ready for you to move in and that's what we expect you to do, at least until your birthday. After that..." He shrugged, but his meaning was clear.

Convince me.

THE LONGER LUNCH LASTED, the more Rand fought a growing anxiety. He hadn't realized how much he dreaded seeing the Rocking T again. He'd loved the old place when he was a kid visiting his great-grandpa, but it hadn't been important to him in terms of family history or stability. No one had ever spoken about the ranch or its future. Now they couldn't talk about anything else and he was beginning to feel more and more defensive.

Kit was rattling on about the herd of longhorns, which Rand was surprised to realize still existed, when eighteen-year-old Travis arrived for lunch with his cousin Jason Cox, the minister. Tall and good-looking like his father, Travis greeted everyone courteously if coolly, grabbed a ham sandwich and disappeared.

Kit sighed. "That boy," she said. "I just don't know what's got into him lately. This time last year he was a delight and now he seems barely able to stay in the same room with us."

Jason reached for the mustard. "It's a phase," he

said. "His heart's in the right place. He was helping out over at the church with the kids."

"There's a bit more to it than that," Boone said quietly. "Kit babies the boy."

A shiver shot down Rand's spine; he had heard these words before. His father had said them to his mother, over and over again. In retrospect, Rand suspected his father might have been right. His mother *had* babied her only son, but his father had retaliated by being too tough. Too remote. Too cool.

The result had been years of boarding school and a resulting estrangement that just seemed to grow and grow and grow. During holidays and vacations, he'd spent as little time at home as possible, preferring the Rocking T, his aunts and uncles, the homes of friends, even camp.

He'd always thought that if his parents really loved him, they wouldn't have stood for that. Now he surprised himself by offering unsolicited advice.

"Don't let Travis get away with this, folks."

Everyone looked at him in surprise.

"Sorry to stick my nose into your business but I know where that kid's coming from."

"Because..." Jason's tone was sympathetic. "You've been there, huh?"

"Yeah, I've been there." Rand hesitated, afraid he'd sound like a crybaby but concerned enough for his cousin to risk it. "I know it'd be easier to let him have his way, but don't. And don't land on him like a ton of bricks, either."

"Then *what?*" Kit's frustration was evident. "What's left?"

"Keep him close," Rand said, "and...love him. Make sure he knows it, because at this point I can guarantee he's not any too damn sure of much of anything."

Max stared at him, wide-eyed. Her hand touched his, resting beneath the table on his thigh, and he started.

Embarrassed, he said, "I guess that's enough free advice for one day. Are you about ready to go, Max?"

"I'm ready when you are."

"Then let's hit the road." He stood up, drawing her with him by the hand still clasped in his.

"Thank you," Kit said softly.

"Ah..."

"No, I mean it. That's the first time you ever opened up with us that way, Randy. It's been obvious over the years that you don't like to talk about personal things. That you'd do so now..." She smiled suddenly at Max. "I guess your new wife is already having a good effect on you."

Max's high cheekbones pinked. "I can't take the credit," she protested.

"Sure you can," Boone countered. "That's why men get married—so their wives can steer them in the right direction."

His smiling glance met his wife's with such intimate understanding that Rand had to clear his throat.

"Whatever," he said. "I'm willing to give Max credit. Thanks for lunch and...everything."

Boone rose. "Call if there's anything we can do.

The phone's working, the refrigerator has been stocked and Lee's expecting you.''

''Sounds like you've thought of everything.''

''We tried to. I'm sure your folks mentioned this, but we're all planning to descend on you for your birthday.''

''They mentioned it. We'll see you then if not before.''

After the newlyweds were gone, Kit turned to Boone. ''I like her,'' she said. ''I *do* think she's good for him. They remind me of us, darling.''

His laughter was incredulous. ''I don't see *that*.''

''Then you didn't look close enough. I saw a…a hunger in her eyes. I think it's a hunger for home. It's a hunger I felt the first time I saw the Rocking T.''

''Kit…''

She lifted her chin, determined not to give in to all the old emotions seeing Maxine had dredged up. ''I think she'll find that home at the Rocking T, with Randy.'' She sighed. ''But despite what I said before, I…I'm so terribly afraid you're right about him. He intends to sell the ranch, just as you did once.''

Boone leaned across the table, his gaze locked with hers. ''But you convinced me I was wrong.''

''Yes, but it was a close call. I hope and pray Randy will wake up in time. He hasn't stopped to consider what that place means, not only to all of us but to him, too. And what it's going to mean to Maxine, poor little thing.''

''Maybe when he sees it again—''

''Maybe. Oh, Boone, if only!'' She closed her

eyes and clenched her hands into fists, willing it to be so.

"A piece of this puzzle is missing," Boone mused. "It's almost as if...Randy needs the money."

"No way," she scoffed. "With the fortune he inherited from Meg's grandfather?"

"You'd think so. Nevertheless, I may just take the time to do a little checking of my own."

She shrugged. Boone was on the wrong track in this instance, but if he wanted to waste time and money digging into Randy's life, let him.

CHAPTER TWELVE

TOPPING THE RISE above the Rocking T near Showdown, Texas, Rand pulled the rental car to the side of the narrow paved road and killed the engine. His hands shook and his whole body trembled as he stared down at the ranch headquarters.

"My God," he said. "I haven't been here in years, but it looks exactly the way I remember it. I thought it would be…different."

"Different how?" Maxi pulled her gaze away from the neatly arrayed buildings and corrals and fences to face him. He was pale beneath the light tan.

"Worse," he admitted. "Run-down, or maybe deserted-looking." He sucked in a deep breath. "Guess we might as well go and see what we've got ourselves into."

Maxi nodded, already liking what she saw. Take away the sports-utility vehicle parked near the barn and the tractor behind one of the outbuildings and they could be driving through time to another century.

The sprawling two-story white house dominated its surroundings, but the big red barn also compelled attention. Everything was freshly painted and neat.

A couple of horses peered curiously past the log corral beside the barn and long-horned cattle grazed peacefully on both sides of the road.

Rand drove beneath a wooden arch with Rocking T burned into the dangling wooden sign. He parked next to the walkway leading to the house, then crawled out slowly, his head swiveling so he could take in a panoramic view. Maxi followed, feeling a strange excitement.

She was a city girl and lacked any desire for country life, or so she'd believed. But she sensed a peacefulness and simplicity here, an air of self-reliance that she immediately attributed to Thom T. Taggart. A yearning to know that kind old gentleman pierced her with unexpected sweetness. She'd never even seen Thom T.'s photograph, but she already loved him.

Rand was going to betray Thom T. and all the other Taggarts. A man who could do that wouldn't find it hard to swindle an old friend and leave his lover to face the music. Straightening her shoulders, Maxi vowed not to allow herself to be swayed from her mission.

At that moment, a man emerged from the house. Grinning, he came down the walk to meet them, his stride easy. In his late thirties, he wore no hat and his brown hair was thinning.

"Randy." He stuck out his hand. "Boone told me you were coming."

"Good to see you, Laddy."

Startled, the man shook his head. "Nobody's called me that in years. It's 'Lee' now."

"Sorry. I haven't *seen* you in years, so I didn't

know." A smile lifted one corner of Rand's mouth. "Nobody calls me 'Randy' anymore, either, at least until I get around the family."

"Okay," Maxi said, "it's Rand and Lee." She smiled at the newcomer. "I'm Maxine."

"I know." He took the hand she offered. "I'm real glad to meet you. C'mon in, folks. The books are all spread out for your inspection." He led them back to the house. "Rachel must have told you that I'm an accountant in my other life."

"I think she mentioned it." Rand guided Maxi before him, his hand warm on the small of her back.

Lee opened the door and stepped aside. "Welcome home, folks." He indicated that they should enter ahead of him. "Old Thom T. always knew you'd come back, Randy—*Rand*."

Rand's fingers dug suddenly into Maxi's back. She wanted to turn so she could see his face, but he was directing her inside. There, she stopped short.

Victoriana surrounded her: dark wallpaper; rich, though threadbare, Oriental rugs, and heavy wooden furniture. But more than the components of the room made an impression; she was struck by the feeling that she, as much as Rand Taggart, had come home.

She uttered a soft, "Ohhh."

Lee gave her a quick, approving grin and she realized he hadn't seemed comfortable with Rand's lack of reaction.

"Great old place, isn't it." Lee crossed the room to a huge rolltop desk that dominated one wall. "The books are in there." He nodded at one of two doors. "Bedrooms are upstairs, Maxine. The kitchen's that way.'' He pointed. ''Kit stocked the refrigerator herself. No chance of you starving to death. I've given the men their orders, so you won't have to worry about the stock or the day-to-day details of runnin' this place. Unless there's something else, I'm out of here.''

Rand shook off his stupor. ''You're living in the foreman's house?''

''Yes, but that's not where I'm headed. I'd scheduled a trip to Dallas a couple of weeks ago but put it off when I heard you'd be comin'.'' He reached for a tan Stetson on a hat rack near the door. ''I'll be back in time for your birthday, though.''

''But—''

''Rand, this trip is pleasure, not business. I've got a gal in Dallas and I'm not as lucky as you are—she hasn't said yes yet.'' Holding the hat, he turned to Maxi. ''Real glad to meet you,'' he said in his Texas drawl. ''You'll be happy here.'' He winked. ''Thom T. said so.''

He was gone.

Maxi turned uncertainly toward Rand, wondering how he was taking all this. His expression was uncommunicative.

''Now what?'' she wondered.

He shrugged. ''I suppose we should bring in our suitcases and get settled before we look around.''

''All right.'' She hesitated before adding, ''Rand, you seem so...'' She licked her lips. ''Shaken.''

He shrugged it off. ''I'm fine,'' he said brusquely. ''C'mon, let's get at it.''

This time he led the way and she followed uncertainly.

RAND HALTED before the door to the right of the stairway. "You take this room," he said. "It was Thom T.'s."

Her eyes got that stubborn look. "No way. You're the master of this house. You take it."

"No, you take it." He didn't want it; he *really* didn't want it. This whole place vibrated with the spirit of the old rancher who'd inhabited it for so long. Rand didn't need to sleep in his bed, as well. "I'll take that room." He pointed to the door at the opposite end of the hall.

"I'll take that one."

"Dammit, Max, that's where I always slept when I was here. Don't be such a pain."

"I'm not the one who's a pain." She snatched her suitcase from his grip before he knew what she intended. "I don't care if you sleep in the barn, but I'm not sleeping in Thom T.'s room—coward!"

She marched away from him, shoulders straight. He watched with jaw clenched. He could take one of the other bedrooms; there were three of them. But her final word rankled.

Because he *was* a coward. Dammit, he was all shook up just being here again. Maybe he *didn't* have the guts to sleep in the room of the man he was willing to betray.

To hell with that. He kicked open the door and plunged into the room before he had time to lose his nerve. After dropping his suitcase just inside the door, he walked with reluctant steps to stand beside the old-fashioned four-poster.

He'd been in this room before, of course, but he'd never realized how small the bed was. This couldn't be any bigger than a modern double bed, much too tiny to share with any degree of comfort.

Depending on the two people sharing it...

Thom T. had shared it with his wife, universally known as Miss Agnes both before and after her marriage. She'd died long before Rand came on the scene, but he'd heard a lot about her and the way she'd tamed the wildest man in this part of Texas.

Saved him from an early grave was how Thom T. himself recounted it to his wide-eyed great-grandson.

Rand laid a hand on the heavy dark bedspread, imagining that he could feel Thom T.'s energy beneath it. Thom T. had been born in this bed and he'd died in this bed. Other Taggarts almost certainly had, too.

Now I'm master of the Rocking T, as Max put it. At least for a little while....

Rand let his head drop forward until his chin rested on his chest. He should have known that plans made in Chicago and Mexico and Boston wouldn't hold much water when faced with Taggart reality.

"Rand?"

Her soft inquiry made him jump and pull his hand away from the bed guiltily. "What is it?" His voice was a croak.

She took a few steps into the room.

"Can I give you a hand, or shall I go on downstairs and...and...look around?"

"I'll go down with you," he said. "I can unpack later. Are you hungry?" He followed her into the hall, glad to get out of the room.

"I could use something to drink." She gave him a quick, mischievous smile. "Knowing your family, there's got to be a pitcher of tea in the kitchen." Then she looked really confused, because of course she *didn't* know his family on such short acquaintance.

She was right about the tea, though. Over icy glasses of the stuff, Rand felt himself calming down, getting hold of himself again. While Max checked out the contents of refrigerator and cabinets, he stared out the window at the horses idling in the corral.

Laddy—make that Lee—had thought of everything.

"We've got enough food here to last at least six months," Max declared, closing the last cupboard door.

"It won't go to waste," he said. "Lee can always use what we don't get to."

"Yes." She no longer sounded excited and happy, just guarded. "How about steak with all the trimmings for dinner?"

"I thought your specialty was baking cookies."

She drew her eyebrows together. "I'm a woman of many talents. As you very well know, I didn't grow up with a silver spoon in my mouth like some people I could name."

"Don't get personal, Max. I've got enough problems without that."

"You certainly do." She sighed. "What do you

say we call a truce? I don't mean to be a bitch, but…being here and knowing full well what you intend to do is making me a tad uneasy."

"Jeez, Max, I don't intend to torch the place."

Her steady gaze never wavered. "You might as well…or plunge a knife into someone's heart. It comes down to the same thing. Everybody's hoping against hope—"

"That's enough. You're in this as deep as I am, so don't go all sanctimonious on me now."

She followed him into the parlor. "I'm *not* in as deep as you are, because I wasn't born a Taggart."

He whirled to face her, armed only with his guilt. "You're a Taggart *now* so back off." He turned to the door. "I'm going out to look around. You coming?"

"No, and you shouldn't go either, not until you've checked out the books."

"There's plenty of time for that. If you're in such a hurry, do it yourself."

"I just might," she hollered after him.

He slammed the door.

Not because he was mad at her; he wasn't. She was right, and every word she said cut him to the quick. But she hadn't changed his mind.

He had responsibilities that required money in large amounts. He was doing what he had to do.

Thom T. would surely understand that.

RAND WAS USED to having Max around. That was the only reason he couldn't get into his tour of the grounds. He wanted to see everything through her eyes, he finally admitted. This would all be new to her, while it was achingly familiar to him.

Despite his lack of pleasure in what he saw, he was impressed. Lee was doing a helluva job. Standing next to a corral holding two fat and sassy quarter horses, Rand found himself hoping that Lee would be able to keep his job when the new owners took over.

Hay and grain filled the barn; saddles and bridles gleamed from sawhorses and hooks in the tack room. Tools hung neatly on walls, and stalls had been recently mucked out.

Rand lingered by the corral, until finally the bay gelding wandered up for a closer look-see. Absently he stroked the animal's head, thinking that perhaps he should turn the horses into the pasture but then deciding against it. He and Max might want to go for a ride; hell, they'd have to do something to pass the days until his birthday.

He gritted his teeth. He knew how he would like to spend those days: stretched out on that too-narrow bed with her beside him. That was something else to which he'd grown accustomed: her presence in his bed. But that was agony, as well—agony that would only be appeased by possession of the body he'd merely glimpsed.

His stomach rumbled and he straightened. She hadn't joined him, so perhaps she'd started dinner. He could sure use a nice rare steak washed down by a bottle of cold beer.

He turned and made his way across the quiet yard to enter the house. He saw her at once, hunched over the rolltop desk. At his entrance, she glanced up, excitement breaking free.

"Rand, come take a look at this!"

His heart sank. "Don't tell me something's wrong with the books. Dammit, I don't want to have to tell Rachel—"

"No, no, you don't understand. The books are in perfect order." She smoothed her hand over the page.

"Then what—?"

"Lee's done a fabulous job running this place. It's worth double what it was when Thom T. died."

"It is?" Frowning, he leaned over to see the numbers she indicated.

She nodded. "The longhorns are doing great and the buffalo—"

"Buffalo? What buffalo?"

She laughed. "You didn't know you raised buffalo?" she teased. "Well, you do, and very profitably at that. You sell them mostly to meat-specialty shops and exclusive restaurants."

"No kiddin'!"

"You also breed and raise quarter horses. They're doing well, too, especially the ones your father takes on for training."

He felt suddenly light-headed. "I'm in business with my father?"

"You sure are." She pointed to a figure at the bottom of the column. "*That's* what the Rocking T is worth," she announced. "That's what you were ready to throw away until—"

Something came over her then. Her eyes widened

and she drew a quick breath. Slamming the book closed on his finger, she stood up. "I'll go start dinner," she said, voice tight.

"Not so fast." Extricating his finger, he followed her. "When I told you to check the books yourself, I didn't think you'd really do it."

"Why not? Because women aren't supposed to know one number from another?"

"Well...no, not exactly. Maybe sort of."

She stopped short and faced him. Following too close, he bumped into her; automatically he grasped her upper arms to keep her from stumbling.

"I'm sorry," he said, not sure if he was referring to what was patently an insult or for running into her.

"No, you're not." She shook off his grasp. "As it happens, I'm very good with numbers. And as it also happens, you're not."

"How do you know I'm not?"

"Didn't you tell me?"

"Did I?"

"I hate it when people answer questions with questions." She planted her hands on her hips.

"Do you?" Natural good humor had surfaced. Trading quips made him feel better than he had since setting foot on this place. When she started to berate him, he caught her chin with his fingers and planted a quick kiss on her mouth.

His lips tingled; his fingers tingled. He wanted to tingle all over. "Sorry," he said in a husky voice. "I couldn't resist." And realized that once again, he'd made an open-ended comment: couldn't resist kissing her or answering a question with a question.

She looked too rattled to continue sparring. "Whatever," she said, turning away. "I'll get those steaks started."

Now who's the coward? he wondered.

DINNER WAS A SUCCESS, if she did say so herself. The steaks were perfectly broiled, with baked potatoes and a green salad to round out the meal. Maxi enjoyed being in a kitchen again and found herself humming as she worked.

Even more, she enjoyed watching Rand consume the meal. He was free with his compliments to the point of producing blushes.

She, who never blushed about anything, even the first time she posed in barely there lingerie—

This situation was becoming dangerous. As soon as they finished eating, she tried to shoo him from the room so she could call Helen for a shot of reassurance. Instead he shooed her.

"You cooked," he said, guiding her toward the door with hands on her shoulders. "It's only fair that I clean up."

"Are you sure you know how?"

"Now you've gone and insulted me," he said sadly. "You'll eat those words, lady."

And probably a lot of others, she thought, hurrying to the parlor. Once there, she eyed the telephone on the desk. Pulling a business card from her pocket, she took a deep breath, lifted the receiver and quickly dialed the jail.

The line was busy. She paced for a couple of minutes, then dialed again. Same result.

Maybe she could call R. Renwood Keever. A moment's thought to remember his phone number and she dialed once more. His machine picked up: "...with a client or out of the office..."

Disgusted, she hung up. She didn't trust Keever anyway. She'd just have to try to reach Helen later.

Okay, she'd been putting it off, but she really should call her agent. Taking a deep breath again, she reached for the handset but then pulled back. He'd just yell at her and she really didn't need that right now.

Out of sorts, she paced to an ornate table set next to a rocking chair beneath a long lace-curtained window. The last rays of a setting sun streamed through, illuminating a leather-bound volume that took up nearly the entire tabletop.

She laid a hand upon the book, drumming her fingers on the embossed leather cover. She was having trouble keeping her animosity toward Rand in full flower. He certainly didn't seem to be the despicable person Helen had described. Could she be wrong?

Maxi's heart leaped with hope, however unreasonable. Maybe—

Her drumming fingers came down on the metal clasp of the book and the clasp fell away. Startled, she turned to pick up the book, hoping she hadn't harmed it. When she laid it on her lap, it fell open to a center page and she looked down at an old photograph of a woman.

A young woman with a solemn face and dark eyes

that, more than a century later, still sparkled with intelligence. She wore a simple dress adorned by a magnificent cameo brooch. Elegant though faded handwriting beneath the photo said that this was Rose Taggart.

Rand's footsteps in the hallway brought Maxi's head swinging around. He came into the room talking.

"I not only cleaned the kitchen, I found us some dessert in the freezer. How do you like—" He stopped short. "What is it?"

"This picture—" She touched it with her fingertips. "I hope you don't mind that I opened this old photo album."

"Of course not." He crossed to her side, looked down and began to smile.

"Well?" she urged. "Who was Rose Taggart?"

"My great-great-great-aunt. She's the Taggart who really started things around here."

"What things?"

"Ever hear of Showdown Days?"

"I don't think—" And then she remembered. "That's where a whole town re-creates some kind of legend about a gunfighter and a lady, right? I saw something about it on television a couple of years ago."

His grin widened. "That's the one, and that's the lady. Rose started it all. She was engaged to the sheriff, but she ended up running away with a gunfighter named Boone Smith. Trey comes in on that branch of the Smith family, although it took Thom T. to figure out the connection. Our branch comes through Rose's brother, James."

Maxi stared at him, enchanted. "This is so incredible," she said.

"What is?"

"That anyone would know so much about his family."

"Poor Max." He draped an arm around her shoulder and knelt beside her, his face was very close to hers.

She wanted to pull away but couldn't. "I told you how I feel about pity," she said stiffly.

"And I told you it's not pity, it's sympathy." He kissed her temple. "And a whole lot more."

She clutched at the book as if it offered some protection from her emotions. "Meaning what?"

"Oh, Max," he sighed. "You know what it means as well as I do."

"I don't."

"Okay, play dumb." A smile twitched at the corner of his mouth. "I want you, Maxine Taggart. I want you in my bed but not lying there buttoned up to the chin and stiff as a poker—been there and done that." He bracketed her chin with his fingers and tilted her face toward him. "I want to spend tonight, and every night we're together, making love to you, honey."

She'd been melting beneath his persuasive tone and touch right up until he'd said *every night we're together.* How long would that be? Until his birthday a week from today, most likely.

"No," she told him, but she didn't pull away; he

didn't think she could. "Th-that's a bad idea. We agreed—no sex."

"Adults are allowed to change their minds."

He leaned over and kissed her. Plunging his tongue into her mouth, he gave free rein to the passion he'd longed to unleash for what seemed like a lifetime. She fought her response; he sensed it in the way she accepted without giving. Undaunted, he took his time, positioning her face exactly where he wanted it and pulling her deeper and deeper into his embrace.

The book hit the floor with a solid *thud* and she gasped. The next thing he knew, she was slipping down on her knees to face him, her arms wrapping around his neck to draw him closer. The sweet suction on his tongue announced her late arrival at this party.

They kissed until they were both gasping for breath. Only then did he slide his lips away from hers and nuzzle his way down her throat. Fingers threaded through her hair, he held her away while he found her breast, then he took a straining nipple in his mouth, shirt, bra and all.

Her soft panting breaths urged him on and he lowered one hand to fumble at the buttons of her shirt. Her flesh was exactly as he'd expected it to be: firm and toned but also resilient and warm. Once he'd dragged her plain cotton bra aside, he took the rose-hued nipple in his mouth.

She groaned and for an instant arched her back to press her breast more fully against his seeking mouth. But then she withdrew again, her nipple pop-

ping free with a forlorn little sound as the suction of
his mouth was broken.

He covered her bare breast with his hand, unable
to deprive himself of the feel of her. "What is it?"
he managed to ask.

"I don't want to do this," she stated, tugging the
edges of her shirt together.

"I think you do."

"I don't care what you think, Rand." She rose and
staggered a few steps away, holding the edge of the
table for support. "You don't want me, plain Maxine
Rafferty—"

"Taggart."

"Whatever. This is proximity at work, nothing
else."

"You don't know that."

"Don't I?"

He shook his head. "What if I told you I—" He
stopped; he wasn't ready to go any further.

"That's what I thought." She licked her lips. "I'll
pass on that dessert. See you tomorrow, Rand."

"Maybe not." He spoke softly. "I've grown accustomed to sharing a bedroom with you, Max, and
I like it. If you change your mind..."

"I know where you are," she finished for him, her
tone dull. "Don't hold your breath, okay?"

HE DIDN'T HOLD his breath, but he didn't think of
anything else, either. By ten o'clock he was pacing
his bedroom like a caged tiger; at eleven he stared
at the door as if it were the enemy. By eleven-fifteen

he couldn't stand it any longer and charged out into the hall without any plan at all.

The first thing he saw was Max, sitting on the top step of the stairs with the photo album on her lap. Their glances met and locked. Slowly, without ever looking away, she put the book on the floor.

When she stood, he saw that she was wearing that awful white Mexican nightgown. She licked her lips. "I've decided..." A shiver went through her. "I've decided you m-may be right. I know this is the wrong thing to do, Rand, but..." She appeared almost desperate. "Why me, if it isn't simply proximity?"

"Why you?" He searched his heart and answered as honestly as he could. "Because you're sexy and gorgeous. I didn't see it at first, but I do now. Because you're smart and funny and gutsy. Because I..." He couldn't go on.

She wouldn't let him off the hook. "Because you what?"

He drew a deep breath. "I like the hell out of you, Maxine. Maybe it's even more than that, or will be. I don't know for sure. I do know that I care more about you than any woman I've ever met." He forced himself to add, because he wouldn't take advantage of her, "Is that enough?"

She considered, and after a moment, a smile flickered around her lips. "No," she said, "it isn't enough. But I'm weak..." She took a step toward him.

He reached her in a few long strides, swept her into his arms and against his trembling chest. Then he turned and carried her into the bedroom.

CHAPTER THIRTEEN

IF RAND HADN'T COME out of his room and seen Maxi sitting on the stairs, she might actually have given in to all the things she was feeling and knocked on his door. Those "things" had in fact driven her from her bedroom—his bedroom when he was small. Knowing that had finally made it impossible for her to stay there.

For a long time, she'd sat on the stairs, listening to Rand pace behind a closed door. Then the door had opened, as she'd known it would. He'd walked out, picked her up in his arms and carried her away.

The interior of the room was dark, illuminated only by moonlight streaking across the dark carpet. Rand halted in that silvery glow to look down at her.

"Max," he said in a husky voice, "you're beautiful."

She wasn't, not like this: no makeup, hair slicked back, glasses perched on her nose. But he sounded as if *he* believed it to be true and a shiver of gratitude shook her.

"You're beautiful, too." She said it shyly, because she felt so vulnerable. All her life she'd strived to make herself attractive and to show off her assets—until now. She'd thought her plain appearance would protect her from Rand, yet here was a world-class-gorgeous man looking at her, speaking to her plain self as if she really were the most beautiful woman in the world.

His laughter sounded giddy. "I guess that's a compliment." He hoisted her higher in his arms. "Max, I knew we'd get to this point, but I sure was getting tired waiting. We're good together and we're gonna be even better."

He carried her out of the moonbeam and to the bed, where he deposited her in the shadows. Without self-consciousness, he began to undress.

She heard a smile in his voice when he said, "We've got almost a whole week. I don't want to waste any more of it."

"Neither do I."

He joined her on the bed and reached for her. She went to him willingly, happily. His skin felt smooth beneath her reaching fingertips, his body all silky muscle. What a strange sensation, to be swathed in fabric while he was naked.

But not vulnerable. He took charge with a hungry kiss that left her weak and wanting. When he reached for the hem of her voluminous nightgown, she maneuvered around to make it easier for him to lift it over her head.

Then they both were naked and straining together, exchanging heated kisses and caresses. Their breaths mingled, and after a few moments, she couldn't have said what she felt and what she felt in him. As her blood heated, her equilibrium retreated.

The thought of pulling back never entered her

mind. She'd known what she wanted when she'd come out into the hall; she just hadn't had the nerve to walk straight to *this* room and tell him so. Instead she'd waited, and this was her reward....

This drugging rapture, invading her veins like liquid fire. He trailed his hand down her hip, his touch light and teasing. Everything he did, every touch, seemed perfect to her, designed to lift her to a fever pitch—and succeeding. Eager to possess and be possessed, she resented the few seconds lost while he retrieved a condom from the bedside table.

"Hurry *up!*" She tugged on his shoulder.

"Hey, I'm doing this for you. Left to my own devices—" He tumbled over and grabbed her. "I wouldn't want anything between us, Max, Maxi, Maxine, baby, darlin'."

"You're being sensible." She curled her leg over his hip, tightened her muscles and pulled him closer. "I'm glad one of us is." His hardness touched her softness and she gasped. "Randy!"

"Ah...yes." He was over her with a quick motion, his knees sliding between her thighs. Braced on his arms, he entered her with slow deliberation. Once firmly and deeply joined, he leaned down to draw a puckered nipple into his mouth.

Exquisite pleasure bubbled through her. She'd never been so completely engaged in the act of love, never felt so willing to relinquish control. There was nothing he could do that she wouldn't welcome, as she welcomed the acceleration of his deep thrusts.

She clutched his shoulders, meeting his strokes fiercely. This man had ducked beneath her defenses and connected with something she hadn't even realized was there inside her.

That something was love, she acknowledged with a flash of insight that made this climax the sweetest she'd ever known.

THROUGHOUT A LONG NIGHT, they made love, slept in each other's arms and made love again. At dawn's first light, Rand stifled his groan against her tousled hair.

"I don't understand what you've done to me," he whispered, "but I wouldn't want you to think I'm up to this performance level on an every-night basis."

"No?" She cuddled closer. "And here I was thinking that by Saturday we could make love…my math's not so hot, but I was thinking maybe seventeen more times?"

"In six days? I'd be dead!" But he didn't pull away in horror, just cupped her breast and ducked to take the tip into his mouth.

The glorious taste of her filled him, made him stiff all over again. She was the sexiest woman he'd ever encountered, the wildest in bed and the most deeply satisfying. An unexpected contentment warmed him.

He could get used to this—maybe on a permanent basis. They were already married, after all. What if they decided to…explore the possibilities?

RAND NEXT awakened at full light. For a long time he lay there next to a softly sleeping Max, wondering why he felt so damn good.

In the city, he ordinarily slept late, but as a kid visiting Grandpa, he'd been expected to pile out of bed at dawn. Like all the Taggarts, he hadn't wanted to disappoint the old man so he'd hauled himself up grumbling at dawn's early light.

Rand couldn't remember the last time he'd felt such a sense of anticipation as he did this morning. He hadn't been here in years. Maybe he'd forgotten the power the Rocking T held over him.

Or maybe the power was Maxine's—Max, wonderful Max, sleeping with her head on his shoulder and one slender hand curled on his chest. He picked up that hand and pressed it to his lips. Her mouth curved into a smile, but she slept on.

How special she was. When he'd first embarked on this crazy scheme, he'd been grasping at straws, with no real idea how perfect she was to play the part of his wife. But they weren't playing any longer. She *was* his wife in every way.

Maybe he'd keep her...or try. Of course, if he decided to do that, he'd have a whole lot of explaining to do to her.

Slowly and carefully, he slid his shoulder and arm free. She sighed and her lashes flickered—amazingly long lashes. Then she turned over, snuggled in the tangle of sheets and slept on.

Moving quietly, Rand grabbed fresh clothing from the bureau drawer and crept out of the room. He'd shower down the hall so as not to disturb her. She needed her rest as much as he did.

And she didn't have memories of a crusty old grandpa to bedevil her awake before her time.

WHEN MAX OPENED her eyes, he was gone. She sat up abruptly in the bed, trying to get her bearings.

He was definitely gone.

Taking a deep breath, she leaned back on a pillow, a satisfied smile curving her mouth. She didn't think he'd gone far. After last night...

For several moments she lay there luxuriating in recent memories. Rand was so—

Crooked. Rand *was* a crook. For her sister's sake, she must never forget that. He was also a con man, so why was it so hard to admit that he was simply stringing her along? Last night had nothing to do with love or even affection—on his part, and also on hers if she had any sense at all. It was simply sex.

That thought brought her lurching out of bed.

If he'd said a word about his financial problems, perhaps she would feel different about him. But he'd never opened his mouth on that subject, and now she was supposed to believe that one night of great sex changed anything?

Beneath the stinging spray of the shower, she reminded herself that she must be more on guard than ever. He seemed to instinctively find her weaknesses and exploit them, but he hadn't turned aside her determination to clear her sister. One good tumble couldn't make her forget a lifetime of obligation.

Could it?

She was still rolling up the sleeves of her plaid shirt when she entered the parlor and stopped short. Rand sat on a velvet sofa, turning a VCR tape over and over in his hands. He looked up, his expression tense.

She felt a stab of alarm. "What is it? What's wrong."

"Nothing." He put the tape aside as if glad to be rid of it. His smile dissipated all the clouds. "How are you, honey?"

The endearment brought a flush of pleasure. "I'm fine," she said. "Is that coffee I smell?"

He nodded. "You sit down. I'll get it."

She did, wondering why it felt so good to be waited on by this gorgeous man. He treated her like a queen, while she—

"Here you go." He set the mug on the table beside her. "One spoonful of sugar, just the way you like it."

He even remembered how she liked her coffee. She was in a ton of trouble here.

He sat down across from her, his own mug cradled between his hands. "Max," he said softly to get her attention.

"Yes?"

"Last night...was incredible."

Her heart fluttered painfully. "It was...good."

"Good?" His laughter was incredulous. "You've been great ever since you got on that airplane in Chicago. Jeez, that seems at least a hundred years ago."

It did to her, too. Had there ever been a time when she didn't know him?

His expression and tone turned serious. "I've been doing some serious thinking. This seems as good a time as any to confess that I've not been entirely straight with you."

She sat bolt upright in her stiff velvet chair, resisting the almost overwhelming desire to shout *No!* at the top of her lungs. Could she handle his secrets now with her emotions still trembling so near the surface? If *she* was dishonest with him—and she was—she wanted him to be equally dishonest. It made the whole thing cleaner somehow.

But she couldn't say that and he wasn't looking at her anyway, instead staring down at the cup between his restless hands.

"Okay," he said suddenly, "this is what's really going on with me, what I've been trying so hard to keep from you and everyone else. I *have* been careless with money."

This was news?

"But not that careless." He shifted restlessly on the sofa, as if he couldn't get comfortable. "To explain how I could be as stupid as I was, I need to go back a long way. I had two real close college friends and we stayed close after we left school. One was Brian Kelly, who got married and went to work for the Boston Police Department. The other was Bill Overton, who went into his family's business. Coconutty—ever hear of it? They make things out of coconuts, stuff like suntan oil and flavoring and candy, all kinds of things."

Hearing Bill Overton's name said right out loud startled Maxi so much that she gasped. Was Rand really going to hand her the key to his own downfall and Helen's vindication?

"Bill was always a fast talker," Rand went on, "a kind of con man. I knew it, but we were buddies and he never turned that on me. Eventually we more or less went our separate ways. Until he contacted me a couple of years ago, inviting me to invest in the family company he'd just inherited. The idea sounded good to me, and I've got to admit, it never even occurred to me to question his honesty. I didn't know any reason I shouldn't trust him.''

He sighed and put his cup on the floor between his feet. She started to tell him to be careful, he'd kick it over and make a mess, but she didn't want to distract him from his story.

He hung his head. "Bill was about to take his company into Internet marketing,'' he said. "Why not? Other completely unlikely companies were doing the same, like that cod liver oil company in Texas. He had answers to all my questions, but I still hesitated. I'd already gone through at least half of what Great-grandpa Randall had left me, plus…I had ongoing obligations.''

His lips tightened. "Just about the time all this was going on, Brian the cop was shot to death in a drug bust. He didn't have much family—he'd gone to college on good grades, not family money like Bill and me. Somebody had to give his widow and two kids a hand. In my own defense…'' He grimaced. "Damn, I'm not trying to make excuses, but I was distracted. Bottom line, I sank several million I couldn't afford in Bill's big venture. And when he needed more, I provided that, too.''

Maxi sucked in her breath. "A sure thing, I suppose.''

"Oh, yeah, for Bill. A couple of months ago, he skipped with all the loot. Seems he'd been embezzling from the beginning, salting everything away in some Caribbean backwater—at least, that's what the law thinks." He grimaced. "I'm not the only one who got taken, but I was the biggest fool in the bunch, if you go by dollars and cents. There was a big to-do about it in the papers. Fortunately none of the investors were named. I don't think anyone in my family even knows the name of my holding company, thank God."

"Why thank God?"

"I'd just as soon my family and everybody else in the world don't hear what a damn fool I've been." He sounded properly disgusted. "Maybe now you understand why I need this ranch so much. In all likelihood, I'll never see another penny of the Coconutty investment. If I know Bill, he'll never set foot in this country again—and why should he? He's got what he wanted."

"Bottom line—you still intend to sell the ranch," she said faintly.

"I have no choice." The grim lines of his face deepened. "You know the worst part of it? Bill and that blond showgirl wife of his are lolling on some tropical island, drinking mai tais, while he laughs at the mess he left behind. I'd give anything I own— anything I have left, anyway—to get my hands on him for five minutes. Just five minutes…"

Maxi's stomach clenched into a knot. How much of this was true? Was *any* of it true?

He looked straight into her eyes. "You believe me, don't you?"

"W-why wouldn't I?"

He shrugged. "I don't know. You just had a funny expression on your face."

She improvised. "I was having trouble taking it all in. Are you sure you're not leaving anything out?"

He looked surprised. "Like what?"

"I don't know…maybe like…is there a woman involved? I mean besides the showgirl wife."

He frowned. "What the hell are you talking about?"

"You must have had a girlfriend mixed up in there somewhere."

"Jeez," he said. "No. Not only no, but hell no. I haven't dated anyone steadily in more than a year."

"But I thought…" She faked a frown. "I thought you mentioned someone special in Chicago."

He shook his head. "That wasn't me. I was in and out of Chicago to see Bill, but there was never time for anything else. I don't know any women in Chicago, aside from Bill's secretary, and I don't even remember her name. I do recall she was good lookin', but I got the strong impression she only had eyes for the boss."

Already fractured by doubt, Maxi felt the bottom fall out of her tight little world. She stared at him wordlessly.

"Now that you mention it…" Rand considered. "I understand the police questioned her after Bill split. I got the feeling they weren't real happy with her story. I don't know if anything came of that, but last I heard, they were no closer to nabbing the guy than they were on day one. Although if he's still getting legal advice from the same shyster lawyer, it should be easy to nab him.''

Maxi thought she might be sick. She had to call Helen and get the truth.

''You look funny,'' Rand said, and he didn't mean funny-haha. ''Are you sure you're all right?''

''I'm fine.'' She wasn't; she just said that.

''You're upset about the ranch,'' he guessed. ''Look, Max, after that near-death experience with the hijackers, I've got to admit I've done some serious thinking. Finding myself back in the bosom of my family is enough to give me pause all by itself, but that's all—*pause.* When the time comes, I'll do what I have to do.''

When the time comes, I'll do what I have to do. The words reverberated along her nerve endings because they went double for her.

AFTER A QUICK BREAKFAST, Rand went out to saddle a couple of horses for their daily ride, while Maxi darted upstairs to call Helen. With hands that trembled, she dialed the jail.

Only to discover that Helen had been released on bail the previous day.

Thank God! She dialed Helen's apartment.

Helen answered breathlessly on the first ring.

''Helen, it's me, Maxi.''

''Oh.'' Such disappointment in a single word.

''Don't sound so happy to hear from me.''

''I am happy, Maxi, but I was expecting someone else.''

''Obviously. How did you get out of jail?''

"*He* paid my bail."

"He who?"

Helen hesitated, then said, "Rand Taggart, of course."

Maxi sat down hard on the edge of the bed. "That's a lie," she said flatly.

"Why—why—!" Helen sputtered. "Of course he did. You were the one who guessed that he and I—"

"He and you what? And don't tell me any phony stories about how he led you on and then left you to face the music alone."

"Why, Maxine Rafferty! How can you turn against your only sister this way? Who have you been talking to—that wretched lawyer?"

Obviously R. Renwood Keever hadn't told Helen that Maxi was spying on Rand. "It's not important how I know," Maxi said. "I just do. Bill Overton paid your bail. He's the one you're involved with."

"Not the way you mean," Helen huffed. "Rand Taggart bailed me out, I tell you. There's nothing between me and Bill."

"Oh, Helen! I wish I could believe you, but I don't. Bill Overton's using you. He's already married."

A clearly audible gasp preceded hot words: "*He's not married!* He said when this was over, he and I would go away and—"

Helen shut up abruptly, but it was too late. Maxi knew.

"Helen, how can you do this? You're not the kind of person who'd try to frame an innocent man."

"Rand Taggart is *not* innocent! If you only knew

how he's treated Bill, lording it over him because of all his money. So what if Bill takes a little? Rand Taggart has plenty more where that came from.''

"You don't know that, not that it matters. Bill Overton is the crook. I can't believe you helped him get away with millions.''

The silence lengthened. Then Helen said, ''Bill didn't exactly get away with millions. There's the matter of a certain little safe-deposit key.''

Maxi wanted to cry with frustration. ''If you've got Bill's safe-deposit key, you have to give it to the police immediately.''

"Why? It doesn't belong to them.''

"Helen, listen to me. Give the key to the police before Bill shows up and *takes* it. You'll be protected if you do.''

"I don't need protection—not from Bill. He loves me. He wouldn't—''

"He would! He almost has to, if he doesn't want to explain you to his wife.''

"How many times do I have to tell you, he's not married!''

"He *is* married, and as long as you have that key, you're in danger. He could show up at your door any minute and—''

"Why should he show up here when I'm meeting him in Las Vegas.''

Maxi froze. "Oh my God, when?''

"None of your business!''

"I'll come home to Chicago Sunday night.'' After Rand's birthday. ''I'm sure I can talk sense to you if—''

"Too late."

"Helen!"

"Don't yell at me. I know what I'm doing. But if it would make you feel any better…"

"What?" Maxi grasped at straws.

"M-maybe you'd like to meet me in Las Vegas. It's not that I'm worried or anything—I'm not, I'm truly not. I know Bill loves me…."

"You don't know that at all. I can hear the worry in your voice."

"That isn't worry. It's just that we've been apart and I don't know what's been happening with him." Helen hesitated. "He isn't married, Maxi. I know he isn't."

"What if he wants the key but not you?"

"I'll never believe that…but just in case… I would feel better if you were there, Maxi. You're my sister. I can trust you when I can't trust anyone else."

"Of course you can trust me, but—"

"You'd never betray me. Not me, the sister who practically raised you, who kept you out of foster homes, who—"

"That's enough." More than enough. Maxi felt sick all over again.

"I *want* you to know everything because I trust you. Bill's registering at the Double Play Hotel and Casino under the name Brian Kelly, which I think was someone he used to know. I'll be flying in at eleven Saturday night. I should be at his hotel by midnight with the key."

"Don't do this."

"I have to. If you love me, meet me at the airport

at eleven and we'll go to the hotel together. That way you can see for yourself that Bill and I love each other. Will you do it?''

Maxi groaned, thinking about Rand, thinking about the danger to her sister. ''I don't see how I can,'' she said at last.

''I don't see how you can't. You owe me.''

With a click, the line went dead, and with it, Maxi's hopes.

MAXI WRESTLED with her dilemma all day: her sister or the man for whom she'd developed such deep feelings. Maybe she could sneak away long enough to meet Helen in Las Vegas and still be back in time for Rand's birthday showdown...or maybe she should confess everything to Rand. But that would surely risk her sister's future. It seemed as if every choice would destroy one of the two people she loved. Even doing nothing was a choice.

Whatever she did, could she live with herself afterward?

She argued with herself constantly. There was no guarantee Rand could do anything even if she told him. Plus, the police would surely get involved and Helen would be back in jail, this time perhaps for good.

The most telling reason of all to keep quiet was that Rand would hate her forever.

Of course, when all her secrets were revealed, he'd hate her anyway. Was there the slightest chance he wouldn't *have* to find out? Maybe after his birthday, after he'd gained—or lost—his inheritance, she could simply disappear and no one would ever have to know the extent of her duplicity.

Ah, but it was hard to think of simply going away—so she wouldn't. Nor would she continue to wrestle with her conscience. These days were too precious. She had plenty of time to decide what to do, she conned herself into believing.

Each day she and Rand grew closer. They shared long lovely horseback rides and explored every nook and cranny in the house and barn. Best of all, they were completely alone...almost like real honeymooners.

It was heaven, as long as she clung to her vow not to *think*.

If her days were heaven, the nights were paradise. After dinner, they'd sit on the front steps talking and looking at the stars until, with an exaggerated yawn, he'd hold out his hand to her.

And she...she always took it. In his arms, she was happy. Only later, while he slept beside her, did her secrets overwhelm her.

But inevitably Friday rolled around. Maxi still didn't know what she was going to do, having flip-flopped at least a dozen times. When they strolled to the corrals after breakfast, she was still in a quandary.

"You're distracted," he said.

She sighed. "I'm sorry."

"It's okay. Maybe you'd rather talk than ride."

"God, no. I mean, I look forward to our rides."

He halted suddenly, bending down to drag something from the fringe of weeds growing beside the barn. Straightening, he offered it to her with a smile.

It was a Rocking T branding iron, rusty and forgotten. She took it from him, tears welling in her eyes. It looked so unloved and unappreciated, this symbol of family history.

"Hey!" He lifted her glasses from their perch on her nose, the glasses she didn't need except as part of her disguise. "What's the matter?"

"Nothing. Really." She swallowed hard and forced a smile. "How about giving back my glasses?"

"Your eyes are too beautiful to hide." He tightened his hold on her, the glasses dangling from his fingers as the branding iron dangled from hers. "Don't let anything make you sad, Max. We don't have time for that."

"We don't have time for much of anything."

"We have time for kisses," he said.

And so she kissed him, and it became one of those long, leisurely kisses they shared these days on a regular basis.

And she hated herself for it.

THEY RODE OUT much later, over rolling green hills and past grazing herds of curious longhorns. These surroundings were already becoming familiar to her. A couple of riders in the distance lifted their arms in greeting and she waved back, knowing they were Rocking T riders giving the newlyweds a wide berth.

Circling back on an unfamiliar rutted trail, they pulled up their horses on a small hillock overlooking the ranch buildings from the back. Maxi drew in a deep breath of clean fresh country air. Bracing her hands on the saddle horn, she stood in the stirrups to glance around.

She was actually starting to like horses and feel comfortable around them. Within another month she might actually—

Her hand froze in midmotion above her horse's neck. She wouldn't be here for another month and neither would Rand.

Lifting the reins, she started to turn her horse, when something against the trees caught her attention. "Is that a graveyard?" she asked.

"Sure is." Rand, in faded jeans and well-worn boots, looked as if he'd never traveled a step outside of Texas. "Most of the Taggarts are buried there, starting with Jesse Daniel, who was Thom T.'s great-grandpa. My grandpa Travis is there—he died before I was born—and lots more Taggarts."

She twisted toward him in the saddle in time to see a hunger in his face that had never been there before. Whatever he might say, Rand Taggart's heritage was important to him.

And he was going to *sell* it?

Maybe he wouldn't have to do this awful thing if he could catch Bill Overton red-handed and recover what was rightfully his. There was a chance, wasn't there?

If Maxi talked, that is.

CHAPTER FOURTEEN

"RAND." Maxi drew a shuddering breath. "I've got to talk to you."

Rand put his dish towel on the kitchen counter and looked at Max with relief. She'd been tense and taciturn ever since she'd seen the family cemetery. Maybe she was one of those people who couldn't handle death, even at a distance. If so, he'd be disappointed, but he'd also be relieved to know what was bothering her.

"I'm all yours." He sat down on a wooden kitchen chair and eyed her expectantly.

Thinking: he *was* all hers. This past week had been total joy. Each day he grew to know her better...to like her more. Having her in his bed was bliss, but having her beside him all day, every day, was a special kind of pleasure he'd never expected.

Was he falling in love?

He'd never used the *l* word in connection with anyone not related by blood, not even privately. He enjoyed women, both intimately and otherwise, but he'd never met one he thought he could be happy with for the rest of his life.

Until now.

The object of this newfound affection swallowed

hard and licked her lips. Whatever was bothering her must be a beaut.

She took a deep breath. "You're going to hate me," she said in a despairing voice.

His chest constricted. "Why would you say a thing like that?"

"Because it's true." Nervously she wrung out the dishcloth and spread it over the rim of the dishpan to dry. "I haven't been—" she took in another deep breath "—quite honest with you."

"That's okay," he said, feeling the first pangs of alarm. "I wasn't quite honest with you, either, until a couple of days ago. Tell me now and whatever it is, we'll forget it."

"I don't think so." She pulled out a chair and sat down, a picture of dejection. "See, it's…I think you should know, uh, that…"

Her uncertainty alarmed him even more. She'd never minced words before. "Honey, just say it," he urged. "I'll understand."

She lifted her downcast gaze. "First you have to make me a promise."

"Of course."

"Don't be flip. This is serious. You have to promise you won't call the police."

His alarm escalated. "Why would I call the police?"

"Because I know where Bill Overton is—or rather, I know where he's going to be tomorrow night."

Rand almost fell off his chair he was so shocked. "How the hell would you know Bill's plans?"

She licked her lips. "Because Helen Reed is my sister."

Who the hell was Helen Reed? He didn't know any Helen— And then he remembered. "Bill's secretary? *That* Helen Reed?"

She nodded miserably.

The truth crashed into him like a runaway stagecoach: if Max was the sister of Bill's secretary, then her appearance on that airplane in Chicago had been no accident. And when she'd agreed to marry him, that was no accident. And when she'd asked if he'd ever made moves on Bill's secretary, that sure as hell was no accident, either.

She shrank back. "I knew you'd be mad."

"Mad? Me, mad? Why would I be mad?" He sprang to his feet, awash in a flood of horrifying possibilities. "What kind of a two-faced double-dealer are you, Max?" He banged a palm flat against his temple. "I thought Bill made a fool of me, but it was nothin' to what you've done."

"Please, Rand, let me explain." She leaned forward, her movements jerky. "I was just trying to help my sister get out of a jam."

"A *jam?* You call being in cahoots with an embezzler a jam?"

"She's not in cahoots with him—she really isn't. Helen's weak where men are concerned—"

"Unlike her sister, who can marry a guy and sleep with him without batting an eye."

She turned her head away with a strangled groan. "It wasn't like that—it honestly wasn't. How was I to know what would happen when I got on that plane?''

''Yeah, how?'' Couldn't she just look at him and see he wasn't a crook? But the final nail in her coffin of lies was that she'd slept with him. If she didn't trust him, how could she have done that? That question left him reeling. ''Lies. It was all lies.''

A crimson flush moved up her throat and tinted her cheeks. ''I'm telling the truth now,'' she said miserably. ''I...I also stole your briefcase in Mexico. I saw your safe-deposit key, although I didn't realize what it was until later.''

''*You* did that?''

She hung her head. ''Please believe me, I feel just awful about it. But m-maybe there's some way we can get your money back. I'm willing to do anything so long as it doesn't make Helen's situation any worse.''

''Helen, the accomplice to the real crook—that Helen? And you'd help me because...?''

''Because I was wrong about you and I don't want you to have to sell this ranch.''

''Like you care.'' That was cold, but he was too angry to spare her. ''There's something I can do, all right. I can be in Las Vegas to confront that—'' He stopped short. This wasn't going to be as easy as simply confronting Bill. He'd need a confession or some kind of evidence.

What he needed was the safe-deposit key the police were so hot to find. To get it, he needed details.

''Say something.''

''I'm going to Las Vegas.''

"I'll go with you."

"You damn sure will. Do you know when and where they're meeting?"

"Yes, but I won't tell you unless you promise not to involve the cops until I can get Helen out of there."

"Sure, hell yes, why not? Anything you want. You can trust me just like I can trust you."

"You *can* trust me—now. Can't you see I've made my choice?"

"All I see is that you've been working that knife deeper into my back ever since the day we met."

Her head drooped. "I don't guess I can blame you for feeling that way, but I'm going just the same."

"I won't stop you," he said shortly. "So spill it—what's the deal?"

MAXI LOOKED anxiously around the garish lobby of the Double Play Hotel and Casino in Las Vegas, wondering if Bill Overton was already here. "Now what?" she wondered aloud.

Rand gave her a scathing glance. He'd been cold to the point of icy since her confession, speaking to her only when it was absolutely necessary.

"Does Bill know you?" he asked abruptly.

"I met him once or twice. Why?"

"I have to get him out of his hotel suite long enough for me to get in. I need to catch him in the act of taking that key."

"Do you think his wife will be with him?"

He shook his head. "He'll leave her wherever

they've holed up. He won't want to risk having her find out about your sister."

"Helen thinks she and Bill are going to run away together. Any chance of that?"

"None whatsoever. He's crazy about Kristi." His gaze remained chilly, as if he didn't care. "If you asked Bill to meet you in the lobby, would he do it?"

"Yes." The way he'd ogled her the only time they'd met, she was sure of it.

"Could you keep him occupied long enough for me to break into his suite?"

That sounded dangerous to her. Since he obviously wasn't in any mood for solicitous expressions, she just said, "Yes," again.

Her tone apparently displeased him. "You may be a trifle overconfident. Overton's a player. I don't mean to insult you—" He ran his gaze over her dismissively. "I'm mad at you, but my mama taught me to be a gentleman. To be brutally honest, he'd never look twice at you—certainly not long enough for me to get in and get hid."

"That's what you think." What else did she have to lose? Rand might as well know *that,* too. "I can get him out of his suite and keep him out—forever, if that's what you want."

"Yeah, right." He rolled his eyes, adding, "I don't think so."

"I *do.*"

"Dammit, Max, I know the man. I doubt you could coax him across the hall, no offense intended."

"None taken." Which was a lie. She held out her hand. "I'll need some money."

He eyed her suspiciously. "What for?"

"If I'm going to be your decoy, I have to look the part." She sounded confident—very confident.

And it hit him: maybe she had even more secrets than she'd hitherto revealed. Numbly he pulled out his wallet, extracted several bills and laid them on her palm without counting.

She rolled her hand into a fist around the money. "I'll meet you upstairs."

"Is that a promise?"

"Dammit, Rand, I'm not going to run out on you."

Their angry glances clashed. She broke away first.

"I'll see you later," she said.

"Later." He turned and made his way across the casino to the bank of elevators.

Taking a deep breath, she turned in the opposite direction, toward the shops. Almost giddy, she realized that soon he'd know everything...almost.

RAND BANGED on the bedroom door. "It's nine-thirty. Do you *ever* plan to come out?"

"I'm almost ready!"

"You said that ten minutes ago. I'm losing patience out here." *And I never did have much faith this was going to work anyway,* he added to himself.

"Okay, stand back."

The knob rattled; the door flew open and out walked a goddess. Realizing his jaw had gone slack, he snapped his mouth closed, but he couldn't stop staring.

The short red sequined dress bought with his money plunged almost to her waist and clung to what little it covered like a coat of sparkly paint. Fabulously long legs in black stockings ended in high-heeled black slippers, and her face...her face...

Long-lashed golden-brown eyes beneath sleek eyebrows, the kind of cheekbones that couldn't exist in real life, lips as lush and bright as raspberries. Bright hair suddenly looking more gold than brown curled around her face and fell over alabaster shoulders. Her skin glowed like satin, while her breasts rose seductively outside the meager confines of the flashy fabric. When she moved, it was an undulation across the thick carpet.

Even her voice sounded different: lower, sexier. "Do I pass muster?"

Rand could hardly breathe. "You lied to me again."

"Not really." She glanced down at her splendiferous self. "This is the lie. That was the real me at the Rocking T."

"Yeah, and I really am a rocket scientist." He'd never felt so foolish in his life, despite the fact that the past twenty-four hours or so had hit a new high—or low—for personal stupidity. "What are you—a supermodel? You've got that gloss about you."

"I'm a plain old *Violet's Advantage* catalog model, which isn't as super as you might think."

He'd probably seen her photo, he realized with a sickening lurch. He'd picked up a *Violet's Advantage* once while waiting for a date. Paging idly through, he'd rather absently admired the glossy women in silk and satin.

Good old Max had been one of them?

Bewildered by this turn of events, he crossed to the fully stocked bar and poured himself a stiff shot of straight scotch whiskey. ''So what's your name?'' he asked.

The sophisticated air fell away. ''You know my name,'' she said indignantly.

''You model as Maxine Rafferty?''

''Of course. Or at least, a nickname. Most people know me as 'Maxi.'''

''Maxi.'' He had control again. When he turned, nothing trembled but the hand holding the drink. ''That makes sense. You don't look much like a Max at the moment.''

She lifted her chin, her hands going to her hips. It was a pose, he realized; she was more anxious than she cared to show.

''Okay, let's get this show on the road,'' she said.

''We already have. I sent the message to Bill while you were dressing. He'll meet you in the casino in—'' he checked his watch ''—exactly ten minutes. While you keep him busy, I'll break into his place and hide until your sister shows up with the key. You have to keep him occupied long enough for me to get in.''

''Just how do you intend to do that?''

''Don't ask.''

She lifted her chin. ''All right, I won't.'' But he

could tell she wanted to. "You'll make sure Helen doesn't get hurt, won't you?"

"No one will get hurt." He hoped.

"And you'll allow her to leave before you call the police."

"Let's just say I won't make any effort to keep her there. It's Bill Overton I'm after. Look," he added impatiently, "I need you to occupy Bill for at least a half hour. Once you dump him, come back here to this suite and wait. If you hear a commotion, call the cops."

"No cops." She wavered. "What kind of commotion?"

"You know—gunshots, bombs, anything like that."

"Rand! Surely you don't think there'll be gunfire."

"Nah," he said, "I was kidding. Just stay out of the way, okay? If I have to worry about your sister, I don't need you to worry about, as well. Just do your part and we'll pull this off."

He finished his drink. "You'd better head on down. Take the service elevator in back so you won't risk running into him."

She licked those glossy lips. "All right."

He didn't want to soften, but he did. "Scared?"

"Only for Helen."

"Good girl." Damn! He couldn't let her get to him again.

She undulated to the door and paused with her hand on the knob. "Good luck, Rand."

"Good luck...Maxi."
She was gone.

RAND LOITERED near the bank of telephones in the lobby, pretending to read a newspaper but really shielding his face. When Bill stepped off an elevator, it was harder than hell to let his former friend stroll past as if he were king of the world. Once the coast was clear, Rand darted inside an elevator and punched the up button, glad this part of the plan was over.

Watching Maxi wow the throng had not been a pleasant experience. By the time Rand got downstairs himself, she was surrounded by a mob intent on seeing the glamorous model up close and maybe even get her autograph.

Hell, he liked her better as plain old Max—and he *wasn't* jealous.

On the eighteenth floor, he moved out cautiously. Bill's suite was just around that corner. Luxuriant greenery spilled from niches evenly spaced along the wall between doors, offering some cover for his furtive approach to the double doors of 1808.

But he didn't stop there, instead heading for his own suite next door at 1810. He crossed the room swiftly and let himself out onto the balcony in back. With care, he climbed up on the high balustrade, holding on to the building for support.

Las Vegas sparkled below him in all its garish glory, but he wasn't interested. All his attention focused on 1808. A good eight- or nine-foot gap separated the two balconies—and they were eighteen stories high. Still, he figured he could make the jump.

If he tried really, really hard…

Hell, he'd done this sort of thing for a movie when he was only twelve. All he had to do was remember Trey's advice: if you're gonna do it, go all out. Halfway measures can get you killed.

He closed his eyes for just a moment to center himself, opened them again and without hesitation hurled his body into space.

His feet hit the balustrade of Bill's balcony and he fell forward, landing hard on his hands and knees on the artificial turf. For a moment he crouched there between a patio chair and a planter, head down, breathing hard. His hands and knees stung with the force of his landing, but he'd made it. The rest should be easy.

Nobody was going to worry about locking a sliding door eighteen stories up. If Bill had walked outside to admire the view—and who wouldn't?—that door would be unlocked.

Quietly Rand tested the mechanism. The door slid open easily and he stepped inside. He moved stealthily to the entryway and pressed his ear against the front door.

And almost immediately heard someone fumbling with the lock. He ducked around the edge of the enormous planter in the entryway, wiggling deep into the lush greenery. Lighting here was low and dramatic, which would make detection difficult.

Had Bill lost interest in Maxi already?

Jeez, not a chance. Which could only mean—

That was not Bill Overton pushing open the door.

A woman whipped through the arched entry and

slammed the door behind her. Long blond hair swirled around her expensively tanned face and he recognized Kristi Overton. Bill's showgirl wife, small overnight case in hand, was about to surprise her husband. Judging by the expression on her face, it wouldn't be a pleasant surprise.

Pausing, she fumbled at the pocket of shiny skin-tight jeans and shoved a credit card inside. That really worked? If it was that easy, Rand should have tried it himself instead of playing Spider Man.

The doorknob rattled again and Kristi sprang around like a tigress. Jeez, someone else was trying to get in. Rand fought the desire to press deeper into the foliage. Trey had explained that the eye was attracted by motion. It was better to simply hold still and pray.

So Rand did. The door opened and another woman stood there, but this one didn't stride boldly in. She slipped inside as if she expected the police to jump out at her any minute.

It was Helen Reed, early for her rendezvous with Bill Overton. She saw Kristi and stopped short.

Kristi planted her hands on her hips. "And you," she said coolly, "would be Helen Reed if I'm not mistaken."

Helen blinked. She was pretty but not nearly the knockout her sister was. "I…I'm sorry, I thought this was Mr. Overton's suite."

"It is. *I* am Mrs. Overton."

Helen's eyes widened still more. "That's impossible. Bill never told me he was—"

"Well, he is, and I'm her. I think you and I better have a nice long talk. Then—"

"Ms. Reed! Wait up!"

What was this—Grand Central Station? R. Renwood Keever rushed into the entryway, briefcase flapping at his side. Helen let out a little squeak of alarm and fell back a few steps, while Kristi started forward.

"Ah," Keever said, "I see you two have met. I was afraid of that."

At which point he pulled a revolver from his pocket and pointed it awkwardly at the two women. Suddenly Rand's options narrowed to exactly one.

MAXI DISTRACTED BILL for forty minutes before realizing she couldn't stand any more of this, even if he could; he was practically salivating. She had already confided her deep fears for her sister and he had already assured her that Helen was in no real trouble, which Maxi knew was a lie.

If Rand wasn't in by now, he never would be.

Bill apparently noted her change of mood, for he said, "Why don't we go back to my suite for a quick drink. It's much more comfortable than this coffee shop."

"I'd love to," she declared warmly, thinking that if Rand expected her to disappear and let him play hero, he was sadly mistaken. Bill's invitation fit in nicely with her plans.

The elevator was crowded when they entered on the casino floor, but by the time they reached eighteen, only the two of them remained. Beyond an occasional leer, Bill had been a perfect gentleman.

She didn't expect that to last.

At his door, he fumbled for his key card. "Look, I've got at least an hour before I have to, uh, meet a business associate," he said. "That should be plenty of time for us to have that little drink and get better acquainted. As for your sister, I think I've put your mind at ease. Helen was a wonderful secretary, but I never really knew her very well—"

The door swung open and Bill gestured her inside, his expression lecherous. Which was a good thing, because when he was looking at her, he couldn't see Rand round a corner into the foyer and start forward.

But if Bill turned suddenly—

Maxi threw her arms around Bill Overton's neck, uttered a breathless, "I can't thank you enough!" and kissed him.

OKAY, Maxi had done the job Rand sent her to do, but what the hell was she doing here and why was she kissing that snake? Grabbing Bill's collar, Rand hauled him out of her arms and around to face retribution.

It took the discombobulated man just an instant to realize he was in big trouble. His eyes went wide and panicky. "Rand! How did you find me?"

"If I told you, you wouldn't believe it." Rand drew back a fist. "You low-down double-dealing skunk. You robbed me blind."

"I can explain everything!" Bill held up his hands in supplication, palms facing out. "This is all a big mistake. I didn't steal your money, H-Helen did. That's why she has the safe-deposit key. I'm meeting her later tonight to talk her into giving it all back. Then—''

"You lying sack of shit!" Kristi's strident voice announced her arrival from the bedroom, Helen hot on her heels. "*You* did it! You strung this poor kid along just like you always do—and I believed you when you said you'd changed." She looked at Helen for agreement. "How dumb is that? If it hadn't been for Renny—"

"Renny?" Bill appeared horrified.

"R. Renwood Keever, you fool! He called to find out where you were meeting your mistress. Otherwise, I'd still be sitting on that island drinking mai tais and waiting for my faithful husband's return. Of course, Renny also wormed a few details out of *me,* but that's beside the point. Can you believe that shyster followed Helen here with a gun to take that key from her? If Rand hadn't been around—"

"Honey, baby, what are you talking about?" Bill started toward her but veered unexpectedly to lash out at Rand with a wild right hook. His fist landed a glancing blow on the side of Rand's jaw, sending him staggering back into the cocktail table. He went down with a mighty crash.

Maxi rushed to his aid, but Bill straightened with a pistol in his hand before she could launch her attack. He pointed it right at her.

"Hold it! Everybody over there against that wall. All except Helen." He waved the weapon at the cowering secretary. "I want that key."

"I don't have it." She sidled over behind Kristi. Peering out, she added, "How can you do this to me, Billy? You said you loved me."

"I don't love you, you silly bitch. I used you. Now, give me the damn key." He waggled his fingers impatiently. "Helen, I'm warning you—"

Rand, still on his knees, dived for Bill's legs. Bill toppled over backward, the pistol flying across the room to slide beneath a chair. Rand heaved himself up to straddle his former friend, his only desire to get his hands around that lying creep's neck.

One of the women screamed, but Rand was too busy fighting a buzz saw to worry about that. If he could just hold this guy down long enough to—

"Cease immediately and get your hands up!"

What the hell? Rand battled flailing fists. Grunting, he managed to heave Bill over onto his stomach. Holding the frantic man down with one knee in his back, Rand finally looked up—straight into the muzzle of Bill's pistol in the uncertain hands of R. Renwood Keever.

This would damn well be the last time he ever used a necktie to bind and gag a bad guy.

Keever's eyes glowed with a feverish light. "The key," he snarled. "Whoever's got that key, give it to me now or—" He made a slashing motion across his own throat with the pistol for illustration.

Nobody moved a muscle.

"I mean it. Helen, give me that key."

"I don't have it!" She crouched lower behind Kristi.

Who snapped, "Don't look at me. If I had the

damn key, would I have come looking for that bozo?'' She sneered at her husband, now flat on his belly and held there by Rand's knee.

''You, then.'' Keever swung the weapon toward Maxi.

''I don't know anything about a key except what *you* told me.''

''I believe you,'' R. Renwood said. ''As a Mata Hari, you're a total bust.'' His smile was malicious. ''That only leaves you, Mr. Randall Taggart.'' Stepping forward, he pressed the muzzle of the revolver directly behind Rand's left ear.

CHAPTER FIFTEEN

MAXI'S SCREAM nearly split Rand's eardrums.

Apparently it had the same effect on R. Renwood Keever, for his hand jerked even as he fired the pistol. A bullet buzzed past Rand's ear to tear a hole in the wall.

Without waiting to assess the damage, Rand leaped to his feet and lunged for Keever's gun hand. Surprisingly the shady lawyer didn't fight to retain the weapon, just let it go and rushed toward the front door.

It opened in his face, bringing his flight to a premature conclusion.

"Police officers! Everybody halt and get your hands in the air—*now.*"

It was over.

Mostly.

"EVERYBODY *SHUT UP.*"

The cacophony of sound ceased abruptly. With weary patience, the middle-aged Chicago detective who'd led Las Vegas officers in the bust surveyed the little group wedged into the LVPD office. Everybody had been talking at once, with the exception of

Bill Overton, already behind bars. Who might yet join him was anybody's guess.

"That's better," the cop said. "I never saw such a mad bunch of people. Maybe if I let you all get it off your chest, we can get down to business." He faced Maxi. "Who are *you* mad at, lady?"

Maxi glared at Rand. "Rand Taggart. He promised he wouldn't involve the police."

The cop didn't flick an eyelash, just turned to Helen. "And you're mad at…?"

"My sister." Helen's glare matched Maxi's. "I trusted her and she betrayed me to *him.*" She indicated Rand with a stiff forefinger.

"I see. How about you, lady. Who you mad at?"

Kristi rolled her eyes. "My no-good philandering husband, who swore he'd stop cheating the last time I caught him at it."

Helen gasped. "You mean I'm not the first?"

"Honey," Kristi said, "you're probably not the *tenth.* How do you think I got him from his second wife? Bill was born a hound dog and he'll die a hound dog, which doesn't get that damn ambulance-chasing attorney off the hook. I wouldn't even be here if he hadn't tipped me off."

The policeman indicated Keever. "Your turn. Who're *you* mad at?"

The gaunt attorney curled his lip. "Basically," he said to the cop, "you. I'd have got away scot-free if you hadn't shown up. And Overton, of course—I'm mad at him for trying to stiff me in the first place. As for you, *Mrs.* Overton, all I wanted from you was a time and a place. Don't blame me if you insisted on knowing *why*."

The officer swiveled in his chair so he could look at Rand. "You get the last word, Taggart. Before we start putting the facts of this case together, who are you mad at?"

Hell, Rand was mad at everybody. He'd been played for a chump and it didn't sit well. But there was only one real villain.

"All roads lead to Bill Overton," he rasped. "His hand's in everything. What I don't know is, was he the one asking questions about me in Texas or is something else going on?"

"That would be me," Keever said. "Done in all innocence on my part, I assure you. My client, Mr. Overton, wished to know how close you were to catching up with him."

"Not very, until my blushing bride decided to speak up." Rand's indignant glance zeroed in on Maxi. *"And I didn't call the police."*

"Then how did they just happen to show up?" Maxi shot back.

"I can answer that," the cop offered. "We've been tailing your sister since she got out of jail, ma'am. We figured she'd eventually lead us to Overton." His sudden grin seemed out of place until he added, "We just didn't know she'd also lead us to the entire cast of Looney Tunes."

Nobody could dredge up anything greater than a pained smile, so he went on more soberly. "We need to ask a few questions before we let anybody go, but we've got the guy we were after. Now, if you'll just hand over that key, Mr. Taggart—''

Rand fished out the safe-deposit key entrusted to him by Helen once she'd been overwhelmed by Kristi's diatribe. That earned him a shocked glance from Maxi, which he ignored. "I've got to be back in Texas by tomorrow night," he said. "It's important."

"That's doable." The policeman reached for the telephone, adding, "God willing and the creeks don't rise."

RAND AND MAXI arrived at the Rocking T Ranch in a driving rainstorm at ten o'clock on the last day of September. They'd barely spoken since leaving Las Vegas. Maxi was beginning to wonder if he ever intended to speak to her again.

Topping the rise above the ranch house, he slammed on the brakes and said, "Shi—oot!"

"What's wrong?" She braced her hands against the dashboard.

"Look for yourself. They're all here, every last one of 'em."

Several cars were indeed parked beside the house. "You knew they were coming for your birthday," she pointed out, wanting to wish him a happy one but doubting he'd take it in the spirit offered.

He drove on. "I was hoping that when they realized we weren't here, they'd wait in town." His tone hardened. "What the hell. I'm doomed anyway. Let's get this over with."

Maxi yearned to protest, but what was there to

say? He was probably right. Even if he wasn't, she'd still be in his doghouse—and he didn't even know her final and most potentially damaging secret. Lips pressed in a tight line, she waited until he braked behind all the cars there ahead of them, then she leaped out and ran through the rain for the door. Inside the house, she stopped short.

Kit, Rachel, Meg and Clementine looked up from the large photo album open on a table before them. Kit said, "At last!" and Meg started forward.

"Maxine, we've been so worried. Where on earth did you and Rand disappear to?"

"We—" Maxi struggled for an explanation that didn't include, *We went to Las Vegas, caught a bad guy who'd bilked Rand out of all his money and completely obliterated any chance we might have had for a future together.*

Meg put an arm around Maxi's shoulder. "Never mind that now. You're soaked. Come dry off and then we can sort all this out."

At that moment, Rand entered. Rainwater streamed from his face and hair and his shirt clung to his chest and arms. Elemental and almost frightening, he walked through the room without so much as a greeting for the women staring at him openmouthed.

"My goodness," Meg said helplessly. "I guess we've got more to sort out than I realized."

Taking Maxi's arm, Meg steered her toward the stairs.

MAXI LEANED over the bathroom sink, tears of defeat mingling with the rain wet upon her cheeks. What a mess...and it wasn't over. Now she had to face a roomful of nice people who would, in the end, be forced to deny Rand his due.

It was all her fault.

The sooner this ended, the better. After drying her face and hair, she folded the towel and put it back onto the rack, took a deep breath, squared her shoulders and walked out into the bedroom.

Meg sat at the foot of the bed, smoothing a hand over the quilt. She looked up with a smile. "One of Rand's ancestors made this quilt," she said.

To Maxi's horror, tears began to roll down her cheeks again. "I'm not surprised," she managed to say. "Everything here...has some special meaning...and I...I..."

Meg took the weeping woman in her arms. "There, there," she said, patting Maxi's shoulder. "Nothing can be this bad."

"Oh, no?" Swallowing back her grief, Maxi brushed angrily at damp cheeks. "It's worse. Rand's furious with me and I don't blame him."

"If he loves you, he'll get over it."

"Yes, *if*." Maxi said the final word hopelessly.

"You love him, don't you?"

"I..." Mouth gone dry, Maxi stared at Rand's mother. Dared she say so out loud?

"Why do you hesitate?" Meg asked gently. "You were in that bathroom crying over him, and that wouldn't happen if you didn't care...a lot. You love him, Maxine. You should be proud to say so."

"Meg..."

"*Do* you love my son?"

"Yes." It was barely a whisper. "But..." She couldn't add what she felt: *Not that it will do me any good.* As long as a single chance was left that Rand might get his inheritance, she wouldn't let him down.

Maybe there *was* something she could give him for his birthday.

"Meg," she said impulsively, "I need to speak to Jesse privately. Would it be all right?"

"Of course. I'll get him." Meg's lovely blue eyes revealed curiosity, but she didn't ask any questions, just went to fetch her husband.

"Meg says you want me."

Maxi turned from the window and the continuing rain outside. Rand's father stood just inside the door, tall and hard and eyeing her with caution.

She nodded. "Thanks for coming." She swallowed hard, aware of his coolly assessing look. "It...it's about Rand."

"What about him?"

How to say this? With no time for finesse, she spoke bluntly. "How do you feel about him, Jesse? Is he a complete disappointment to you?"

The tall Texan recoiled. "What the hell are you talking about, girl? He's my son and I love him. Yeah, I've been disappointed in him from time to time, but I've been damn proud of him, too. Where do you get these cockeyed ideas?"

"From—"

"Damn! That really torques my jaw." He took a couple of steps forward, hands clenching at his side.

"Why would you think such a thing, Max? Surely you don't believe it."

"No," she said, "I don't, but Rand does. Maybe it's time you told *him* how you feel."

Seeing the shock on this hard man's face, she wondered if she'd screwed up yet again.

RAND DRIED HIMSELF in the bathroom off the screened-in back porch, and he was steaming. Let Max—make that *Maxi*—have the upstairs. He didn't want to run into her until he had to.

Towel covering his head, he rubbed vigorously, but not vigorously enough to muffle his father's voice.

"What the hell's goin' on, kid?"

Slowly Rand lowered the towel. "What makes you think anything's going on?"

"I didn't just fall off a turnip truck," Jesse said bluntly. "But let's take first things first. You and Maxine disappear, then show up again not even talkin' to each other. I'd say something's goin' on, all right."

"We were in Las Vegas," Rand said shortly. Stripping off his soaking shirt, he looked around as if he expected to find a fresh one.

Which he did, in his father's hands. He took it and pulled it over his head. Emerging, he said, "Thanks."

"Yeah. So what's your beef with your wife, besides the fact that she talks when she should be listenin'?"

Rand let out a pained breath. "If you must know, she lied to me."

Jesse considered for a moment. "And your point is?"

Rand couldn't believe it. "You don't think that's important? What if Mom lied to you? How would you like that?"

"She has and I didn't." Jesse hooked thumbs through the belt loops of his Wranglers. "When she left with you, she told me she'd made a mistake and the marriage was over. She hadn't and it wasn't, but she put all three of us through hell before *that* little lie got found out."

"That's why you two lived apart all those years? What in hell made her do that?"

"Jealousy." Jesse's gray eyes narrowed. "What did you think?"

"I thought it was me," Rand said slowly. "I thought you didn't...want a son."

Jesse's face contorted with what could only be pain...and something harder to pin down. He turned away, hesitated, turned back awkwardly. "Every man wants a son," he said. "I...loved you and your mother both, and I wanted you both to be happy. She swore that in Boston, you were. I was too damn pig-headed to push it the way I should have."

"I never got over that separation," Rand said. "I never felt as if I measured up to what you wanted in a son."

Fire flared in Jesse's eyes. "Never measured up? Damn, boy, you've always measured up, just not in the areas I'd have picked for you. I wanted you to follow in my footsteps and instead you took after your mama's side of the family. That was a big disappointment, but I didn't love you any less for it.''

Rand couldn't believe this was his father talking. All choked up, he managed a weak, ''Dad...''

Jesse grabbed his son in a big, embarrassed bear hug, then quickly let him go. ''Now, about you and that wife of yours—'' He spoke gruffly, as if uncomfortable with this display of emotion.

Rand said, ''We've got...just call 'em problems.''

''There's only one problem that's insurmountable.''

''I'm not sure I want to hear this.''

''You're gonna hear it whether you want to or not. Hell, now I've started spilling my guts, it may be hard to stop me.'' Jesse grimaced. ''I reckon you know what I'm about to say anyway. If you love her, you can work it out.''

''It's not that easy, Dad.''

''I didn't say it was easy.'' Jesse cocked one eyebrow. ''*Do* you love her?''

Rand's head sagged and he let out a weary sigh. ''Yeah, I love her,'' he said, giving up his last pretense of objectivity, ''whoever the hell she is. I just don't—''

''Everybody's waiting for you, Randy.'' Clementine's blithe voice brought both men spinning around. ''Time to pay the piper.'' She winked, grinned, disappeared back down the hall.

Rand and Jesse exchanged questioning glances, then followed her to the parlor.

LIKE A REAL-LIFE VERSION of a Hollywood movie, all the usual suspects gathered in the parlor for the final act of the improbable drama set in motion years earlier by Thom T. Taggart: Boone and Kit, Trey and Rachel, Jesse and Meg, Clementine, plus Rachel's brother, Lee, and her son Jason. Rand and Maxi sat side by side on one of the hard Victorian sofas, not touching, not even looking at each other.

Expecting a spotlight to pin them where they sat at any moment.

Boone cleared his throat. "We had plenty of time to figure out how to go about this while we waited for you two to show up," he began. "I've been designated master of ceremonies, so I'll start by saying we're all relieved you made it back before the witching hour." Everybody smiled and nodded except the "you two" he was talking about.

Undeterred, he continued. "Before we get on to more important things, we'd like to clear up a few little, uh, discrepancies, Randy."

"Great." Rand slumped. "Lemme have it."

Meg said, "Randy!" in that mother voice meant to simultaneously convey disapproval and encouragement. "We just feel you have a right to know that *we* know everything."

"Everything?" That was Maxi's croak.

Meg nodded. "Let's see, we know Randy's been supporting the widow and children of his old friend Brian Kelly. You even moved them into Grandfather's Boston town house."

Rand shifted uneasily on the hard sofa and Maxi couldn't stop herself from reaching out to touch the hand resting on his knee. He gave her a startled glance but didn't pull back. Perhaps he felt as she did, that they were momentarily united against the world whether they liked it or not.

"I didn't want to tell you about that, Mom," he said. "I know how much you love that place. I didn't think you'd appreciate my turning it over to strangers."

"When you were doing a kindness for someone who deserved a break? Oh, Randy..." Meg looked close to tears. "I'm proud of you, honey."

Rand seemed completely unprepared for this response. Before he got past that, Jesse spoke.

"We also know you were the one who jumped the hijackers on that airplane in Mexico," he said. "And Maxine helped, am I right?"

"Yes, but how—"

"Your uncle Boone still has a few contacts," Jesse said wryly. "Does the name Larry Evans do anything for you? Insurance...Dubuque?"

Rand groaned. Next they'll bring up the embezzlement, Maxi thought. This is awful.

But instead, Clementine was saying, "And of course, there's that business about Maxine really being Maxi Rafferty, world-famous lingerie model."

Maxi's stomach dropped. She hadn't expected anyone to know *that*. "How did you find out, Clemmie?" she asked.

"I recognized your picture in the catalog. I didn't say anything then because I figured you and Randy must have your reasons for keeping quiet."

Rand threaded his fingers through Maxi's and

hung on tight. "What else you gonna hit us with?" he said to his assembled loved ones.

Trey, who'd watched the proceedings silently, grinned. "When we started comparing notes, I felt duty-bound to mention that camp for disadvantaged kids you started and still support in northern California."

Rand expelled his breath in an annoyed *whoosh*. "How the hell did you find out about that?"

"I've known for a while. It's the Taggart connection. Someone asked if I was related to *that* Taggart and come to find out, I am."

Maxi felt numb. Why on earth did Rand act as if he was ashamed of his many good deeds? He seemed to cherish his shaky reputation and shy away from his philanthropy.

And then, because she knew him now with her heart, she understood. He wanted to be loved unconditionally, not because of what he did or didn't do or for the size of his bank account.

He would be in for a real surprise when he realized how many people truly cared for him. That knowledge warmed her when she needed comfort most.

"Anything else?" Rand looked and sounded beleaguered.

Boone glanced around with arched eyebrows and Maxi sensed Rand holding his breath just as she was. "Apparently not. In that case, it's show time. Clemmie, punch the on button, hon."

IN THE QUIET ROOM, Rand watched his great-grandfather smile across time. Before Thom T. could open his mouth, the first silent tear overflowed.

"Howdy, Great-grandson," the old man in the tailored Western suit began. "I'm a' hopin' you're watching this on your thirtieth birthday, surrounded by a lovin' wife and a bunch of young'uns. There's nothin' more important in the whole world than family love and loyalty. Us Taggarts have survived all that's been throwed at us because we always believed that. I know you won't let anybody down, yourself included. I've knowed all along that you'd come through when the chips were down."

Someone was sobbing. Rand suspected it was Kit, who knew Thom T. better than anyone, with the possible exception of Boone and Jesse. *Much better than I did,* Rand thought. *And now it's too late.*

At least some hope remained that he'd get control of the ranch. They didn't know about the embezzlement so they couldn't know how badly he needed money. They might still decide to approve his inheritance. All was not lost.

Thom T. continued, gently urging. "It's never too late to do the right thing," he said, as if privy to Rand's thoughts. "I know you. You were a good boy and now you're a good man. I'm proud to pass the Rockin' T into your care. Take it to greater glory, boy.

"Just remember that wherever I am, I love you."

The screen went blank. There wasn't a dry eye in the house.

MAXI COULDN'T REMEMBER the last time she'd cried—before today. Patting away her tears for what seemed like the tenth time, she glanced at Rand. He, too, had been moved to tears by the old man's final message.

Rand cleared his throat. "Now what? As Great-grandpa would have said, I feel like I been drug through a knothole. If you've got any more little surprises, let's get 'em out of the way now."

Boone glanced at Jesse and Meg. "Do we?"

"Just one." Jesse spoke directly to his son. "We talked this over among ourselves while we were waiting, and as far as we're concerned—" He looked around at all the suddenly solemn faces. "You've complied with the conditions of the will. You're hitched, and God knows you're a productive member of society. We were worried at first that you just wanted this place so you could sell it, but I think most of us have changed our minds about that and the rest are ready to take a chance *because we love you.* Congratulations, son. Unless someone's changed his or her mind, the Rocking T is yours."

Maxi sat there holding her breath, her emotions in turmoil. The Taggarts loved and believed in Rand. Could he continue to deceive these wonderful people in so cruel a way? He turned and their gazes met. She wanted to plead with him, but no words came.

"I'm sorry," he said, "but I've got to do this."

Do what? Stick to his original plan or tell the truth while there was still time, admitting that he intended to sell the ranch regardless of anyone else's feelings? She longed to influence his decision but knew that wasn't possible. She'd already so damaged her credibility with him that nothing she could say would make any difference. He was on his own now.

He turned to their fascinated observers. "You've been straight with me so I'm going to be straight with you. Max and I met on that hijacked airplane. Our so-called marriage was nothing but a scam to get my inheritance, which I fully intended to sell."

Meg looked as if he'd kicked her. "Why, Randy? Why would you go to so much trouble just to sell the Rocking T?"

"I need the money, Mom." His words were leaden. "It's...a long story."

"We got plenty of time," Jesse said quietly.

"Okay, then. Here's the short version. I expect you remember Bill Overton."

Meg's eyes narrowed. "And not fondly. What does he have to do with any of this?"

"I invested in his company, Mom, and he embezzled everything. That's why Max and I went to Las Vegas—to catch that thieving lying pile of—" He broke off midtirade with a rueful laugh. "You get the picture. He's in police custody now, but who knows if I'll ever see a cent of those millions."

Kit, the eternal optimist, said, "But you might."

"I might also win the lottery."

Clementine frowned. "Then you're not really married?"

"We're married, all right, but that was just a technicality to meet the conditions of the will. I wish I didn't have to tell you this. I'm not proud of what I tried to do, but it's time to be honest."

Maxi couldn't let him shoulder all the blame.

"Neither of us is proud of what we did," she said quickly. "You see, my sister was Bill Overton's secretary and she's mixed up in the embezzlement. Only, she told me Rand was behind it and I set out to get something on him to clear her." Her shoulders slumped. "I couldn't have been more wrong. I deeply regret what I've done."

"But you *are* married," Clementine returned stubbornly to her point.

"Yes." Rand bit off the word. "But we're telling you it was just part of the hoax."

Meg frowned. "How can it be a hoax when you *are* married and you *do* love each other? That sounds real to me."

"When we love—?" Maxi couldn't help glancing at Rand.

All he did was bluster. "What makes you think we're in love?"

"Because," Meg said sweetly, "Maxine confessed her feelings to me and I understand you, Randy, did the same with your father. Surely neither of you is still lying."

Maxi and Rand looked at each other then, *really* looked at each other.

"Dammit, Max, he forced it out of me."

"Your m-mom caught me at a weak moment."

"I wasn't lying."

"Neither was I."

Clementine said, "For heaven's sake, you two act as if this is news. It's only obvious you're meant for each other."

"Yeah, right." Rand lifted Maxi's cold hands to

his mouth and kissed them. "Say you love me now, Max, and I'll believe you."

"I love you, Rand." The icy shield around her heart began at last to thaw. "Do you love me?"

"God, yes!"

"The rest of it can wait, then."

Kit laughed with sheer relief. "That settles that. You're in love, you're married and Randy won't sell the Rocking T out from under us, right?"

Randy grinned and pressed Maxi's hand against his chest. "Sounds right to me. Maxi?"

Maxi closed her eyes. She'd rather take a beating than confess to yet another deception. Maybe if she let things ride she could deal with this final deceit later....

Or maybe not. Maybe if she didn't risk everything by speaking up, this secret would come back to ruin what she was so close to finding with this man.

"Maxine?" Boone, ever observant, demanded her attention. "Is there something else?"

She could be no less honest than Rand was. "Yes," she said, "there's something else." Her stubborn lips would barely move to form the words. "Our marriage..." She gazed at Rand, pleading with him to understand. "It's not real, Rand. That wasn't a government official who married us. It was an actor I met on a modeling assignment in Ensenada a year or so ago. We're not married and never were. I was pulling a scam of my own to help H-Helen."

This final confession threw everyone into an uproar, but Maxi only had eyes for Rand. He looked as if she'd hit him over the head with a baseball bat.

Then his face cleared and he sighed. "It figures," he said, and pulled her into his arms.

He kissed her, and at the touch of his lips she believed at last that everything would be all right. With or without the Rocking T, with or without the Randall fortune, they would make it.

She'd never ask for anything more, she swore to herself as she returned his kiss. When he lifted his head, she said, "I'm sorry I've cost you your inheritance, darling. If only there was something I could do."

"Maybe there is." Boone glanced at his watch. "Hey, everybody quiet down!" When they did, he went on. "It's a quarter to twelve on September 30. If Rand and Maxine really want to marry, we've got a minister in the family, right? Jason can perform an emergency ceremony, with the legalities to come."

Maxi twisted in Rand's embrace. "Could you do that?" she asked the bespectacled Jason.

"Only if you're both willing to swear that this marriage is the real thing."

"It's real, all right," Rand said without hesitation.

"The marriages I perform last a lifetime," Jason warned, "until death do you part."

Maxi grinned. "Not to be melodramatic, but we've already faced death a couple of times together. So yes, I'm willing to swear."

Rand nodded. He didn't seem able to stop smiling.

Jason looked sternly from one to the other. "Be very, very sure. I'd take it real personal if you disappointed me."

"Get on with it already!" Rand kissed Maxi's

temple. "Here, I'll make it real plain." Gazing into her eyes, he declared, "Ms. Maxine Rafferty, I love you. Will you marry me, once and for all, now and forever?"

"I certainly will, Randall Taggart, and the sooner the better. Because as it so happens, I love you, too."

Assorted relatives applauded enthusiastically. Jason glanced at his watch again, then stepped to the middle of the parlor and pointed to the spot directly in front of him.

"In that case, you two lovebirds stand right there and everybody else can serve as witnesses."

"Hurry!" Rachel squeezed her son's elbow. "It's five minutes of midnight!"

"Relax, Mama, we've got plenty of time," Jason assured her. "Y'all ready? Here we go… 'Dearly beloved, we are gathered here—'"

JASON'S "YOU MAY kiss the bride" came on the first stroke of midnight. Holding his wife in his arms, Rand felt his heart lighten with each chime of the grandfather clock, until he thought it might take wing.

This was so much better than anything he'd dreamed of. He'd never actually expected to find real love, although he'd always known he would eventually marry. He wanted a family of his own, a son. He remembered his father's words: *Every man wants a son.*

Loving applause bathed them and Max hid her face against his chest as if suddenly shy. Boone held up his hands for quiet.

"Are we all in agreement, then, that the conditions of Thom T.'s will have been met?"

Nods and more applause provided the answer, and Clementine called out, "Speech! Speech!" The cry was soon taken up by the others.

Rand was glad to oblige. "I've seen the light," he assured them. "It occurs to me that I've been a bit secretive over the years—"

Clementine booed loudly, hushing only at her mother's pointed glance.

Rand went on. "I'm going to do better, honest. I'll start by swearing I'll never part with the Rocking T, assuming that's okay with my wife?"

"More than okay," Maxi agreed happily. "I love this place, too."

"In that case—" Rand grinned broadly "—I repeat. The Taggart family heritage is safe with me. Of course, I may have to sell off everything on four legs to keep it going. And one final promise..." He met Maxi's laughing gaze. "From here on out, my new wife handles all our family finances. Have I learned my lesson or what?"

Everybody cheered.

EPILOGUE

THE THIRD TIME was a charm.

Rand and Maxine made it all nice and legal a month later. Once again, Taggarts gathered at the Rocking T ranch house, this time for a champagne reception to honor the newlyweds.

Clementine kissed her brother's cheek, then her new sister-in-law's. "This is so romantic," she sighed. "Are you going away for a honeymoon now?"

"Yes, but we're not telling anyone where."

Rand and Maxi exchanged intimate glances. They'd agreed that the only place to honeymoon was the place where they'd "married" originally: Ensenada. This time things would be different.

A lot had happened since Rand's birthday. Helen had agreed to a plea bargain and would escape jail time by testifying against Bill Overton; she'd also made up with her sister, to Maxi's relief. Kristi was divorcing Bill and couldn't have cared less what happened to him. The crooked attorney, R. Renwood Keever, was well on his way to disbarment, and law enforcement officials were optimistic about recovering the bulk of the money Bill had misappropriated. And Maxi had made peace with her agent, promising

him that after the honeymoon she and her new husband would sit down together and discuss her future—if any—as a model.

None of this unduly concerned Rand at the moment. He and Maxi would be all right, with or without the Randall loot. For the first time in a long time,
he had faith that everything would turn out okay—
especially with Maxi holding the checkbook.

Across the room, Jesse called for attention. "What
we need right about now is a toast," he announced,
lifting his champagne flute. "To the newlyweds."

"Hear, hear!"

"And to Thom T. Taggart."

Rand raised his glass. "Without Great-grandpa's
meddling, Maxi and I would never have found each
other."

"Amen to that." Maxi kissed his cheek and cuddled against him. It was so wonderful to belong to
someone, really *belong*.

"To Thom T."

"To Thom T.!"

Off to one side, Clementine sighed. Rand's sister
was staring at her champagne flute as if counting
bubbles.

Rand heard her mutter, "Thanks for nothing,
Great-grandpa. Without you around to help me, I'll
probably be the first Taggart in history to end up an
old maid."

"No, you won't." Holding Rand's hand, Maxi
slipped her free arm around her sister-in-law's waist,
speaking with certainty. "When the right time comes

for you, I just have to believe Thom T. will have that covered somehow.''

''Absolutely,'' Rand agreed. ''Look what he did for us—got us hitched and turned me into a rancher all at the same time. He'll do the same for you, Clemmie, someday, somehow.''

''Someday, somehow,'' Maxi echoed, filled with wonder. Not only *hitched* but *happily hitched!* Who'd have thought it?

Dead or alive, Thom T. really *could* work miracles, and nobody would ever be able to convince her otherwise.

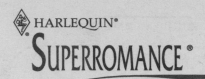

HARLEQUIN®
SUPERROMANCE®

You are now entering

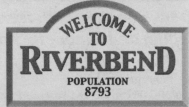

WELCOME TO
RIVERBEND
POPULATION
8793

Riverbend…the kind of place where everyone knows
your name—and your business. Riverbend…home of
the River Rats—a group of small-town sons and
daughters who've been friends since high school.

The Rats are all grown up now. Living their lives and
learning that some days are good and some days
aren't—and that you can get through anything
as long as you have your friends.

Starting in July 2000, Harlequin Superromance brings
you Riverbend—six books about the River Rats and
the Midwest town they live in.

BIRTHRIGHT by **Judith Arnold** (July 2000)
THAT SUMMER THING by **Pamela Bauer** (August 2000)
HOMECOMING by **Laura Abbot** (September 2000)
LAST-MINUTE MARRIAGE by **Marisa Carroll** (October 2000)
A CHRISTMAS LEGACY by **Kathryn Shay** (November 2000)

Available wherever Harlequin books are sold.

HARLEQUIN®
Makes any time special ™

***Don't miss
an exciting opportunity
to save on the purchase of
Harlequin and Silhouette books!***

Buy any two Harlequin or
Silhouette books and save
$10.00 off future Harlequin
and Silhouette purchases

OR

buy any three
Harlequin or Silhouette books
and save **$20.00 off** future
Harlequin and Silhouette purchases.

***Watch for details
coming in October 2000!***

PHQ400

HARLEQUIN®
Makes any time special ™

Silhouette®
Where love comes alive ™

HARLEQUIN®

Bestselling authors

MARY JO
PUTNEY

MERLINE
LOVELACE

GAYLE WILSON

*Cordially invite you to
enjoy three sparkling
stories of unexpected love*

Bride
BY ARRANGEMENT

*One timeless classic and
two brand-new tales*

Available August 2000

HARLEQUIN®
Makes any time special ™

Visit us at www.eHarlequin.com   PHBBA

HARLEQUIN®

SUPERROMANCE

COMING NEXT MONTH